Secrets
of the
Amazon

BRIAN ATHEY

Am´azon (ă), n. Fabulous race of female warriors in Scythia; female warrior (lit. & fig.); masculine woman

Prologue

*"...to establish a defence on the
ground of insanity, it must be clearly
proved that, at the time of
committing the act, the party accused
was labouring under such a defect of
reason, from disease of the mind, as
not to know the nature and quality
of the act he was doing ..."*

House of Lords

An accused party, by the name of George, sat in the window seat of the patients' common room, looking out through the bars at the rain washing down the bare, black branches of the trees outside. His head danced to the music in his headphones. In a deserted corner, a television set was loudly playing a repeat of the 1960s black and white adaptation of The Adventures of Robinson Crusoe. Oblivious to the noise, four chemically-coshed inmates were standing around a pool table, staring at the pretty coloured balls and wondering whose turn it was to break.

From the other side of a reinforced glass partition, two staff were observing George. The female consultant psychiatrist asked the male nurse whether there had been any change.

"Not really," said the nurse, "He just sits there all day, listening to his music and chuckling to himself. He's no trouble; seems to be quite happy."

"Hmm. It could be a reaction to the sedatives," said the doctor.

"He hasn't had any. No sedation. Nothing. ... If I didn't know better, I'd have said he's permanently out of it on cannabis," said the nurse.

"There's no chance that he's ...?"

"No chance, doctor," said the nurse, "No way does he get a supply of it in here. And he's only had one visitor; that Murphy bloke brought him the classical music tape. Now *there's* a weirdo if ever I saw one. Wearing latex gloves and a surgical mask on a psyche ward? Belongs in the loony bin, if you ask me."

"Murphy?" said the doctor, "Or was it Murray? Wasn't he the one that George said tried to frame him for the murders, before he changed his plea? Something about a screwdriver?"

"A hammer, wasn't it?" said the nurse, "No, no. ... It was a spanner! That's right. A big, blood-stained spanner."

The doctor leaned forward. She noticed that George's head had stopped bobbing to the music. It was time to turn the tape over in his Walkman. "The insanity defence has been accepted," she said, "Personally, I'm not convinced. I think he was perfectly sane when he did the killings and now he's keeping up a pretence."

Having opened the Walkman and removed the tape, George glanced across the room at the partition. On seeing the blonde woman behind the glass, his breathing quickened and fumbling, he dropped the cassette. For a moment, he remembered how she had tried to kill him. He closed his eyes for a few seconds. When he re-opened them, the flashback had passed.

2

The woman was gone. His tape was back in the Walkman, playing *Dance of the Cygnets*. The significance of this particular piece escaped him. He'd heard it before somewhere, but couldn't recollect the short happy episode in his previous life of misery. Another thing he couldn't recall was how, like Defoe's protagonist, he'd come to be mentally stranded on his personal island, with just his own thoughts for company. Not that it mattered a jot. He was warm and dry, free from physical pain and hunger. Living with the guilt was no problem to him, if indeed he was guilty. A serene smile took over as he looked out of the window, his head swaying gently to the music.

Unknown to George, his fate had been decided by a series of events, set in train on the night of a certain school reunion, almost a year before.

Chapter 1

A Saturday Evening in Early Spring

Alan Murray stood at the foot of the wide staircase. Drawing aside the cuff of his overcoat, he looked at his expensive, green-gold watch, which he had bought very cheaply on his last visit to the Swiss canton of Basel-Stadt. Unfortunately, the Canton where the watch had been made, also gave its name to the local language, Cantonese. His Rolax said just after half-past seven. He screwed up his eyes to read the old grandmother clock across the hall. Roughly twenty-eight minutes past. Squinting, he read the bright red digital display on the burglar alarm panel – 18:30. Yes, it was definitely half past seven, more or less. He'd been ready for nearly an hour. It had only taken him fifteen minutes. A quick shower, followed by an over generous dose of his very reasonably priced deodorant, and Bob's your auntie's meal ticket. Why do women have to make such a fuss about it? They've got the same bodies as men – give or take a few odd bits, here and there. It shouldn't take three times as long to wash what was anatomically a very similar lump of flesh. Did women have toes which somehow collected more dirt between them? Did their armpits sweat more profusely than men's? And just how long could it take to slap on a bit of lipstick and a flick of mascara? A couple of minutes should do it.

He sighed and looked around the hall. The oak panelling next to the large fireplace was finally without its layer of tarry staining, accumulated over decades of coal fires. For a moment, he wondered how the previous occupants could have afforded to heat such a

4

room, only to have the warm air dissipate up the staircase and out through single glazed windows. The ornate stonework around the fireplace shouted loudly that this fire was not solely meant for heating the hall, but rather as an indulgence to announce to visitors that the house-owner had money to burn.

Across the hall, near the door of the old dining room, the last six-foot-wide, smoke-stained, panel section lay propped against the dirty, bare brick wall, which it had hidden since the house was built. A plastic dust sheet was laid on the newly varnished parquet flooring beneath. Standing next to the panel was a trade sized tub of fire-retardant sealant. Alan looked at the fingers of his right hand and tried to scratch off the last of the brown, dried-on carcinogenic muck. He made a mental note to buy a new pair of decent quality rubber gloves to replace the thin latex ones.

For the third time in five minutes, he walked over to the door below the staircase and turned the handle. His push rattled the door but failed, yet again, to make it budge open. He walked in baby steps back to the base of the stairs, but had to steady himself on the banister as he lost his balance. He looked up the stairs and listened. There was still no sign of her.

"Taxi's here!" he shouted, stifling a snigger.

From above, there came the sound of a toilet flushing. A stair creaked and carpet-muffled footsteps hurried down the dog-leg flight.

Sam appeared, dressed in a black trouser suit. Her looks denied her forty-something years of age. The short, wavy, blonde hair framed a face with sparkling green eyes, and a complexion to make a woman of thirty distinctly catty. Samantha's figure might have been suggestive of a regime of dieting and excessive exercise, but was in fact maintained by a fortunate metabolism which had never permitted weight gain. That, and the fact that her appetite for food was far outstripped by her appetite for life.

Her pace slowed as she came to the last few stairs. "Pathetic," she said, looking down at him from the bottom stair. She read his smiling face like the curling pages of a favourite book. "I would have heard it pulling up, or at least the bell would have sounded."

"You know the bell doesn't always work. Besides, you came running. So, you fell for it and I win." His grin was wide, revealing a full set of slightly yellowing teeth.

She stuck out her tongue then said, "Well technically speaking, sweetie, you lose, because April Fools' finished hours ago. Now, have you checked the babies?"

"They'll be fine. The door's locked. The Sparkies will never even know they're down there."

Sam said, "I've made up the spare bed, but I still think that room's a bit damp and musty."

"Well what can they expect, flaming miracles? Springing it on us like that! The room's never been slept in for years. ... I don't even know why we're going, never mind having lodgers nosing about the place."

"Oh, sweetheart. When George called, he was practically begging me to go. Look on the bright side, we'll get to see Dixie. It's ages since we last saw him. Should be a laugh. When we get back it'll be a quick cocoa and pack the Sparkies off to their stinky bed. Give them a full English in the morning, then wave them on their merry way. Come on, we deserve a night out. The time's right. Let's enjoy ourselves. What could go wrong?"

"Huh! Another fine mess you've got me into, Harpo." said Alan, dancing his eyebrows and taking a drag on his invisible cigar.

Sam recognised the true nervousness behind his feeble Groucho Marx impression. "Don't worry. It'll be fine."

"Chickens checked?" grouched Alan.

"Check. Back door locked?"

"Check. Clean panties on?"

She pouted. "Check. If you really want to."

Groucho raised his eyebrows, this time in expectation. "Tell you what. We'll just stay here and have an early night, eh? I'll call and cancel the taxi."

She said, "Stop worrying. Nothing's going to go wrong."

Headlights momentarily illuminated the front window. The bell rang and a car horn sounded outside. Exhaling a deep sigh, he took her coat from the stand and held it as she put her arms in. Then Sam and Alan left their dilapidated farmhouse, never suspecting that their first night out in three years would change their cosy, private lives forever.

The hotel in the centre of Durham had been chosen for the reunion mainly for its location, which was more or less neutral territory for most of the ex-school pupils. Many had moved away from the area for employment. For those who had remained in the county, Durham City was a focal point eminently suitable for the gathering. A venue of such elegance was not to be found nearer to the old school. None of the run-down, ex-pit villages could boast of anything approaching the class of the hotels in the city. The timing of the event, a fortnight before Easter, had been chosen to avoid both term time for Durham University students and the peak of the tourist season.

Sam and Alan arrived at the 'The King's Head' shortly before eight o'clock for their first ever school reunion. Outside, the air was markedly chilly for the time of year and as they entered the sauna, which was the upstairs function room, both stared at the forest of people, then turned to give each other anxious looks.

An ocean of middle-aged bodies exuded damp warmth into the atmosphere. The noise of a hundred conversations was punctuated with occasional bouts of laughter. A few of the men wore dinner jackets. One or two sported denim jeans, but most were dressed in middle-of-the-road, 'best' suits. Near the stage stood a short, very fat man, wearing a tent-sized Hawaiian shirt and tight-fitting shorts. One tall woman stood out from the crowd, in her red Jersey evening dress, which tightly hugged her over-ample bust and various other bulges. A mock snakeskin handbag, and diamond earrings completed the illusion of one-upwomanship.

Second prize in the ladies' fancy dress competition went to a thin, dark-haired woman, wearing a cream dress with a low-cut top revealing her complete lack of any semblance of a cleavage. Through the very lightweight material two brownish pimples stood out, one at each side of her far too open top. From behind it was possible to make out how her pink panties were sticking up her bum crack. Other than red Jersey and window netting, the favoured material for the ladies was black wool polyester mix. Sensible attire was the order of the day. The miniskirts of their schooldays had long since been consigned to the dustbins of East Durham, dumped in the landfill of exhausted limestone quarries. Advertising what was on special offer was no longer necessary nor desirable, except it seemed, in the cases of Red Jersey woman and the pink panty stick insect.

Alan didn't immediately recognise anyone as he scanned the room, but then he picked out a familiar face at the bar, beyond the crowd. "Oh look, there's Dixie," he said.

Dixie seemed to be the only person in the room who was not engaged in conversation. His large bald patch shone above his overgrown eyebrows, which crowned a pair of tired looking eyes, below which, his face seemed to consist of layers of bulldog baggy wrinkles. The last of his hair was wiry and grey, sticking out in various directions and in desperate need of a cut. He was propping up the bar, in a wrinkled charcoal suit with his shirt collar undone and gaudy Paisley tie pulled to one side. Sweat was beginning to aggregate into small droplets on his forehead. In one hand he held an almost empty pint glass, and in the other a large cigar, with a half inch of ash clinging precariously on the end. Like Alan, Dixie was searching the room for a familiar face. The sweat droplets gathered to form a small stream which ran down into his eyebrow. Wiping his forehead, Dixie switched on his full smile when he caught sight of Alan's raised hand. As Dixie raised his hand to wave, a shower of ash landed on the shoulder of his jacket.

Alan and Sam struggled through the crowd towards the bar. There was puzzlement on all sides as they excused themselves for barging through the throng of people they must have known well, twenty-five years before. Some looked familiar but their names were too deeply buried for anything like instant recall. A tall, plump woman with a round face stopped Alan and insisted on kissing him on the cheek. "Lovely to see you again, John," she said.

Alan miraculously recalled her name. "Anne, you're looking well."

With hairlines receding, most of the men had started turning grey, with the noticeable exception of one man with a full head of dense black hair. As Alan and Sam pushed past him, he smiled in recognition and said, "Hi Alan, catch you later, mate."

Alan, caught off guard, could only reply, "Er, yeah, Okay."

The black-haired man continued his conversation with three women as Alan and Sam reached the bar and the safe refuge which was Dixie. In their schooldays, John Dixon had been Alan's best friend for many years. The pair had left school and studied at the same university, both reading Mechanical Engineering. For two years after graduating they had both lived at home, but then Dixie had moved South for his new job. Since that time, they had kept in touch by letters. In the intervening years, Alan and Sam had attended Dixie's wedding, the christenings of his two sons and the funeral of his wife, Alice.

Dixie smiled, leaned forward and kissed Sam on the cheek, then shook Alan's hand vigorously.

"Jesus! They're all so old!" said Alan.

Dixie laughed, having experienced the exact same emotion at the previous reunion, four years before. "And you're not?" After another laugh, he said, "Come on, what are you having?"

Alan reviewed the beer pumps and decided on Yorkshire bitter. Sam chose a pint of the same. As Dixie pocketed his change an over-amplified noise of microphone tapping rocked the room, followed by the obligatory "One Two, One two." and some ear-piercing feedback. All eyes turned to the small stage at the end of the room. As the spotlight switched on, the man paging Mr. Juan Tuwantu, proved to be instantly recognisable as the ever-popular George Wilson, still sporting a full head of bright ginger-red hair. It was George who had been the main driving force in organising the reunion. He was also responsible for persuading Alan and Sam to accept two lodgers for the night. As George abused the public-address system, Sam's mind drifted back some years.

Back in sixty-six, George had been Sam's steady boyfriend for two months until he tired of missing out on the carnal pleasures which she had denied him. Despite their difference of opinion regarding pre-marital sex, they had remained platonic friends until ten months later, on a Friday night after a dance at a small local club. Sam and George had been among the regular crowd of under-age and newly legal drinkers at the club. On that particular Friday, she made a point of dancing with him for most of the night. During the last 'smooch' dance she squashed her developing breasts into his chest, gave him a pathetic little-girl look and flashed her mascara. George took the bait, ate the hook and started to reel himself in. He asked if she would walk to the bus shelter and stay for a chat while he waited for his bus.

For some weeks before, Sam had been pondering on her parents' troubled marriage. They had stayed together for the sake of their only child. Recently their quarrels had become louder and longer, but still

11

without any physical violence until one Saturday morning when her mother appeared, sporting a black eye, badly disguised with foundation and face powder. Up until then, Sam had believed a white knight, Sir Right, would appear on the scene, sweep her off her feet, marry her and make lovely babies. She had saved herself for the perfect man she knew would some-day be hers. That Saturday morning, she saw her father in a new light. He'd been her mother's Mr. Right all those years before. *How could it come to this!* Sam vowed to herself never to marry. She was to be the mistress of her own destiny, strong and independent, an Amazon, taking men on her own terms. To this warrior, there was no longer any reason to save herself for some mythical, saintly Mr. Right, so that afternoon she started to plan her first campaign.

Ginger George was to be her first conquest. Since their parting he had gained in popularity, becoming a more worldly-wise individual with the reputation, deserved or otherwise, of being something of a stud. According to the grapevine he had deflowered two girls in the last three months. They hadn't been mentioned by name, but everyone guessed who they were. Sam decided to let him educate her in the ways of lust, only to cast him aside after luring him into love.

So it was on that cool Friday night in June, that the re-united couple walked hand in hand to the bus shelter, the Amazon and her sexual tutor. Giving up her virginity proved to be memorable not so much for any great pleasure, but more for the relief of a relatively painless introduction to womanhood, unexpected of the clumsy extrovert George. Tipsy Sam encouraged him to go all the way as he stroked and kissed her into easy submission.

In the scrub behind the bus shelter they made what passed for love. Having heard horror stories of 'knee trembler' couples becoming embarrassingly unable to decouple, Sam insisted on lying on her back. Afterwards, as George rose to his feet, almost apologetically, he asked if she was alright. Sam didn't reply. In the darkness, he turned his back on her as he pulled up his jeans. She had been blinded by staring up towards a street light. She heard his zip close, then caught a glimpse of his madly grinning face as he turned towards her. Standing up, she paid for his services with a smile and a kiss on the cheek, then pulled on her knickers. They had been off for just under two minutes. As she stood up, she felt the need to clean up. She pushed her handkerchief up her skirt and into her knickers. Without saying a word to George, the Amazon strode out into the light from behind the bus shelter, determined that he was not to be her white knight. This would be their first and only sexual encounter.

George emerged from behind the shelter in time to see Sam as she disappeared from sight, walking quickly in the direction of her home. He waited ten minutes for his bus. As he offered the fare, he looked at the small blood stain on the back of his right hand. That night George went home, a very happy, but slightly puzzled boy.

The next morning Sam awoke still feeling sore. She retrieved the blood-stained handkerchief and knickers from under the bed, where she had hidden them. Her mother would never believe that her period was a fortnight early, so the offending items would need to be thrown out. Samantha knew that her mother kept a close eye on the number of items she had in the wash, so she decided to buy a replacement pair of knickers

13

that day. She could easily bluff her way out of the loss of a handkerchief. Her secret was safe. Over breakfast, the only comment which passed about the previous night was when her mother asked if Samantha was alright, as she'd been in the lavatory and bathroom for a long time. Samantha dismissed her mother's concern with a story about school dinners. For the rest of the day Sam was self-consciously worried that she might be walking differently as she tried to avoid aggravating her soreness.

Sunday was, as usual, a somewhat lost day. Samantha's mother baked and cooked for most of the morning. Her father had the best part of a gallon of aperitif at the Working Men's Club before coming home to blame his wife for everything wrong with the Sunday dinner, the hippie drug culture and the rubbish, modern music on the jukebox at the club. Sticking rigidly to his Sunday routine, he wolfed down his awful dinner, burped, slurped his burnt rice pudding, then left the dinner table and fell asleep, snoring on the sofa for three hours.

Samantha and her mother stuck to their own routine of washing up after Sunday dinner, followed by their short walk through the dene. Mrs. Black's relaxed conversation disguised a moral lecture on the evil of drink with a few sideswipe references to her husband's state. Sam eventually realised that her mother was warning her about the loosening of a girl's guard while under the influence of alcohol. A thought flashed past Sam's consciousness. Had her mother seen the knickers? Suddenly more attentive, Sam listened as her mother explained, in more detail than Sam cared to know, about how she had been persuaded to give up her own girlhood after a visit to a pub. *Good*, thought Sam. Her secret was still safe.

As she loaded the washing machine on Monday morning, Mrs. Black wondered where the cheap pair of knickers had come from. They didn't look as if they had been worn, merely crumpled and creased. Things were starting to make sense. She wondered if her baby was growing to be a woman a bit too quickly for her liking. She decided to adopt a policy of watching and waiting. It was no good discussing her concerns with the Floyd 'bloody' Patterson of the village.

At school, Sam had double biology in the morning. With the year's coursework finished, the class was simply catching up on some practical work which filled up the remaining lessons before the end of term. As she waited for the teacher to come round to look at her dissection, she thumbed through a new textbook which had been left on the bench by an earlier class. The curriculum had changed such that human reproduction was covered in the fifth form. The book fell open easily at the relevant chapter. The basics were familiar to her, but she lacked detailed knowledge of the process. As she read on, her mouth dropped open slightly. The middle of the month wasn't the best time to 'do it' to avoid pregnancy. It was the best time to conceive. One male gamete was enough! Oh God, she'd had thousands of Ginger's inside her, all searching for her perfectly ripened ovum! Why hadn't she insisted that Ginger should use a johnny? What if she was pregnant? She leant down and reached urgently inside her school satchel for her diary to check her dates, just as Mr. Hunter arrived. He was pleased to find his missing textbook, but less than happy with her dissection. She would have to do much better if she was to get a good 'A' level grade. Sam ignored his comments. Her mind was set on her diary. When Hunter left, she counted the days, closed her eyes, and mentally screamed, *Shit!*

For the rest of the week Sam noticed that her mother seemed more attentive than usual. At tea, it was almost as if she was waiting for Sam to speak. At breakfast, there was always an enquiry about Sam's health, "You alright, love?" To which Sam would always reply "Yes, mum."

The following Friday night Sam went to the club as usual. She hadn't told any of her friends about her previous week's little adventure behind the bus shelter. When George failed to turn up at the dance she began to wonder if he was trying to avoid her. Was he worried that she might be pregnant? Perhaps he'd moved on to sexual pastures new without a single thought for her. A mixture of pride and a pragmatic will to avoid attracting attention to her possible condition prevented her from asking where he was that night. None of her friends volunteered the information, or even mentioned his name. She left early, walked home, went quietly to bed and cried softly as sleep came slowly to comfort her.

Throughout the weekend the thought of pregnancy was never far from the forefront of her mind. The next week at school dragged on as Wednesday, the due date of her period, approached and passed without its desired result. On Thursday morning, her mother seemed to be more attentive than usual. At teatime Mrs. Black decided to give her favourite daughter a cuddle and asked whether she was alright. Samantha assured her mother of her good health.

"Tonight's the last night for the fair," said Mrs. Black, "Fancy a look along? I'll get you a hotdog."

"Yeah. Okay," replied Sam, unable to think of anything but her predicament.

By Friday morning Sam was dazed with worry when she woke to find that she still hadn't started. After breakfast, she went to the lavatory and felt a strong urge to be sick, but as she leant over the toilet bowl nothing came out. So this was it! Morning sickness! How was she going to tell her mother?

All morning at school she had a headache, felt dizzy and kept tasting the reflux of stomach acid. By eleven o'clock the back of her throat was becoming sore after retching unsuccessfully in the toilets. Finally, in her last lesson before lunch she regurgitated her morning's cereal onto the floor of room 15. The assistant caretaker was summoned to clean up and Sam was escorted to the sick bay. Sitting on the bed with a plastic bowl on her lap, she reflected on the cause of her sickness. She remembered reading in a magazine somewhere that morning sickness could last all day for nine months. If this was the price of a quick fling, she vowed that this would be her last. She also vowed to make Ginger George pay for what he'd done.

Sam left school shortly after the others had eaten lunch. By the time she arrived home her stomach was making loud gurgling noises and she needed to hurry to the lavatory. She wondered if diarrhoea was a common side effect of morning sickness. Gradually over the afternoon her tormented stomach settled down and lost most of its pain. At six o'clock she felt much better. The headache had gone and her stomach no longer wanted to be emptied in either direction, so she resolved to go to the club to confront Ginger George. She bathed slowly, dressed quickly, then carried Ginger's unborn son and heir to the club.

As Sam entered the hall, she spotted George at the side of the dance floor. He was standing there, alone, eyeing up a group of girls who were dancing intimately with their handbag partners. Like most other hungry predators, George was looking for any weakness which could be exploited. It took just ten seconds for Sam to stride purposefully across the hall to him, give him a stare which said, *I'm going to cut your balls off!* then grab his arm and lead him outside.

Ginger was taken so much by surprise that he had no time to say anything or decide whether to resist her urgent arm pulling. When she led him to the alley behind the club, he thought his luck might be in again that night. "I'm pregnant!" she blurted in a loud, desperate whisper, looking around to make sure nobody else was within earshot. "I'm three days late, and I've had morning sickness all week."

"That's nothing to do with me. I didn't put you in the club."

"Are you trying to say I dreamed it all? You seduced me behind the bus shelter a fortnight ago. Took advantage of me. And now you just don't want to face up to your responsibilities. I suppose that's why you weren't out last week. Couldn't face me, could you, knowing what you'd done. Well you've really knackered up my life for me, thanks very much."

She was starting to cry. He tried to interrupt but she continued through her weeping, "I'll never be able to go to college now. I could have been a research chemist at ICI or somewhere, but you've put the blocks on all that. I'm going to end up on the bloody social, pushing a pram with your kid in it, and where will you be? Oh no! It's nothing to do with you."

At this point Sam's tears were flowing freely. She had an ache in her groin which only added to her sorrows. Ginger put one arm around her to comfort her. She whimpered, "Bastard!" but still let him hold her.

With his free arm, he reached into his pocket. She expected him to pull out a dirty handkerchief for her, but when his hand re-appeared it was holding a three pack of condoms. Ginger released his hold around her shoulders and handed her the packet.

"Count them," he said, "The missing one's still behind the bus shelter."

Sam took the packet, opened it and found that there were two left. Still thinking of her condition, she suspected that he was probably telling lies.

"I never saw it. Anyway, you could've used the other one last Friday on some other poor unsuspecting innocent," she said, wincing as her stomach pain increased. "You weren't here."

George began to explain, in succinct Anglo-Saxon, that he had been taken ill with diarrhoea the previous Friday, probably after eating a dodgy hotdog. As he spoke, Sam ignored his explanation, held her stomach and took in a deep breath.

He said, "Are you alright?" He didn't know what to do. It was the first time he'd seen anyone suffering from morning sickness. He took back his pack of condoms and offered her a dirty handkerchief, which she refused.

As she wiped her eyes with a clean tissue, he asked, "You really are up the stick, then?"

She laughed and cried as she suddenly realised what was causing her latest, more familiar, abdominal pain. They walked back to the dance hall, the Amazon laughing intermittently, the sexual tutor more puzzled than ever before.

* * * *

Sam had a tear in her eye and a gentle smile on her face as Alan's laugh brought her back to the reunion. Ginger George had just resurrected a joke which must have been hilariously funny in the 1930's, but which now drew a mixture of laughing, booing and cries imploring him to leave the stage. When she looked again at the friend, whom she had misplaced but never lost, Sam had the urge to shout some obscenity at him, but she controlled herself, realising that some of the people around her would have grown up to be first class stiffs. Besides, he'd never wilfully hurt her in his life. She still had a soft spot in her heart for her first conquest.

"Hasn't changed much, has he?" said Alan, raising his voice above the row.

"He's done very well for himself," replied Dixie, equally loudly. "He's regional director for Royal Hotels, you know."

"Just goes to show," Alan shouted, "Leave school after 'O' levels and rule the world."

There was obviously no malice in Alan's remark, but as the noise in the room abated a little, Sam said, "Getting a bit elitist aren't we, Murray. Just because he never went to university doesn't mean to say he's thick, you know. I mean, he did get better 'O' levels than you and me. It wasn't his fault that his parents couldn't afford it."

Dixie said, "It was his father who put the blocks on 'A' levels for Geordie. He wanted him down the pit and earning, so he wouldn't have to put in so much

20

overtime himself. Frank was a bit of a bastard. Oh, sorry Sam, I mean … well you know. Anyway, he gave Geordie a right belting when he got the sack on his first day."

Dixie paused to have a long mouthful of beer, then smiled and added, "The way I heard it was that Geordie actually managed to smuggle a match down and light up at the bottom of the shaft. How he didn't set off the firedamp, well, God alone knows."

"Oh yes, I remember his dad," said Sam, wrinkling her nose as if tasting something nasty, "Not a very nice man, but as far as I remember, George told me that he got sacked for fighting on his first day. He said that he smacked the deputy with his shovel and told him to stuff the job. Of course, George reckoned the deputy had him sacked as revenge for being given a good beating by a teenager. But then, Ginger was always prone to a bit of bragging, when it suited him."

"That sounds more like George," agreed Alan, "Ideal material for the diplomatic corps – gunboat department. Mind you, he was bloody big for a sixteen-year-old, so maybe he did bray the deputy."

George was still speaking into the microphone. "So, he says, *Of course I have, you don't think I always smell like this, do you?* Hey! Enjoy the night. Let's have a big hand for Big Bri's Mobile Discotheque!"

The noise level in the hall rose in a crescendo of clapping, whistling and foot stamping. As it died away the short, fat, balding disc jockey waved from behind his console and started his sixties night with 'Younger Girl' by 'Lovin Spoonful'.

Big (around-the-waist) Brian had been told in no uncertain terms that his sound level was to be kept to a maximum of 'marginally above background', otherwise the well-built, red haired man would see that he never worked again and also disconnect him from his testicles and other, valued equipment. Big Bri eyed the slider marked 'Master Level' on his console, longing to increase it above two. The fingers of his right hand caressed the fader as he rehearsed moving it up. It was so unnatural to have such a powerful system limited to background level, like a caged tiger. He knew that with a flick of his finger he could have caused structural damage to such a dump as this crumbling hotel. With the control set below three, there was a risk that the audience would be able to hear themselves talking. He resolved to leave it at two for the time being and gradually increase the level over the night until a real disco sound could be achieved.

As he watched the arrogant, red-haired bastard walk away from the stage, Bri caught sight of a beautiful lady in red and forgot all thoughts of sound levels for a few seconds. He admired her overflowing bosom and raised his stare to make eye contact. Her gaze seemed strangely distant as she gave him a half smile. He replied with a wink and a pout of his lips. She ran her forefinger down her cleavage and caressed her left breast as her shoulders danced to the music. Judging by the way she was coming on, Bri thought that maybe he might need to hang on to his 'other equipment', so he decided to keep the level at background for the present. Shortly, the track finished and it was time for his opening address. Bringing up the mic level, he introduced himself.

George made his way to the bar as 'Lovin Spoonful' played. After tasting the foundation of five makeup-covered cheeks and shaking six clammy hands he arrived at the bar just as Hawaiian Brian garbled five seconds of unintelligible noise into the microphone, followed by what sounded like "Yeah!"

The senior sexual tutor greeted his middle-aged Amazon with, "Your mother couldn't come, then? Sent you instead? You look just like her when *she* was eighteen." The music started again.

Sam smiled and her tears welled up as they embraced. Once again, she felt her breasts pressed against his chest. She aimed her kiss at his lips, but he diverted her such that he kissed her cheek leaving her to suck amorously on the bottom of his chin. Grabbing a handful of red hair, Sam repositioned his head such that she could have tongued his tonsils, and gave him a real smacker. "Keep some for me, you dirty old bugger," Alan complained to his over-sexed partner. This worked like a bucket of cold water on a pair of copulating dogs.

George pulled back, shrugged his shoulders and gave Alan a look which said, *Not guilty, Mi'lud*. Alan's body language reply said, *Case Dismissed*, as he supported Sam from behind. His better half was not behaving like the lady he had known since childhood. She was definitely wobbly, which was quite surprising as she'd had less than a pint of the strong beer. He assumed that she must have had something to steady her nerves before leaving home.

"How long has it been?" asked George, combing his hair with his outstretched fingers. He was staring into Sam's green eyes. "It must have been seventy-one when I saw you last – you've hardly changed."

"You mean I'm not bald and grey with a face like a prune?" said Sam, obviously fishing for another compliment.

"Well that was what I was expecting," said George, gaining a friendly slap on his head from Sam's left hand.

Alan stepped forward and shook George's hand, saying, "Good to see you again, mate."

Dixie merely nodded at George in recognition, held up his half empty glass and asked, "George?"

"Pint of Durham Ale please, John … Have you been kissing the girls, Alan?" said George, pointing out a lipstick mark on Alan's cheek.

"Oh, I got snogged by Anne Brown," said Alan.

"I hope not, mate. She's been dead for about ten years, now. Comes to us all, I suppose," said George.

Dixie had been listening to the conversation and now turned away from the bar to join in. "Anne Brown was the weedy one, I suppose she'd be called anorexic nowadays, poor bugger. The big fat one's Anne Wood, capable of re-stocking a minor planet from her mega-womb. She caught me last time and I had her all night, telling me how she'd had eight kids before she was thirty. By forty she was well on the way to a couple of footie teams. The worst of it was that she kept calling me 'Alan'. Just be thankful you got away with a peck on the cheek."

"Sure you're not exaggerating just a little bit there, John?" asked George, accepting the pint.

Alan asked George, "Who's that guy with the black hair? He recognised me, but I've no idea who he is. He looks familiar, but I don't think he was in our year."

George shook his head and said, "Don't know. He's probably one of the girls' husbands. Maybe he just thought he recognised you. Looks like a rug to me."

"He called me Alan, so he must know me. And I'm sure I know his voice from somewhere. It'll come to me."

"He might be somebody's boyfriend," said Sam, "Or maybe he was just trying to pick you up. I'd be careful in the gents if I were you, love." As she said this, Sam nipped Alan's bottom, causing him to jump and knock George's arm, spilling an inch of beer from his glass onto the carpet.

"Still mad as ever then, sexpot?" asked George, half smiling and shaking his head slowly at Sam.

"A bloody fruit cake," said Alan.

Sam stared at George, trying to work out what it was that was wrong about him. His smile seemed forced, not the natural grin of old. She remembered him as a much more carefree young man, never serious for more than a minute. He seemed to be troubled, or perhaps it was simply the effect of a lifetime's wear and tear on the smile muscles.

"Oh, by the way, Sparky and Joan couldn't make it. So you won't have guests for the night, after all. Family emergency or something," said George.

Alan and Sam smiled at each other before Alan said, "Oh, what a pity, we were really looking forward to seeing them."

George said, "Ron and Joan are alright. They're really lovely people. I couldn't have organised this without them and their address books. You didn't have a problem putting them up, did you?"

"Oh, no!" replied Sam, "We would have loved to have had them for the night. Only, our guest bedroom got flooded last week and they would have had to sleep on the sofa-bed. Not very comfortable. It's a bit embarrassing, really." Sam watched George, tilting her head to one side, smiling and flashing her eyelashes as she waited for his reply.

George recognised Sam's performance from years before. Long buried images emerged from deep within his brain. Yes, now he remembered her subtle technique for bullying him into silence. Sensing her lie, he asked, "Much damage?"

Alan came to the rescue of his damsel in distress, spoiling George's fun by changing the subject. "Only the bed clothes and mattress. Same again, George?"

George turned to Alan and replied, "Just a half, please, mate. Can I pinch your missus for a dance?"

Without waiting for a reply, he took Sam's hand and guided her through the crowd to the dance floor. They jogged on the spot for a minute, then George pulled her past Big Bri, through a side door, marked 'Staff Only', into a long service corridor, where well-worn, burgundy carpet gave way to well-worn, bleached, plastic floor tiles. Only the bass notes of Big Bri's amplifiers could be sensed as the door closed behind the couple. They walked down the narrow corridor to a point where a window on an outside wall was running with condensation.

"I've got to talk to you!" said George, "I really need you …"

Sam interrupted. "It was nearly thirty years ago, George. Kid's stuff. A one-night stand. It meant nothing. It's far too late to start thinking about all that again. We were never an item, never could have been. Alan and me, we go together. We're happy."

"I'm dying!" said George, grabbing both of her shoulders, then almost immediately releasing his grasp as he saw the shock on her face.

For a moment Sam was stunned into silence, then she looked into his eyes and laughed. "Very good! I remember the last time you tried that one. You thought you might be dying, so how about a quick one for the road. You were dying alright, dying to get into my pants." With a smile, she put her hand between his legs and started to rub. "Okay then, Romeo. Can you get a room?"

As she finished speaking, Sam noticed that George's expression hadn't changed. He was still deadly serious.

"Come on Ginger, stop messing about. Let's go somewhere else. What do you mean, you're dying? So, what are you dying for? No, I mean, what are you dying of?"

Sam stopped smiling as she noticed his eyes beginning to fill.

"Astrocytoma." He covered his eyes and bowed his head, as if to hide his embarrassment at crying.

She stopped her crutch massage and said, "What? An astrocytoma? No! You're joking? You *are* joking. Yes, you're joking. Come on, George, enough's enough. It's not funny. Brain tumours aren't funny, George.

She waited for him to burst into laughter. He'd never been cut out to be a poker player. Soon he wouldn't be able to keep his face straight. That's why he was covering up.

The look on his face, as he uncovered his eyes told her how wrong she had been to doubt his sincerity.

"No, George," she said, shaking her head, as she tried to take in the reality. The hand which had cradled his balls now moved to gently stroke the side of his head. "But it should be operable. The cure rate's ninety percent, if you catch it early enough," Sam's speech slowed as she completed the conditional part of her statement.

Her shoulders dropped and she shook her head slowly. The look on his face told it all.

"I went to the quack last month and it was already too late. Surgery's out."

"But you must have known something was wrong. Didn't you have headaches?"

"I put them down to stress."

"What about chemo and radiotherapy. It might respond."

"I'm not going to have chemotherapy. It doesn't work with what I've got, and the side effects ... I don't think I could ... If I've got to die, I want to go with some dignity. And as for radiotherapy, it sounds like they'd have to fry my brain before it had any effect, so they didn't offer it. They can't operate 'cos it's too far gone and in the wrong place. That's why I need you, Sam. I've got to get on the trial."

"I'm sorry sir, this area is for staff only," said the waiter, who had approached unnoticed by the pair, "I'll have to ask you to return to the function room, please."

"What!" said George, "We're trying to have a conversation here!"

"I'm sorry sir, it's fire regulations."

George calmed down a little and said, "Sorry, son. Give us a couple of minutes." He stuffed a fiver into the waiter's waistcoat pocket.

At this, the waiter transferred his tray of hors d'oeuvres to his right hand and took the note from his pocket. "I'm sorry, sir, I can't accept this, but could you please return to the room as soon as you can. Thank you."

George took his fiver back. "Okay, thanks. Two minutes, Okay?" The waiter walked off in the direction of the function room. There was a short blast of noise as the door opened, then relative silence as it flapped shut.

"What were you saying about a trial?" asked Sam.

"Methyphenax Four. Phase one human trial starts next month."

"How do you know about Methyphenax Four?" said Sam.

"I've got to get on the trial. Please, Sam, I'm begging. They gave me six months, at most! Please!"

Again, he took hold of her shoulders as if to start shaking her, but then released his grip and held his hands together, pleading.

"George! How? I can't. I'm sorry. We don't work for Falmer's any more. Anyway, they don't even organise the trials. They subcontract the whole job to an external test house. It's a blind trial. They choose

29

the subjects. I don't even know which test house is involved."

"What? Don't you still have contacts with them? Are you saying there's no chance?"

"Have you had a second opinion on surgery?" said Sam, "They don't always get it right, you know."

George hadn't been listening. "Maybe you could get me some. If you could get me three month's supply, I'd be alright." His eyes were like golf balls, sticking out, wide open. His fuse was about to blow.

"George, I don't have access to it. It's a new treatment which could make them billions. They don't leave them lying about like aspirins. I didn't even have clearance for that area."

"So, it's a tablet, like aspirin. You don't need to inject it?"

"I can't get any, George. If I could, you know I would, but they have extreme security with all new developments, and this one's a real hot potato," said Sam, realising that he was holding on so tightly to her left hand that it hurt. She cuddled him, trying to calm him, and tearfully added, "It might not even work. Get a second opinion on surgery."

After a minute of running her fingers through his thick, red, wavy hair, she released him, gave him a kiss on the cheek and hurried up the corridor before her feelings could flood out. By the time she reached the staff-only door she was completely composed, almost. As Sam pushed the door, George shouted, "Don't tell anybody!"

When George re-joined Alan and Dixie, they had taken a table near the bar. Sam was nowhere to be seen. "Where've you hidden her then, George?" asked Alan.

"Don't know where she's gone, maybe she's gone to powder her nose," said George, looking tired and very unhappy.

"Are you alright, George?" asked Dixie, "Not on any powerful painkillers, are you?"

George's first thoughts were that Sam had told them of his illness, but then he realised that Dixie was referring to the half-finished pint he had left, and the newly poured half.

"No, I'm just not drinking a lot nowadays. Have to watch my weight," he replied, thinking how long it would be before he had to swap codeine tablets for a morphine pump. He didn't want to die, drugged up to the eyeballs in a hospital bed, unable to shit unaided. He didn't want to die alone, with no friends to mourn his passing. He didn't want to die in long, drawn out, physical or mental pain. Most of all, he just didn't want to die from this bloody awful lump in his head.

George sipped at his half-finished pint of warm Durham Ale, determined to get his hands on the new, miracle cancer drug. He needed more time to work on Sam, so he plotted his simple scheme to become her lodger, in place of Ron Sparks. "Must call and book a taxi for later," said George as he rose. Then he pushed his way through to the main door leading to the staircase.

"Now I see who that is. It's One Eyed Wanda, isn't it?" said Alan, nodding in the direction of Red Jersey woman, who was approaching rapidly. "I didn't recognise her at first. Whew! She's grown a bit, hasn't she?"

31

"You're right there," said Dixie with some admiration, "Her centre of gravity's certainly got higher since she was at school. Actually, she'd look quite attractive if she got rid of that lipstick and wore some sensible clothes."

Wendy Simpson approached, swinging her mock snakeskin handbag.

"Hello," said Alan with a burp, "Wendy couldn't come, so she sent her mother, eh?"

"What?" said Wendy.

"It must be forty years since I last saw you, and you haven't changed a bit," said Alan.

"I sincerely hope not, Minty. I've spent a fortune on this body over the years. The only thing I couldn't get sorted was this," said Wendy, turning her head and pointing at her glass eye. She seemed to be far more interested in Dixie, to the point of almost ignoring Alan while smiling affectionately in John's direction.

Alan, slightly embarrassed at her frankness, picked up on her use of his old nickname. "Hah! Nobody's called me 'Minty' since we were at school."

Wendy turned to Alan and said, "Well, to tell the truth, I can't remember the last time anybody called me 'One Eyed Wanda' either."

Alan blushed and didn't reply. *Surely, she couldn't have heard his remark?* He took another mouthful of beer.

Wendy asked Dixie, "Where's that bastard, Wilson? He was here a minute ago, wasn't he?"

"I think he went out to make a phone call," said Dixie.

Wendy pushed and pulled at her bust in an effort to make herself more comfortable and said, "The sod only told me it was tarts and vicars, wait till I get my hands on him! I squeezed into this bloody dress and it's giving me hell. It's years since I last wore it."

At this, Alan and Dixie burst into laughter. She looked affronted for a second, then joined in, exclaiming, "The ginger bastard!"

As Wendy sat down next to Dixie, Alan offered to buy her a drink, then left for the bar to get her orange juice.

"Your wife not with you tonight then, John?" she asked.

Dixie took a deep breath then said, "She died fourteen years ago – Cancer."

"Oh, I'm so sorry, John. That must have been awful!"

"Well, you know, it was really bad at first, but time heals. Alice and me, we had a great life together. She never saw the kids growing up, though. Pity. She was really special, you know. I'll never forget her, but then again, you can't live in the past, can you?"

"No, of course not. I know how you feel, John. I've lost three husbands. Well, not lost them exactly. … Divorced them actually. They were all wrong for me. You found anybody else, John?"

"No, not really. Never bothered looking," said Dixie, trying to avoid staring at her overexposed bust.

"It costs nothing to look, John," she said, taking a deep breath, which expanded the objects of his gaze.

Alan returned with the orange juice, which he handed to Wendy. Then, turning to Dixie, he said, "There's a mystery tour bottle party later, do you fancy it?"

Dixie looked up and said, "Sorry. A what? A mystery bottle party? What's that? Some sort of murder game, or something?"

"No," said Alan, "You take a bottle and then go on a mystery tour by minibus somewhere for a party. Sounds like a laugh. Are you on for it? There's only fifteen seats and it's first come, first served."

"No, it's not really my sort of thing. I'd be a bit of a wallflower. You and Sam go, I'll just stay here," said Dixie.

Wendy coughed and gently kicked Dixie's ankle.

"Unless you fancy going for a ride, Wendy?"

"Love to, John. You're on," said Wendy with a smile, raising her eyebrows, as if in ecstasy.

From nowhere, Sam appeared and shouted, "Wendy Robson! How are you doing?"

Wendy stood up and the two embraced. Then for the next hour they swapped life stories, huddled in a corner at the next table, away from the prying ears of the males. An occasional cry such as "Never!" or "No, he didn't" punctuated the whispered conversation with associated shrieks and laughter.

A slightly happier looking George Wilson re-joined Alan and Dixie at their table and commented on the ladies' noise with, "The last time I heard that racket I was driving past a poultry farm."

Wendy noticed George's return and broke away from her clucking to threaten him. "I'll sort you out later, Wilson."

"Promises, promises, Wanda," he replied with a wink and a very rude hand gesture.

"Are you going to the party, George?" said Alan.

"Oh, a party, why not? Where's it at?"

"Don't know. It's a mystery tour."

"Well that sounds very interesting," said George, nodding, "This place will be dead after eleven. Anyway, who cares where it is, as long as there's transport, something to drink and a crust to eat."

"Oh, you'll need to take a bottle," said Alan, "God knows how we'll get home, but if the worst comes to the worst we can always crash on the floor, I suppose. Done that plenty times in the past."

"I don't think you'll need to worry about getting home, mate," said George, with a restrained laugh.

Alan swayed, steadied himself with two hands on the table and ignoring George's quip, scanned the room in search of the black-haired man.

Chapter 2

The driver of the Royal Hotel's minibus stood talking to the night security guard of The King's Head Hotel. Both were looking up at the sky and the quickly moving clouds. Both agreed that it was a daft idea to go on a mystery tour, at this time of year, on such a night, with the wind from the North. Then both grinned knowingly as the first of the eleven passengers walked through the glass doorway via fresh, cold, spring air to mount the fifteen-seater. The last person to board was the red-haired man, who nodded to the driver as he passed. The driver replied with a thumbs-up, winked at his security guard friend, and hurried to his cab.

The journey to the mystery party took fifteen minutes. As the street lights of Durham disappeared, the view outside of the minibus was cast into almost total darkness. The full moon struggled to penetrate the thick cloud layer. To compound the effect of blackness outside, the driver had been instructed to keep the interior lights on full. Speculation about the destination heightened as the passengers guessed at local landmarks, half seen as the moonlight broke through momentarily. The route did not include any large towns or villages. An occasional row of street lights would appear in the darkness as the minibus raced past small isolated groups of houses.

From the back of the bus someone tried to organise a sing-song, but this dissolved into anarchy as the choice of song brought total disagreement. Sam told Alan to sit down and be quiet. Nobody wanted a sing-song. Alan muttered something about 'boring old farts' and flopped down.

Sam looked around the bus at the other passengers, wondering what kind of lives they had enjoyed or endured. She recognised Theresa Griffiths in one of the front seats next to her husband. He was a very portly man with thinning grey hair, a rounded face, and a narrow moustache along his top lip. Sam had gathered from her earlier conversation with Wendy that Theresa had taken to calling herself "Teri" after marrying the strait-laced policeman, Peter Green. Sam giggled to herself at the thought of 'Theresa Green'. Theresa had always been a stuck-up little bitch, just because she lived in the officials' houses while all the others were from colliery or council houses. Maybe she had mellowed with time and discovered how to look straight ahead instead of down that snooty nose of hers.

In the seat behind Teri Green sat the ageing hippie, John 'Rat' Foster. Nobody knew how he had acquired his unsavoury nickname. At school, he had never been known as anything other than 'Rat', even to the extent that some of the teachers had used the nickname. Political correctness had not been heard of back in the sixties. Teachers at the old school ruled with an iron fist, using verbal and physical abuse to control the pupils. 'Rat' Foster had taken more than his fair share of beatings from the more sadistic members of the teaching staff. His drug taking had been common knowledge throughout the school and the reaction of the older, prejudiced teachers had been to try to beat the habit out of him. It was Rat who had introduced Sam to the pleasures of cannabis in her last autumn before university. She paid for her first drug experience by choosing Rat as her third conquest. It happened at a going-away party, in a bed under a pile of coats. This time it seemed to last for an hour, due to the effect of the cannabis. In reality, Rat could only hold back for a few minutes, but Sam had still felt some pleasure without any associated pain. Despite her mind swimming with the drug, she had insisted on taking the precaution of using a condom.

Sam turned her head and her eyes focussed on the man sitting across the aisle from Rat. He was facing the rear, staring directly at her. On his thin face was the smile that the weasel saves for the baby rabbit. She didn't try to hide her dislike of Malcolm Burke, smirked at him and turned to Alan.

"Who invited Burke?" she whispered.

Alan just shrugged his shoulders then put his arm around her. "Probably the same person who invited Lesley Connor and her girlfriend. I was talking to Burke in the bog. Said he didn't really know why he came tonight. Has to get up early for his sister tomorrow. As far as I remember she was called Angela or Alison possibly. Dopey sort of kid, she was. Sort of a piggy look about her. Always seemed to be scared of boys."

Sam wasn't listening. Her gaze fell on Lesley, the lezzy. "No need to ask which one goes on top there," whispered Sam, "Did you see her friend? She's like a Russian shot putter."

Dixie and Wendy were sitting together halfway down the bus. She had chosen the window seat, on his left, to keep him on the side of her good eye. "Did you really mean it?" she asked.

"Mean what?" said Dixie, showing complete bewilderment at the question.

Wendy leaned over and whispered in his ear. "That I might be attractive. You know, if I got rid of my lipstick and dressed properly."

Dixie turned and looked her in the eye, still mystified.

"My second husband was deaf. I learned lip-reading and signing," she said.

"Right," said Dixie, nodding in recollection of his earlier conversation with Alan, "Right."

"Well?" asked Wendy.

"What?"

"Did you mean it?"

"Yes, of course I did."

"Even with this?" She turned her head to expose her prosthetic eye in his direction.

Dixie took her hand and said, "I always fancied you at school, you know."

"Oh no, not the one about marbles!" she laughed.

"No, seriously! I really did, but I was so shy I never dared say anything. I suppose it was an inferiority complex."

"Yes, you always were the quiet one, weren't you? Strong and silent."

Wendy's right hand slid across Dixie's left thigh.

Alan shouted from the back, "We've gone round in a circle. There's the cathedral."

In the distance, the floodlit cathedral and castle were visible, towering above the light pollution of the city, through the left-hand side windows of the bus.

The minibus slowed and negotiated a tight corner. The cathedral and castle disappeared from view as the engine revved loudly in a low gear. Branches of overhanging trees caught the sides and top of the vehicle as it was driven slowly down a steep, bumpy track. Springs creaked with every pothole in the road. Gradually the sound level of murmured conversation rose as it became clear that this was to be the location for the mystery party. The springs stopped creaking as the bus reached a level parking area and drew up beside a large, old, stone-built farmhouse.

The minibus door opened and the passengers began to disembark. The house cast a dark shadow in the moonlight, then a cloud drifted to block out the light completely. Teri Green let out a short scream as a hand reached out to touch her. The moonlight switched on again as the cloud drifted away and Teri saw that it was Peter's hand. In the shadow, Lesley Connor tripped over something at knee height. Her friend caught her just as a security light switched on and bathed the area in front of the house in its harsh glow. This revealed a large terracotta plant pot filled with dead flower plants and weeds. A bell sounded inside the house.

Alan and Sam jumped to their feet at the back of the bus. Sam looked out of the window at their home and cried, "Oh no! No! No! No! Not here! No chance!"

Seconds later, when he realised where they were, Alan joined in with, "No, we can't have it here. The house is a mess and we're just not prepared. We haven't got any food in, no drinks, no glasses, no music, no toilet rolls."

Despite all their protestations, Alan and Sam were forced to accept that they were to host the surprise party. Their excuse of having no food was countered by two large hampers being unloaded from the boot of the minibus. Bottles clinked as a third hamper was unloaded. The portable party had arrived, and the couple had no option but to open their front door to it. This was a great disaster to Sam and Alan, but an even greater relief to the other nine party-goers who were freezing in the cold night air.

Alan was first to enter the hall. He switched on the lights and disarmed the burglar alarm as the minibus pulled away. George looked around at the ancient oak panels and said, "Wow! This is incredible. It's like a manor house, isn't it? How old is this place, Alan?"

"What do you reckon?" Alan threw back the question, suddenly sobered by the unwelcome role as party-giver.

"Seventeenth or eighteenth century?"

"Miles out. It's a late nineteenth century ringer. It was built by a gentleman farmer who made a fortune out of coal. He fancied himself as lord of the manor, so he built himself a manor house," said Alan, "Everybody, it's warmer in the kitchen, if you want to go through."

Five minutes later the party was slowly getting under way in the kitchen, the only place in the house where outdoor clothing was not required. The room was mock medieval, with an oak beamed ceiling and Yorkshire flag floor. A very large, solid wooden table stood in the middle of the room. Alan picked up and closed his DIY encyclopaedia.

Along one wall, modern kitchen units had been fitted. In a corner stood a solid fuel stove, providing comfort for the people huddled around it. One by one, they began to loosen their outdoor clothes and retreat from the overpowering heat. Best suits, black wool, polyester and red jersey were revealed once more as overcoats were piled onto the table.

There were only three chairs in the room. Lesley Connor sat in one, at one end of the large table. Her shot-putter stood guard behind the chair. The Greens occupied the remaining chairs. Teri seemed to be looking around for a waiter. Peter was looking down at the chair, as it creaked under his weight.

The hampers contained a cold buffet of Cordon Bleu quality, at odds with the paper plates, plastic glasses, napkins and disposable cutlery. Sam and Wendy set about laying out the buffet on the uncoated end of the table. George and Dixie opened bottles of wine and handed out beer cans from the third hamper. Alan disappeared to the living room, carrying his book.

Teri asked Sam "Have you really got no wine glasses? It's not the same in plastic." She was holding a plastic tumbler half full of white wine.

"There might be one in that cupboard, but don't tell everyone," whispered Sam.

George handed Sam a plastic tumbler peace offering, and asked, "White, Red or beer?"

"White, please," said Sam, accepting his apology. "Some mystery party!"

George filled the tumbler, put the wine bottles on the table and said, "Guided tour time. Come on."

"You're not going to get heavy with me, are you, George?"

"No, I promise. Just a look around."

With that, the pair left the kitchen and returned to the hall, where they had entered the house.

"Alan's done a hell of lot of work in here. The panels would have been a death trap in a fire, so he had to take them down, line them and treat the wood. The floor needed stripping and re-varnishing."

"What's through there?" George interrupted, pointing at a door off the hall.

"That's the old dining hall. We haven't started on it yet. It's filthy."

"What about that?" said George, pointing at another door.

"The living-room."

George wasn't interested, but instead turned to the staircase and said, "Let's see the upstairs."

They both walked over to the foot of the staircase. George suddenly turned and tried the handle of a door near the stairs. It rattled, but didn't open.

"What's in here?" he asked.

Sam hesitated. "Nothing, just a store cupboard."

"I'm sure I heard something in there," he said.

"Old houses sometimes play tricks on your ears. Come on, I'll show you the upstairs."

They climbed the stairs and upon reaching the top, Sam switched on the upstairs corridor lights, saying, "The toilet's the first left, here. Our bedroom's just over there. The other four bedrooms are off to the right there. We've only part decorated two of them. The others are pretty much as we found them."

"So, what's along here?" asked George turning down the left corridor past the toilet.

"The bathroom's next left. On the right is the upstairs sitting room. It's got a beautiful view down to the river. It's really peaceful and the wildlife is great to watch."

Sam opened the sitting room door and switched on the light as she entered. George followed her in and stood for a few seconds taking in the cosy feel of the room, even though his breath formed a freezing mist. At one end of the room was a coal fire, set ready for lighting. The opposite wall was taken up with bookshelves, untidily stuffed with books of varying sizes. Near the bookshelves stood a desk and a table. The desk surface was covered with open books, papers, office files and a computer. Almost the entire outside wall of the room was taken up by four pairs of tall French windows which opened onto a narrow balcony. The curtains were open, revealing outside, large snowflakes gently drifting Earthwards.

George walked over and stared out of the window. "So, do you own all that land out there?"

"Oh, no. We've just got the garden out front and a couple of acres. Alan's wild garden. The farmer kept all the fields around the house. Oh, and the drive's ours as well."

George turned his gaze on Sam. "I'm sorry for burdening you with my problem," he said, quite composed.

"George, I really wish I could help, but it's all under lock and key."

"It was wrong of me to ask. It's just that I get so depressed about it. Sorry. I sprung the party on you to get more time to talk. I thought I could persuade you to get me the stuff, but now I think I really will get a second opinion on surgery. Let's enjoy the night. You only live once, eh?" His laugh was forced, hollow and short-lived.

"Let's join the others," said Sam. She had no wish to rub salt on this particular wound.

George noticed a large, framed photograph on the wall near the door. It depicted a serene country garden, full of colour with delphinium, foxglove, aconite and lupin, rising above a sea of shorter blooms. Roses were climbing the walls of a stone-built house. George said, "That's pretty. Where was it taken?"

Sam said, "It's our front garden in the summer. We had the picture enlarged and framed to remind us what the place looks like when it's in full bloom. Cheers us up in the darkness of winter. Shall we go?"

They left the upstairs sitting room and turned left towards the top of the staircase. In the hall, downstairs a door slammed closed and a key rattled in a lock. Sam beckoned to George not to take the stairs but to continue down the dimly lit corridor. "This way, it's a short cut," she said.

"I thought you said your bedroom was down here?"

"It's alright you're quite safe, that is, if you want to be." She gave him a weak little girl smile. At the end of the corridor was a doorway which opened on to a small landing with one narrow staircase descending and another much narrower one leading upwards.

"The servants' staircase," Sam said, "That goes down to the kitchen, but they slept in the attic. It must have been a different world. We found sacks of old straw up there. I think they might have used it for bedding. The rooms up there are quite warm though, heat rises and all that. Do you fancy a quick look up? It won't take too long."

In the kitchen, as the servants' staircase door opened it nudged Wendy Simpson out of the way. George was the first to appear in the room, and apologised to Wendy. Sam followed, still clutching her plastic glass of white wine.

Rat Foster was standing near the back door peering out of a small window. "It's snowing," he said, but no-one acknowledged his observation.

Alan appeared at the hall doorway and invited everyone to come through to the newly warmed living room, where there would be seats for all. As the others left for the comfort of the living room, Dixie and Wendy remained in the kitchen, taking possession of two of the chairs near the stove.

Sam and Alan's small collection of music CDs proved to be a great disappointment to the party guests. Most of the music was either modern jazz or classical orchestral, neither of which appealed to Rat Foster, who had been appointed DJ for the night. He resorted to choosing the music with his eyes closed and ended up playing a CD with Tchaikovsky's Piano Concerto Number 1 and the greatest hits of some old Scandinavian rocker.

As the Berlin Philharmonic belted out *Finlandia* Rat said, "I give up. Snowing or not, I'm going outside for a smoke."

Most of the gathered company knew that Rat's idea of a smoke would not entail the use of tobacco, but no-one bothered to comment as he left the living room.

"Haven't you got any decent music – sixties stuff, maybe?" George complained to Sam.

"We don't really have time for a lot of music. We've got some old vinyl records."

"Anything's better than Beethoven for a party," said George.

"Sibelius," Sam corrected, "I'll go and find the records."

"I'll help you look," said Alan, "I think I know where they are."

The couple left the room and crossed the hall to the store cupboard door near the stairs. Alan unlocked the door and they both entered and descended the stairs. The cellar was divided into two by a modern white painted block wall, containing a heavy white PVC door. Alan opened a cupboard, found the box containing the vinyl records and brought it to the bottom of the stairs.

"Did you check them?" asked Sam.

"Yes, they're fine, but we might lose the backup supply."

"Let's have a look," said Sam, opening the white PVC door.

They both entered the room, unaware that someone had followed them down into the cellar. Sam walked over to the desktop computer and shook the mouse to clear the screensaver. The display showed a diagram of the small biochemical plant in the room. Along the bottom of the screen was a status bar showing a sequence of green lights with one rogue, flashing red light. As Sam clicked on the red light a new window opened.

"What do you think?" she asked.

"Battery volts are low. We'll have to get a new one, but it'll be okay for now. It should still have enough juice to start the set. Just hope we don't have a power cut," replied Alan.

"I was looking for the downstairs toilet," said a voice from behind in a southern accent.

Alan and Sam turned simultaneously with matching looks of panic on their faces. Peter Green was standing there, mouth open, his eyes darting around the room, taking in every detail. Sam regained control before Alan and said, "We haven't got one. You'll have to use the one upstairs."

She tried to turn the fat policeman away in the direction of the door, but he just stood rigid, staring at the stainless pipework and tanks in front of him.

"That's a hell of a central heating boiler. Looks very high tech. Bet it costs a fortune to run."

"Yes, it does. The toilet's upstairs," Sam said.

Peter kept looking at a large tank with a glass inspection window.

"Hang on. It's not a boiler at all, is it? What's happening in there? It's fizzing."

"Actually, it's a fermenter," said Alan, earning a look of annoyed incredulity from Sam.

"Oh, you make home brew? I do a bit myself, but mine's not high tech like this. I just put a beer kit in the bin, add two pounds of sugar, pitch the yeast, then keep it warm and wait. What are you making, lager or bitter?"

"It's lager," said Alan, as Sam came up with, "Bitter."

Alan said, "You know the way the Americans drink lager and call it beer? Well this is a sort of bitter lager beer, but we like it, and that's all that matters, eh?"

Peter's gaze fell on the top left-hand corner of the computer screen, at the box, labelled 'Fermenter Temperature'.

"Is that your bin temperature? Thirty-one degrees! Surely that's far too high? You'll kill the yeast, especially if it's a lager yeast. You should be keeping it below fifteen for lager yeast," he said.

"Oh, I can assure you, it's a special high temperature yeast," said Alan.

"Really? Where do you buy it? I've never come across high temperature lager yeast."

Sam came to the rescue. "We send away for it. It's only available by mail order."

"Madison's?" said Peter, nodding.

"Sorry?" said Sam.

"Madison's mail order brewing supplies. I always use them."

"No, some other firm. What was the name?" Sam said, looking at Alan.

"Er, it was … oh yes, Smith's mail order brewing supplies," was Alan's lame ad lib.

"Have you got a catalogue?" said Peter.

"No. It got pissed on by the cat," Sam answered quickly.

"So, where's Smith's then? Have you got an address for them?" asked Peter.

"Somewhere down South. Er, Folkestone, I think. Do you know Folkestone?" asked Sam.

"Well, it's funny you should say that, I know Folkestone really well. My parents live just outside. They retired there ten years ago. They used to pop over to France for day trips, but they can't really manage it now. I don't recall seeing any home brew firms called Smith's, though."

There was a short silence. Sam gave Peter a smile and tried flashing her mascara. The ex-policeman frowned and gave her a perplexed look.

Finally, Alan broke the silence. "Alabama," he said, like a grand master declaring checkmate.

"Alabama?" said Peter.

"Yes. Have you ever been to Alabama?"

"No, why?"

"It was Folkestone, Alabama, in the deep South. It's a special high temperature *American* bitter lager beer yeast, only available from Smith's in Folkestone, Alabama. You're sure you've never been to Alabama, have you?"

"Afraid not. But never mind, I'll look them up on the World Wide Web and get their address. I've got one of those modems, you know. Brilliant. Very useful."

Sam said, "We really must get back to the others, they'll be thinking we've got lost."

Before Sam could guide him out of the room, Green noticed a small stainless-steel tank labelled "THC". "What's in that little tank?" he asked.

"It's a super clearing agent, Tri-Hexyl Chloride. Makes the final beer sparkling and perfectly clear," said Sam.

Alan looked at her in awe of her incredible talent for keeping a straight face while telling whopping great lies. He anticipated the policeman's next question and had his answer ready – Smiths of Folkestone, Alabama.

Unfortunately, the policeman's piggy eyes picked up another part of the plant.

"That looks like a still. You're not distilling, are you?" he said.

"Yes, Why not?" Alan said, showing some irritation at the wrong question having been asked.

"It's illegal."

"Well it's not really a still. It's more of a concentration enhancer, just to make it a little bit stronger. It uses hydrogen-hydroxyl ion displacement," said Sam.

"Hmm, well that's a new one on me. Are you sure it's legal?"

"Oh yes!" said Sam, laughing confidently.

A small pump, somewhere in the labyrinth of pipework whirred into life for a couple of seconds. As it stopped, the computer beeped and a box appeared on the screen. Sam managed to stand in front of the screen and hide the message before piggy eyes could get a glimpse. She reached behind her back and tapped the space bar to clear the message.

Sam looked Green straight in the eyes, without a trace of a smile. Her breathing was deep and noisy. "It's a hobby! Would you deny anybody the pleasure of flower arranging, pigeon racing, brass rubbing, tangerine desiccation or even precision home brewing? It's a hobby, and we enjoy it, so what's wrong with that?"

Peter jumped back in surprise. "Oh, nothing, it just looks very complicated. I didn't mean to pry. Just seems like a lot of work for a pint of beer. But fair enough, each to his own. Shouldn't you be getting back to the others. They'll be wondering where you've got to."

Sam pressed home her attack, pointing at a motorised valve. "Don't you want to know what this bit's for?"

"Shush!" said Alan. He had noticed, what his partner had missed – that Peter's body language was screaming loudly that the policeman was about to disgrace himself at any second.

"Upstairs, you said?" Peter confirmed, as he hurried out of the room and hauled himself, wheezing, up the cellar stairs.

As soon as Peter was out of earshot, Alan said, "Nosey bastard. Typical copper. Still, I think we got away with it."

"You think so?" said Sam, "He could be trouble. Let's just see what happens." The couple then left their biochemical plant room, locked up and took the old vinyl records up to the living room.

An exhilarating walk in the snow, a dose of skunk and the arrival of vintage sixties vinyl transformed the miserable Rat back into a swinging disc jockey. The living room reverberated to the sounds of 'Aftermath' by the Rolling Stones. As if attracted by the change in musical style, Dixie and Wendy entered the room looking slightly dishevelled, like teenagers after a snogging session.

By the time that Jagger was belting out 'Under My Thumb', Lesley, her girlfriend and the Greens were all up, attempting to dance in the middle of the large room. Dixie and Wendy joined in with their own brand of close coupled waltzing.

Sam, who had been reminiscing with George, decided to go to the kitchen to open another bottle of white wine. As she left, Malcolm Burke looked around the room, then rose to his feet and followed, unnoticed by all except George.

In the kitchen, Sam bent down to take a bottle from the fridge. Before she could decide which bottle to open, she felt a hand on her bottom. "You'll have to wait till they've all gone, sweetie," she said. She turned with a smile on her face, pouting for Alan. The smile was immediately erased as she found that the hand belonged to Malcolm Burke.

"It's been a long time, Sammy," he said, crowding her against the open fridge.

"Not long enough, Burke," she hissed, pushing him away.

"We've got unfinished business."

"Okay. You want some more, do you?" She laughed as she closed the fridge.

In the hall, George Wilson approached the kitchen door, wondering why Burke had followed Sam. His suspicions had been aroused as he'd observed the stares earlier in the evening. The noise from the living room subsided to an amplified hiss as the stylus followed the groove between tracks. From upstairs came the muffled sound of a female voice shouting "You've had what?"

As George reached for the kitchen door handle, the front door bell distracted him. In the living room, the next track had just started. The noise was so loud that nobody could have heard the bell, so George went to answer it himself. There was a rumble of distant thunder as he opened the large oak door, revealing a young couple, who almost collapsed into the hall. Their clothes were covered in wet snow. The young man was wearing thin trousers and tee-shirt, while his companion wore a full-length coat. Their faces were dripping with water, their hair and eyebrows still covered in melting ice. Entering the house, the young girl began to cry. Her male friend started to talk, but he was shivering so violently that his speech was almost completely garbled. Individual words like 'Car', 'Stuck' and 'Freezing' told the story. George forgot all about his Burke-stalking and switched to emergency hospitality mode, quickly escorting the couple into the warm living room. Wendy released her grip on Dixie and took over from George, mothering the youngsters. Wet coats were removed, towels found, hair dried and seats commandeered near the fire.

Rat turned the music down while the young couple started telling the story of their battle with the blizzard. They had become stuck on the hill on the main road half a mile south of the track leading to the old farmhouse. The young girl, Catherine, told of how she and Bob had been heading for Chester-Le-Street from Barnard Castle, when the snow had started. Conditions had deteriorated rapidly until everything was white before they eventually slid to a halt on the hill, unable to make any progress, having gone off the road.

George, who had been listening attentively to the young girl, suddenly remembered about his earlier quest and looked around for Sam. She and Burke were still missing. George smelled a rat and decided to investigate, but before he could rise from his chair, Sam appeared in the doorway. She gave a perplexed look at the newly arrived couple, but then ignored them and made her way quickly to Alan.

She whispered in his ear, "Have you got a minute? It's Burke. He's had a little accident."

Alan's reaction was as lightning-fast as that of a man who'd been drinking since eight o'clock – his reply an urgent whisper, "What? Where is he?"

"Back stairs," said Sam.

As they crossed the hall to the main staircase Alan asked, "What happened? Is he badly hurt?"

She said, "I'm pretty sure that he's not in pain."

Alan's brain was in the slow lane. "Well if he's not in pain and he's not badly hurt, what's the problem?"

"Well, I don't think he's ever going to feel pain again. I think I've killed him."

"What!" cried Alan, loudly. Then in a subdued tone, "What happened? Maybe he's not actually dead. Maybe he's just unconscious."

They quickly climbed the stairs and hurried along the upstairs corridor through the doorway to the servants' staircase. Burke's body lay on the landing, at the foot of the attic stairs, his eyes wide open and his head facing almost completely backwards in a pose which could never be sustained in life. A large purple bruise had appeared on his neck, where a bone was trying to burst through his skin. There was a small pool of blood next to his right hand. The end of his thumb was missing.

Alan leant over the body, placed his fingers around the wrist and felt for a pulse. He then checked for breathing before looking up and shaking his head at Sam.

"If he's not dead, he must be very uncomfortable," she said.

"How did it happen?"

"He tried to rape me again. Caught me unawares in the kitchen then forced me up to the attic, the bastard."

"Again?" asked Alan, "What do you mean *again*?"

"It was ages ago, just after we left school. He'd been trying it on for weeks, then one night he caught me, pulled me into the bushes and knelt on me while he got ready. I tried to shout for help. He put his hand over my mouth to stop me screaming, so I bit his thumb off. That stopped him."

"But you never told me about it. Didn't you report it?"

"He didn't get very far. It wasn't all that important. Anyway, the police didn't treat it the same in those days, did they? I dealt with him myself. I crunched his thumb up and spat it out at him, then told him I'd kill him if he ever came near me again. Tonight, he used his other hand to keep me quiet, so I bit his other thumb. Then when he backed off, I gave him a little kick and he sort of fell down the stairs."

It would be wrong to say that there was no emotion in Sam's voice. This was no frightened little girl, no whimpering weakling. It was the ruthless Amazon warrior talking, showing no regret or pity, only contempt. The man, Burke, deserved all he had received at her hands.

"I think his neck's broken," said Alan, "Must have been when he fell."

"They'll call it self-defence," said George Wilson, appearing through the open door, "Better call the police."

Alan and Sam looked around in surprise. Alan froze like a rabbit caught in headlights, his jaw dropping.

"No," said Sam, "No cops. We need to get rid of the body."

Alan chipped in with, "No. We can't have the police coming around here. No, no, not a good idea."

"I don't think they would believe us after the last time," Sam said. Alan looked at her with his mouth wide open.

She said, "Six years ago, when we lived near Houghton, a group of fell walkers called at the house one evening."

"Hang on! Houghton must be twenty or thirty miles away from the nearest fells," George said.

Sam shrugged. "They were lost. I don't know. Anyway, one of them went missing after they left. They never found him, but the police questioned us for days afterwards. Even then they didn't believe us, but they had no evidence, so the case was dropped. But during their bloody searches they busted us for hash. If they find out about this, they'll put two and two together and make five. You know what they're like. You've got to help us to get rid of this, please George." Sam finished her helpless little girl performance with a few flickers of her eyelashes.

"I can't, Sam. The police have all kinds of forensic tests nowadays. They'll find out. Then we'll all be in the shit. I'll be an accessory after the fact or whatever they call it. If you don't report it, that will make you look guilty. You'll get life. Alan and me, we'll each get ten years. You'll come out an old woman, Alan an old man and I'll die in jail. Is that what you want?"

Alan said, "What do you mean? Die in jail?"

George replied, "Well, it could happen."

The point had not been lost on Sam, who sensed a mixture of blackmail and barter in George's plea. Smiling, her coded response was, "Okay, George. You help us with our headache, and some-day soon, maybe we could help you with one of yours."

This brought about a complete reversal of George's attitude. He suggested temporarily hiding the body in one of the attic rooms. Sam fetched a sheet from the bedroom to prevent any DNA or fibres getting onto the body as it was being lifted up the staircase. George took the arms and started dragging the corpse towards the attic. Alan followed, holding the legs. As the body was hauled up, the head snagged on each riser and had to be flicked up diabolo-style, by George, to land with a dull thud on the next tread until it finally reached the attic landing. The two men then hoisted the late Malcolm Burke into a small child's bed in a dusty, darkened room, leaving him doubled up.

Alan took an old woodworm-riddled chair from the attic to the bottom of the staircase and jammed it behind the kitchen door to block access to the scene of the death. Sam and George dragged a heavy chest of drawers in front of the landing door after allowing Alan to escape from the back stairs. The three then adjourned to the upstairs sitting room to concoct a story to explain Burke's disappearance. They decided that the best approach would be to feign complete ignorance of Burke's whereabouts. The party would have to be brought to an end as quickly as possible. George agreed to return the following day to sort out the details of the final disposal. Sam and Alan returned to the downstairs living room after calling into the kitchen to pick up more wine. George went to the bathroom, waited for a few minutes, then flushed the toilet and returned to the party.

Young Bob and Catherine were fully recovered from their unpleasant stroll in the snow. Sam, completely unaffected by her own ordeal, introduced herself to the pair and asked if they would like some food. Bob looked slightly disappointed as Catherine smiled and declined saying, "No thank you, we're not very hungry right now. It's very kind of you to let us dry off. I'm so sorry that we've spoilt your party. If we could use the telephone to call a taxi, we'll get going. Thank you."

Sam noticed Bob's chagrin and said to him, "The kitchen's just out there across the hall, if you'd like to help yourself, there's a huge buffet on the table. Shame to waste it. Please help yourself."

Turning to Catherine, she said, "First of all, you haven't spoilt anything. The party's just about over. And, I don't know if you'll get a taxi to Chester-Le-Street at this time of night, but there's a minibus due for Durham, and if you'd like to stay for the night, I'm sure George will arrange free accommodation at the Royal."

For a moment Sam stared at the young girl, thinking back to her own youth. Catherine's hair was the same shade of blonde as her own, except that while Sam's was natural, the young girl's was showing signs of darkening at the roots. As for owning a car at such a tender age, that would be out of the question. Far too expensive.

George arrived in the room, asked Rat to turn the music down and brought Sam back to full consciousness as he announced loudly to everyone, "Well, I'm sure we'd all like to thank Alan and Sam for their hospitality, but we'll have to be getting back to Durham. The bus will be here in a quarter of an hour."

He nodded to Rat, who brought up the volume again, then, leaving for the relative quiet of the hall, he took out his mobile phone to call 'The Royal'. On his way out, George held the door open for Bob, who appeared carrying a large plateful of the gourmet buffet.

"It's only one o'clock!" Peter Green complained to Alan, "And we haven't even sampled your home brew yet."

"Come on, Alan," said Wendy, "It's only just warming up. Tell him, John."

"You've been brewing your own? Let's have a try of it, Al," said Dixie.

"You should see his brewery. It's fantastic! Down in the cellar," blabbed the policeman.

Alan, stuck for answers, looked over to Sam, who smiled and said, "Okay, one for the road. I'll not be a minute."

Crossing the hall to the kitchen, Sam passed George. He was holding his phone to his ear and said, "I've only got one bar."

Sam said, "Really? A big place like the Royal. I thought you'd have quite a few. Public bar, lounge, residents' bar, upstairs bar, downstairs bar."

George said, "On the phone."

Sam said quietly, "Sorry, I thought you were talking to me." She left George to continue his call and went to the kitchen.

George took the phone away from his ear and shook his head. He walked over to the front door and re-dialled, again without success. From the kitchen, came the sound of a door closing. After ten minutes of failing to connect, he decided to try upstairs. This time he got through. A couple of minutes later, in the hall, he was returning his mobile phone to his pocket when Sam re-appeared, struggling to carry two very large, white glazed, earthenware jugs. George stared at the foaming contents. "Home brew," said Sam. As he held open the living room door for her, he felt a few drops of water fall from her hair onto his hand. Looking down, he noticed that her shoes were wet.

Sam filled Peter's plastic glass with the frothy beer as Alan looked on in amazement, wondering how on Earth his partner had concocted something to resemble home brewed beer in such a short time. George took a small tumbler full. As Peter gulped down his first pint, his expert opinion was that the American lager-beer was quite palatable, maybe a little too bitter, and he wasn't too keen on the slight soapy aftertaste. Oh, and it appeared to be quite cloudy. Obviously, that 'Hexyl' stuff wasn't very good at clearing the beer. None of the shortcomings could prevent him from having two large refills, almost completely draining one of the jugs.

Dixie simply accepted the beer and, having taken a sip, diplomatically put his plastic tumbler on a coffee table where it would remain for the rest of the night. Wendy asked Dixie if she could try his beer, but decided not to bother when he slowly shook his head with his tongue sticking out slightly from his open mouth. "Tastes like tea sea fee," he whispered from the corner of his mouth, through closed ventriloquist teeth.

After ten minutes of winding down, Alan and Sam's guests were ready to leave, anticipating the arrival of the minibus by finishing off their drinks. George stood in the hall, ostensibly looking out for the minibus, as he kept an eye on anyone going upstairs to use the bathroom, just to make sure they didn't wander too far.

At two o'clock the minibus still hadn't appeared. George made another call from half-way up the stairs and then announced that the roads were blocked and it would be another hour before their transport would arrive. It was time for party games.

Most of the guests were, like Alan and Sam, just a tiny bit drunk, and in one case, quite stoned. As they had played all of the record collection twice over, Alan suggested that they have a game of *confessions* while they waited for the minibus. Each player would write a personal question on a piece of paper and all of the questions would go into a hat. The first player would take a question from the hat and pose it to the person on their left. This would continue until all pieces of paper had been removed from the hat. Sam left the room to get a hat, returning a minute later, giggling, with a plant pot on her head. "Haven't got a hat," she slurred.

Dixie drew the first question and asked Wendy, "Er, how many sides has a dodecahedron?"

This prompted various discussions about the object of the game while George and Alan argued about geometric terminology. Finally, Rat, admitting his mistake said, "Sorry Wendy, my fault. Might have got it wrong. Okay. A *personal* question, right? Here we go. Er, what was your worst trip?"

"Oh, that's easy, John. Going to hospital to have my eye operation." In the absence of any members of the judiciary, Wendy was the most sober person in the room. She smiled. "I never did drugs."

After a short pause Wendy pulled out a question. "Oh, this is a saucy one! Where did you lose your virginity, George?"

"Behind a bus shelter," he replied.

"A bus shelter?" came in a poorly synchronised chorus.

After a fleeting glance at Sam, George said, "I didn't make a habit of it. Only once." Before anyone

63

could challenge him further, he pulled out another question. and quickly asked, "What was your biggest mistake in life, Teri?"

"Being born in a pit village," was Mrs. Green's succinct answer.

The game continued for ten minutes, but then degenerated into chaos as the rules gradually changed such that anyone could ask any question of any other player as long as no-one else could shout louder. Eventually things began to descend into a sleepy silence. Sam and George were sitting on the sofa. She turned to him, picked up a discarded piece of paper and pretended to read from it in a soft voice. "Why did you get sacked on your first day at the pit?"

George yawned and said, "Well, I lit up when I got out of the cage at the Hutton seam. Jimmy Sands started on me so I brayed him with my shovel."

Sam looked into his eyes and said, "You're not very good at telling fibs, are you? As I recall, you never smoked a cigarette in your life. Couldn't stand the smell."

George gave a little grin then took a deep breath. "You always were the clever bugger, weren't you? Okay. The truth is that on my first shift I got out at the Hutton seam and Jimmy was there. He started slagging off my dad, saying that he was a lazy bastard – that he was sending me down so that he could work less overtime. He said that my father wanted me earning money, so that he could go pissing it against the wall in the big club."

The room light reflected like diamonds in Ginger George's eyes as he continued, "The pit was killing my father. He'd worked down there all his life to support us and his lungs were shot. I couldn't bear to see him coughing up all that crap, so I left school to help out. I could always go to college later, I thought. Funny. It never works out the way you think, does it? Anyway, the rest's history. I lost my rag and gave Jimmy a bit of a slap or two. He came at me with a shovel. I grabbed it and shoved the handle in his face. Broke his nose and got the sack for it. Got a canny belting when I got home. I couldn't tell my dad the truth. He'd have gone and picked a fight. Jimmy would have killed him. He only lasted four years after that. Pneumoconiosis." George held his plastic glass to his lips, toying with the idea of taking a drink. Instead he said, "It's strange, isn't it? When you think about it, Jimmy Sands did me a favour. If I hadn't been sacked, I could have been stuck down the pit, like my dad – coughing my guts up on my way to an early death. As it turned out I can have an early death without the cough and I don't even have to get my hands dirty at work."

Sam gave him a peck on the cheek and whispered, "Meth 4's going to fix you. It's a totally new class of drug. You'll see."

The minibus arrived at three thirty. After picking their way through the slush in front of the old farmhouse, the partygoers climbed slowly aboard,. Peter Green had to be hoisted aboard as he seemed to be incapable of lifting his foot onto the first step. The shot putter obliged with a hearty laugh, shoving the drunken copper up the bus steps. George counted everyone onto the bus and was about to give the driver the go ahead just as Lesley Connor noticed that Burke was missing. After a few shouts of "Has anybody seen Malcolm?" went without answer, George explained that Burke lived in Durham and had probably decided to walk home.

As the minibus left, Sam and Alan went indoors, closing the heavy front door on an all too eventful night, and retired to bed.

"The snow's melting," said Alan as he lay in the dark, "Babies are alright. What did you mean about curing headaches? How come you didn't tell me about Malcolm Burke before now? Are you asleep?" There was no reply.

He turned away from Sam saying, "I don't remember any fell walkers at Houghton. And we never got busted."

Chapter 3

Sunday 2nd April 1995

The fields around the old farmhouse were still virgin white from the previous night, as George negotiated the rough track down the hill. Potholes and slush conspired to give the steering wheel a mind of its own as he fought to drive a straight line. At the bottom of the hill the white Ford estate skidded slightly as he parked near the front door.

George walked over the puddled gravel to the open porch. Not having found a bell-push, he knocked on the solid oak door. This made very little noise, but did succeed in skinning his knuckles on the rough, weather-blasted surface. Suddenly, from within, a loud bell sounded. Its raucous clamour, which had distracted him from following Burke in the early hours, now drilled into his ears and rattled his brain. He reached into his pocket for the codeine, as the door opened and Alan said, "Hi, George. Oh dear, you've got a hangover as well. Went on a bit, didn't it? Come in. Did everybody get back alright?"

Holding a slack handful of pills in his open palm, George confirmed that the surviving partygoers had all been safely returned to their hotel, except for Rat, who was dropped off at his home on the way back to Durham.

As they walked across the hall towards the kitchen, Alan turned to George and said, "It's really good of you to help us out like this. If there's anything we can do for you at any time, just ask."

George coughed as one of his tablets seemed to have stuck in his throat.

They both joined Sam in the kitchen and quickly got down to the business of the disposal of Burke's body.

Sam said, "Why don't we tie a sack of stones around his neck and chuck him in the river? It's only a few hundred yards away."

George said, "No, no. If the sack rotted, the body might float to the surface, or it could be found by anglers. What about an acid bath? That would do the trick, wouldn't it?"

Sam said, "Oh George! Really! That sounds like something a serial killer might do. And besides, where would we get a bathful of concentrated sulphuric? It's not cheap, you know."

Alan floated his idea. "How about just throwing him off a cliff? Then that would explain the broken neck and all of the bruising. And with a bit of luck he'd hit the rocks below and end up unrecognisable. Or, if the tide was in, he might get washed out to sea to feed the fishes and never be seen again."

George laughed and said, "That would make him the fall guy … Get it?"

Alan thought for a few seconds and said, "A fall guy? … Oh yes, right. I get it – falling off a cliff. Very good." Alan wasn't laughing.

George then shot down Alan's brilliant idea. "No good, sorry. We'd have to take him to the coast and dump him without being seen. Then the coppers would be asking how he came to be wandering on the cliff tops twenty miles away after leaving the party."

Alan rose to his feet and went to put the kettle on. "Tea or coffee?" he asked.

"No. You're right," said Sam, suddenly inspired, "You don't need to go twenty miles. There's a sheer drop in Whitehouse Wood. It's only a couple of miles away – on the way to Durham." She paused for more inspiration. "And ... Burke would have taken the shortest route home. And that's through Whitehouse Wood. He lost his way in the blizzard and fell from the top to the bottom, breaking his good-for-nothing neck in the process. Brilliant!"

Alan turned, holding the kettle, and gave a full, toothy grin.

"Lover's Leap," said George, "I know the place. Yeah, sounds good. We'll need to dump him there tonight when it's dark. Only trouble is that it's a full moon. We'll have to wait and see if there's any cloud cover. Meanwhile we need to keep the body cold. The police use temperature to estimate time of death. Seen it on the telly. If he'd been out all night, his body temperature would be quite low by now. Do you have a large freezer we could use?"

"We've got a chest freezer in the cellar," said Alan.

Sam gave Alan one of her looks and said, "It's full of food. Remember?"

George said, "Oh hell! What a choice! Lose a hundred quid's worth of food or lose your freedom for ten years with good behaviour. Let's see, that's about ten quid a year. I know what I'd do."

"Okay, okay," said Sam, "I'll go and sort out the freezer while you and Alan bring Burke down."

"Is that his coat?" asked George, looking at the sheepskin, still on the table from the night before.

"Yes, that's his. He'll need it on him if he was walking home. He could catch his death," said Sam.

The two men went upstairs. Sam took a dustsheet down to the cellar and moved the plastic bottles to one end of the chest freezer, making room for the body. She then covered the bottles with the dustsheet. A few minutes later George and Alan carried Burke's body down the cellar steps and dumped it in the freezer, still doubled up and now wearing his sheepskin coat. Sam closed the lid.

Looking around the cellar, George seemed to be fascinated by the contents of a set of shelves, full of laboratory apparatus. He said, "Wow, what's all the glassware for? This place is like the chemistry prep room at school." His hand alighted on an intricate piece of glass equipment.

"Please be careful with it," said Sam, "It's easily broken."

"What does it do?" said George, gingerly withdrawing his hand from the priceless antique.

"That's an old Soxhlet's apparatus," said Sam, "Used for extracting alkaloids from plant material. We were going to use it as a coffee percolator, but then we bought a cafetiere instead."

"What's this little gadget for?" George was staring down the funnel of a motorised machine with lots of cogs and cams.

Alan said, "It's a pill press. They used them at Falmer's for small runs of tablets. It's an old one which doesn't work, so I brought it home to see if we could use it for anything, but we'll probably just chuck it out. I might strip the motor off it."

Sam nodded and thought how encouraging it was that her partner was picking up the art of telling untruths so convincingly.

The three then climbed the cellar steps and returned to the warmth of the kitchen.

George sipped his tea and said, "We'll have to leave him in the freezer for about six hours, I reckon. Then we'll put him in my boot and drive over to the wood. There's a lane which leads to within a hundred yards of the cliff. We'll need to carry him to the top and then push him off. Or we could just leave him at the bottom. It'll be fairly dark by then, so there shouldn't be any witnesses."

Turning to Sam, George asked, "When do you think you could get the stuff?"

Alan asked, "What stuff?"

"You didn't tell him?" said George.

Sam explained to Alan about George's cancer and that she had agreed to try to get a course of Meth 4.

"But it's…" Alan started.

"…kept under lock and key at Falmer's and we don't have access to the lab," said Sam, "But I'm going to try to get some."

The conversation was interrupted by the front door bell. Alan left the room to answer it. A minute later he appeared with a very worried looking John Foster.

"Hi Rat," said George, "Come back to borrow some Beethoven?"

"I've lost my stuff," said Rat, "I had it when I went out for a smoke, but it's gone. There's about a hundred and fifty quid's worth. You haven't seen a green plastic tobacco pouch, have you?"

"Sorry mate," said Sam, "You can have a look around the living room and hall if you like. George, will you help him look?"

George went with Rat to carry out a search of all of the rooms that Rat could remember being in the previous night.

As the kitchen door closed, Alan said, "You can't give him any of that. It's not assayed. And, the trials haven't even started yet. There could be all kinds of side effects. It could even be toxic to humans for all we know."

"He's desperate. They've given him six months. The pre-clinical work shows its efficacy. A hundred percent success in rodent trials. There's a good chance it'll save him. We can take a little bit from each run and replace it with stearate to make up the weight. Then we make some excuse about the process having a problem and it looks like the yield is down," said Sam.

"If we get caught, Falmer's will sue for everything we've got. That NDA is very specific. We'd probably get jail," Alan said, "I knew we shouldn't have gone to that damned reunion."

"They wouldn't risk a court case. We've got too much on them. It would get very messy for them. George's helping us, and part of the bargain was that he gets the pills. I can't see how we can do anything else," said Sam.

"I'll think of something," said Alan, obviously very unhappy at the prospect of having to steal the new wonder drug.

Shortly, George returned with the broken-hearted Rat, mourning the loss of his excellent weed. Sam expressed her deepest condolences at Rat's bereavement, saying that she would keep an eye out for the pouch.

Alan said, "You might have dropped it in the snow. Should I come and help you look?"

"No thanks. I've already had a good look around outside," said Rat, "Just have to get some more. Cheers!"

Alan walked Rat to the front door and said, "It's not the end of the world, mate. Just think – It'll be cheap as chips when it's legalised. Here, try these for now. It's good shit." With this, he slipped two dozen white pills into Rat's hand.

"Cheers Al," said Rat, "But I wouldn't get your hopes up about them legalising it any time soon. Just 'cos they've had an enquiry. There's too much vested interest in alcohol."

Alan returned to the kitchen and said, "Poor Rat. He's spent his last few quid on the stash and now he's lost it."

"Poor Rat?" laughed George, "He's loaded. He dresses like a tramp and always looks like he can't afford a razor, but I wish I was a few grand behind him."

George tried his tea, which had gone cold. He then left, saying that he would return after sunset to take the body to the woods.

* * * *

At six thirty George returned, parked up and winced as the bell started to ring. Sam answered the door. She was dressed in a disposable coverall with gloves, mop cap and overshoes.

"Where's the doorbell? he asked.

"It's automatic; Al made it; it's supposed to detect an approaching body and ring the bell, but sometimes it doesn't work until you're right up close. Still it saves all that finger work."

What Sam failed to mention was that the bell was designed to be more of an intruder alarm than a conventional door bell and that there were hidden CCTV cameras around the house to monitor visitors.

As they crossed the hall, Sam gave George his protective clothing. At the cellar door George asked, "Where's Al?"

Sam said, "He's just popped out for a walk. The door's open. Could you get Burke out of the freezer? Oh, but put your gear on first. We don't want to leave any forensic evidence. I'll get something to wrap him in."

George went down and started to investigate the cellar. He tried the handle of the PVC door but couldn't open it. He could just make out a high-pitched beeping noise coming from behind the door. As he scanned the shelves near the freezer, he noticed that the pill machine was now missing.

Having put on the protective clothing, he lifted the lid of the chest freezer and saw that the dustsheet and whatever had been hidden by it, had been removed. As he lifted Burke's body, a small plastic bottle, full of a clear, viscous liquid, fell from the coat pocket. He lifted the stiff body out and propped it up against the freezer, then took the bottle and replaced it in the pocket of the sheepskin.

As George stared at the bruising on the neck he wondered if the body was now too stiff. Maybe it was starting to freeze. Six hours might have been too long. He poked at the face and jumped as a voice behind him said, "I don't know what's happened to Al. He should be back by now."

Sam was at the bottom step and continued, "We'll just have to carry him up ourselves. I'll take the feet and go first."

They took the body up the cellar steps, across the hall and laid it against the wall near the front door. George went to his car and opened the tailgate.

"Let's get him into the boot," said Sam, "We can wrap him in this for the journey to the woods. Don't want him catching a cold, or shedding forensics, do we?" She was holding a clean dustsheet and a large skein of thin polypropylene rope.

"Don't you want to wait for Al?" asked George.

"Oh, I forgot, he said we should go ahead without him if he was late getting back from the shops," said Sam.

"I thought he was out for a walk?"

"Yes … He went out for a walk to the shops about an hour ago. Come on, give me a hand to wrap this bastard up," she said.

George said nothing. He silently applied himself to the task in hand as a loud-hailer in his head urged caution. The lady seemed to be protesting far too much. Had she been having an affair with Burke? Had they argued at the party? He'd heard her shouting at him. And what about the fell walker? Had she seduced him and then silenced him for good? Maybe George's first conquest had evolved into a serial killer. Alan was now missing. Was she working her way through all the men who'd slept with her – repaying them as a Black Widow might? Was he to be her next victim because he knew too much, or simply because of their history? As he looked down at the makeshift body-bag, bulging with half-frozen limbs, he knotted the rope around the sheet and jumped out of his skin for the second time in five minutes, as he heard a clicking noise. Looking up, he saw that Sam was pointing a flick knife at him.

"No, no. Don't do it!" said George.

The blade glinted as she raised it higher. "Don't be silly, George. We don't want any loose ends, do we? Lift your head up and hold still, then everything will be just fine."

The blade descended faster than a guillotine. "There, now, that's better, isn't it?" she said, "I don't mind having to burn the old sheet, but all that rope? No way am I going to waste all of it on Burke. It's not cheap, you know."

George froze, looking at the end of the plastic cord, less than an inch away from his right hand. The cut was clean. He said, "What have you got that thing for? It's lethal!"

"What? This little toy?" she said, carefully retracting the blade, "I can't use an ordinary pen knife because my thumbnails are weakened by a fungal infection. So, I've got this instead. Don't worry. It couldn't cut butter." Most of what she said was perfectly true, with the notable exception of the last sentence. The knife blade had been honed to scalpel standard. Butter could have been parted by it, one molecule at a time.

George was still breathing heavily after the shock of being confronted by the knife-wielding serial killer. The chances of ever seeing Alan alive again were getting slimmer by the minute. If she'd knocked him off, then George would be the only person who knew the truth about his homicidal ex-girlfriend. George's first instinct was self-preservation by legging it as fast as he could, but with his reactions dulled by his codeine fix, he doubted if he could outrun Sam to the driver's door. There was nothing for it but to humour her until he could make good his escape. He insisted that Sam should take Burke's legs and go first, so he didn't have to turn his back on her.

On the approach to the entrance of Whitehouse Wood, the tyres of the Ford estate car crunched through the ice, which hours earlier, had been a churned-up covering of muddy slush. Headlights were switched off for the final fifty metres, before the car came to a halt in a small carpark at the end of the lane. The branches of the bushes, like skinny black limbs and gnarled arthritic fingers of a hundred witches, glistened in the eerie light around the car. For five minutes there was no movement, save the witches' fingers shivering in the slight breeze, casting long shadows on the icy ground. Then all faded to darkness as clouds began to cover the moon. George and Sam opened their doors and looked around. Seeing no potential witnesses, they silently opened the tailgate and withdrew the body from the boot.

George took the legs and Sam led the way, holding the head end. The requirement for total silence precluded any exhortation of *Left, Right, Left Right* in order to synchronise their steps. After a few paces, Sam slipped on the ice. George then hoisted Burke's body onto his shoulders and struggled down the path to the bottom of the hill, walking sideways for the steeper parts. Sam followed, carrying the torch. On reaching level ground, they left the path and headed to the bottom of the cliff. As they crushed frosted vegetation under foot, a pungent smell of onions was released by the ramsons, growing in the shade of the cliff.

Sam switched on the torch and picked out a prickly shrub. George placed the cadaver behind the bush and untied the rope holding the dustsheet in place. Sam switched off the torch and helped him to remove the dustsheet from the body. George snapped a few of the branches above the body to make it look as if Burke had fallen through the bushes. Sam stood back while he bowed his head as if in prayer. She jumped back as George turned and vomited, missing her by inches.

They made their way quickly back up the hill as the black witches made another appearance. In the moonlight, Sam and George removed their coveralls and slumped into the front seats of the car. The protective clothing, along with the dustsheet and rope, was bundled into a plastic bin bag, tossed over into the back seat.

She said, "He really was a bastard. A complete male chauvinist pig. Took what he wanted from women and never gave anything back."

George pushed the key into the steering column lock, then looked in the rear-view mirror. He said, "Shit! There's somebody out there."

Sam looked around and could make out the silhouette of a stooping figure against the moonlight. "Bollocks! He's taking down your registration!" she said, "We'll have to get rid of the old tosser."

"No, no!" said George, "There must be a better way. It's still not too late to go to the cops."

After a moment's thought Sam said, "You're right. We can do it the easy way."

"Eh?" said the sexual tutor.

"Come here," the fearless Amazon said, as she reclined her seat fully, "Make him think we're here for something else."

"What, you mean…"

In no time, the Amazon had taken charge and was sitting over her victim. This time her knickers were to be off for much longer than two minutes. She had a vantage point which allowed her to enforce an improvement in her sexual tutor's endurance while checking for the moonlit silhouette in the rear windscreen. The Amazon was on top of her game.

"I think it's an old woman," said Sam as she slowly bobbed up and down. George was far too pre-occupied to comment. After five minutes, the person in the rear windscreen had disappeared and Sam gave George her undivided attention. Twenty minutes later, with the steamed-up windows beginning to frost over, the Amazon was satisfied that they could safely stop pretending to enjoy themselves.

On the way back to the farmhouse George asked, "Shouldn't we have taken some precautions?"

"What do you mean?" she said, "I don't think they'll find him for a while, and we both had gloves on. I'll burn all the over-clothing... Oh, you mean afterwards. You haven't had a vasectomy, then?"

"Well, no. Aren't you worried you might get pregnant? Or have you gone past the what's-its-name?" said George, remembering the result of their teenage encounter.

Sam smiled and paused for a moment before answering. "Chance would be a fine thing. I'm not past the menopause, but I'm still just as infertile as I ever was," she said, "We tried for kids years ago and got nowhere. I checked Alan out myself, and he was fine. So it was obviously my fault. When I was younger, I'd had a mild form of endometriosis, which makes it difficult to conceive."

"You didn't get professional help?"

"No need. I can count tadpoles under a microscope. I didn't see the point of going to the quacks about it. It's very personal and a little embarrassing. Anyway, you've got nothing to worry about on that front."

After a minute Sam asked, "You got any kids, George?"

"No. More's the pity. I really wanted them, but Sheila didn't. I mean, it's very important that two people agree on such a fundamental thing as having kids. I would have loved to have had a family. It would have been great to have watched them growing up; playing football with them; being a dad. It's the biggest regret of my whole life. But she just refused point blank. She wanted me to get the snip, but I wasn't going to have that. That's basically why we parted. Divorced twelve years ago."

"You've been single ever since?"

"Yes. Well, I've had a few girlfriends but none of them impressed me enough to be serious."

"I don't remember you being that fussy." Sam laughed.

"I've matured," he said.

They left the main road and started down the track towards the house.

"You really should get these potholes filled in," said George, as the car bumped from side to side.

"Fancy a coffee?" asked Sam.

"No thanks. I'd better dash. Need an early night. It's work tomorrow," said George, trying not to sound as if he feared for his life at her hands.

Just then the house door opened and Alan walked out, but stopped short of standing on the ice which had formed over the gravel. He gestured for George to come to the house. Seeing that Alan was still in the land of the living was such a relief to George that he decided to stay for a while.

As they crossed the hall towards the kitchen, Alan said, "I've got something for you."

George said, "Oh, that's what you were doing at the shops this afternoon, buying me a present. You really didn't need to."

"What?" said Alan, "Don't be daft. The shops are shut. It's Sunday. No, what I've got for you is definitely not available over-the-counter."

As they entered the kitchen, Alan took a small pill bottle from a cupboard and placed it on the table.

"Methyphenax four," he said, as he stood back with a flourish of his hand, like a magician waiting for applause.

"Where did you get them?" asked George, "I thought they were under lock and key at Falmer labs."

"Ask no questions, matey," Alan replied, his index finger touching the side of his nose.

George took the bottle and pocketed it, saying, "How many do I take? How often? How long does it take to work?"

"Not sure," Sam said, "We're not certain how strong they are yet. Try one every eight hours for the first week. It might be best to ask your consultant for some mild palliative chemo. That way you can explain any shrinkage in the tumour and you won't suffer too many side effects."

The old George returned immediately. Smiling, he said, "Thanks. You don't know what this means to me. A chance to live a normal life and to grow old. Thanks."

"Don't get your hopes up too much. It normally works very quickly, but don't be surprised if it takes a few months to kick in," said Sam. In reality, she had no idea how long it might take to work on human cancers, or indeed whether it would ever work. All research up until that moment had been carried out with animal subjects. Without knowing it, George had been demoted to the rôle of guinea-pig.

Alan said, "Oh, before you go, George. You didn't happen to see a small bottle downstairs, near the freezer, did you?"

George asked, "Why, what was in it?

"Oh, just some medicine. Nothing to worry about. I can easily get some more."

George said, "Well, there was a bottle in the freezer. It didn't have a label on it. Sorry, I thought it had fallen out of Burke's coat pocket, so I put it back before we carried him to the car. It was about so big, full of a clear liquid. Is it important?"

Sam said, "Not at all. Nothing to worry about."

George kissed Sam on the cheek and shook Alan's hand before hurrying back across the hall and out of the front door. Sam followed him to his car and told him to keep in touch and come back any time if he needed more.

In the kitchen, Alan was waiting with two cups of cocoa on the table. He said, "You're quite flushed. Must have been all that humping in the cold night air."

"Humping?"

"Burke's body."

"Oh yes. Humping the body, yes."

Sam sat down and took a sip of the hot cocoa. She said, "What did you put in the tablets?"

Alan put his finger up against the side of his nose and was about to repeat his *Ask no questions* advice, but the look Sam was giving him told him in no uncertain terms that he should answer the question. "Topped it up with lactose and paracetamol. I thought it should taste like medicine."

"Clever boy." Sam congratulated him as an owner might encourage their dog which had just learned how to sit on command.

He said, "You've got a moustache."

She licked her top lip clean.

"What did you put in the home brew?" Alan asked, "It tasted awful and my stomach's been churning all day. I still don't feel very well."

"You didn't actually *drink* any of it, did you?"

"Well you didn't give me any, so I finished off the last bit in the jug. There wasn't much left after Peter scoffed it."

"Oh, you had some of Peter's? Well, for that jugful, my special recipe was three cans of lager, one can of Guinness, last Wednesday's leftover gravy, a good dash of washing up liquid for a nice head and something else, which I can't remember," said Sam, with a laugh.

"You could have warned me," said Alan.

Sam took his wrist and felt for his pulse. After fifteen seconds she said, "Hmm. You're a bit slow. Roll up your shirt sleeve. Back in a minute."

When she returned from the cellar, Sam was carrying a loaded hypodermic syringe, which she discharged into Alan's arm, before he had a chance to pull away.

"Ouch! What's that?" he said.

"Just a little atropine to settle your stomach, sweetie. Can't be too careful." Alan opened his mouth as if to talk, but she placed her finger across his lips to silence him.

Again, she took his pulse, this time for a few minutes. "That's better," she said.

As Alan buttoned up his shirt sleeve, he asked, "Everything go alright in the woods? I was a little worried. Seemed to take you a long time."

"Yes. We dumped him at the bottom of the drop, but when we got back to the car there was somebody spying on us. We waited until they'd gone before we left. Spent a very pleasant half hour re-living old times. Uhm. Very pleasant. I got quite emotional," said Sam, smiling.

"How about an early night and a bit of…" Alan asked.

Wrinkling her nose, Sam replied, "Bit of a headache sweetie. Anyway, I've got a ten o'clock meeting with Steve tomorrow. Sounds important. I'll take this month's production with me. And you've got to get a new battery. Lots to do."

Sam left Alan in the kitchen as she retired for the night.

Alan washed the cups and muttered to himself, "Yes. Maybe I do need a new battery." He looked at the two jugs on the drainer. They still needed washing from the night before, and one contained about a pint of the home brew concoction, which he poured away. He sniffed at the second jug, but couldn't detect anything but stale beer. He peeled off his rubber gloves, washed his hands, turned out the light and went up to bed.

George arrived home, still elated at having acquired a supply of the new drug. His anxiety had evaporated; the surgeon could stick his vanishingly small risk of death on the table, in his bed-pan.

Home for George was one of the older suites in the Royal Hotel, part of his remuneration package as regional manager, since he had lost his house twelve years earlier.

Making his way past reception, George wished the night porter goodnight, then took the lift up to his rooms on the second floor.

Sitting on a sofa, he took the bottle of pills from his pocket and debated whether to start his course of treatment immediately. *Why not,* he thought, *The sooner I start, the sooner I get rid of the awful lump in my head.*

He opened the child-resistant lid and fished out a tablet. Suddenly a series of thoughts crossed his mind. What if Sam and Alan were both working together as serial killers? How had Alan got hold of the drug so quickly? The pill machine. What if Alan had been making pills with cyanide in them, while Sam distracted him with her delightful body?

George couldn't think straight. Maybe the tumour was affecting his judgement. He put the pill to his nose and took a deep sniff. No sign of bitter almonds. He touched the pill on his tongue. It had an intensely bitter taste. He decided not to take the pill, but to have it analysed first. George Mahler at the university would do it. He wasn't a close friend, but he could probably be persuaded with a little bribe.

For a moment George thought how silly he was being. Paranoia had set in. Sam and Alan had no reason to want him dead. He held the pill next to his wide-open mouth, then recalled his earlier concern that he was the only witness who could tell the police how Burke had really died. He put the pill back into the bottle, washed his hands and rinsed his mouth.

Chapter 4

Monday 3rd April

On the Monday morning Sam left for Bishop Auckland to visit her client and ex-employer, Falmer Pharma Labs Ltd.. The weather that day was a little warmer than that of the weekend when the freak blizzard had struck. No longer did the car tyres crunch the ice on the lane, but there was now a swishing noise as they cleared the slush from their treads. The main roads were clear of all evidence of snowfall, except for the film of white dried salt on the tarmac.

Having waved Sam off, Alan stood at the door, worried that she might not make it to the top of the incline. As he lost sight of her car, he returned to the kitchen to wash the breakfast dishes. He pulled on his yellow rubber gloves and started to gently rub off the remains of the cereal into the murky water, wondering whether Sam would like one of those new mobile phones. He'd been impressed with George's model which didn't look too cumbersome. It would give him piece of mind, knowing that if she got into a sticky situation, she could always call home. It would be for emergency use only, of course. The call charges were far too expensive for everyday use.

He planned to visit a few places in Durham to price a new battery for the standby generator and would take the opportunity to call in at some phone shops, which seemed to be springing up everywhere in the city centre.

As he stood, vacantly poking his finger in the plughole to disperse the bits of cereal, he was awoken by the door alarm.

He hurriedly dried his gloves and rushed to answer the front door. *Maybe Sam had got stuck at the main road junction*, he thought. Then he noticed the small plastic bottle of Meth 4 on the table. She'd forgotten to take the month's production and had obviously come back for it. He picked up the bottle on his way out of the kitchen.

Alan opened the front door and found a tall, skinny policeman about to start knocking.

Having just stopped short of punching Alan on the nose, the policeman introduced himself. "Good morning, sir. I'm police constable Latimer. Mr Samuel Black, I presume?"

Reeling back from the copper's right-hand jab, Alan dropped the bottle and said, "Er. Who?"

The policeman took a half step inside the doorway and started sniffing, as if suffering from a cold or trying to get the scent of something or someone. He picked up the bottle and handed it to Alan, then referred to his notebook and repeated, "You are Mr. Samuel Black?"

By now, small denomination coinage was dropping in Alan's brain. He said, "No. Sam Black's my partner."

Then, before Alan could explain Sam's gender, the non-PC PC said, "Oh. Consenting adults, eh? I see. And who might you be, then?"

"My name's Alan Murray," he said, rather timidly.

Alan's only other brush with the law had been at the age of nine years, when he'd been accosted by a great bully of a man. Young Alan had picked up a discarded broken umbrella on his way home from school. He had been waving it about with his friends when the surly, burly copper had stopped him, grabbing his arm in a tight, painful grip. *'Stealing by finding is a criminal offence you little bastard!'* rang in the nine-year-old's ears as he was marched back up the path to where he'd found the piece of rubbish. The next ringing in Alan's ears was caused by the policeman's hand, as he cuffed the youngster. This had left a lasting impression on Alan, who since then, had always tried his best to avoid any confrontation with law officers or others in authority.

As PC Latimer consulted his notebook again, Alan assessed the weakling, skinny, runt of a PC in front of him and decided that this copper couldn't cuff his way out of a paper bag. So, regaining his composure, and with authority, he said, "Look here, my sexual orientation is no business of yours, but for the record, Samantha Black is my long-term heterosexual partner! Now, what's your business here today, my man!"

Alan could hardly believe that he'd uttered such words, but it seemed to do the trick. A properly flustered PC Latimer said, "Very sorry to disturb you, madam. We're making enquiries regarding a missing person. We have reason to believe that the person in question might have spent some time here on Saturday night."

Alan asked, "What makes you think he was here?"

At which the policeman thought, *Ha! Fell straight into the trap!* and, regaining the upper hand, said, "I never said it was a man."

"What?"

PC Latimer then went on. "I only said it was a missing *person*. You said *he*, so you must have known that I was talking about a man and not a woman. How did you know we were looking for a man? Just where were you between the hours of eight o'clock and three o'clock on Saturday night?" The final question was meant to intimidate Alan, but failed miserably.

"Are you for real?" asked Alan, shaking his head.

"Just answer the question, sir," demanded the copper.

"We had a party here on Saturday night. A bunch of old friends came in a minibus. I was here all night," Alan said, getting annoyed with the copper's attitude. He reached for the door and prepared to shut it.

PC Latimer decided to relax his confrontational stance. With no partner to help him out, he was having to play both good cop and bad cop, and was getting a little confused as to whose turn it was next. Having ascertained the whereabouts of the interviewee, the good cop said, "Er, we've had a report that a Mr. Malcolm Burke has not been seen since Saturday night and that he attended your party. Can you tell me when you last saw Mr. Burke, please?"

Alan turned his eyes skyward and rubbed his chin before producing his well-rehearsed line. "I'm not too sure, but I think he left at about one o'clock? I think he said he had an early start, so he must have decided to walk home." Alan shrugged his shoulders for dramatic effect as he performed his *pièce-de-résistance*. "Oh, and Samantha Black is at work."

"I see. When do you expect Mrs. Black to return, sir?"

"She should be back by about half five," replied Alan.

"Thank you, sir. Oh, can you tell me which way's the shortest walking route to Durham from here?" asked Latimer.

"There's a public footpath down near the river," said Alan, without thinking.

"So that would take Mr Burke through Whitehouse Wood?"

"Er. Well somewhere in that direction. Yes," Alan said, regretting having given the copper too much information.

"Thank you, sir. An officer will call back this evening."

PC Latimer decided that he should get the Whitehouse Wood connection to his superiors as quickly as possible. None of the shift had even mentioned the wood as a place to start looking for the missing Burke. This piece of initiative was exactly the sort of thing to get him noticed for a transfer to CID. He was just about to radio in the information when he received a call from headquarters. "Papa five-eight, Papa five-eight, from Delta Charlie, Over," came a female voice from the speaker.

Latimer replied, "Delta Charlie from Papa five-eight. Go ahead. Over."

"Papa five-eight from Delta Charlie. Proceed to Whitehouse Wood middle entrance. Report of a body found. Assistance required. Over," said the voice on the radio.

"Bugger," exclaimed Latimer, not realising that he had pressed his transmit button.

"Papa five-eight from Delta Charlie. Say again. Over," said the voice.

"Delta Charlie from Papa five-eight, Proceeding to Whitehouse Wood middle entrance. Over."

"Papa five-eight from Delta Charlie. Out."

Latimer turned and walked back towards the front door. "Excuse me, sir. What would be the best route from here to the middle entrance to Whitehouse Wood, going by car?"

Alan explained that the shortest route was usually quite congested at that time of day and gave the officer an alternative, longer way to the wood.

Latimer drove away up the incline, with wheels spinning in his haste to get to Whitehouse Wood. At last he was getting his chance to assist CID in a case involving a death, and he had new intelligence that they didn't have.

Alan decanted the Meth 4 into a clean bottle, then hurriedly loaded his car with a set of coveralls, face mask, latex gloves and the empty Meth 4 bottle.

* * * *

While Latimer was practising his rally driving skills on the hill, David Potter was explaining to his audience, "We'll shortly be coming to the well-known, local, geological feature, Lover's Leap. Contrary to popular belief, there's never been any recorded deaths, or indeed, any lovers leaping from the top."

Potter, a short man, dressed in Desert Rat khaki, chuckled and waited for his audience to take in this fascinating snippet before adding, "It's perhaps interesting to note that the crag is not at all a natural feature, but that it was created by human endeavour.

The site was used in medieval times as a quarry, but it was found to provide stone of such low-quality that only a small part of the hillside was ever excavated."

The small group of walkers stopped as Potter held out his right arm horizontally, and in a hushed tone said, "As we turn off the path to the right, we'll see the rock face in all its glory. At the base of the cliff we might well be lucky enough to see a family of long tailed tits around the patch of gorse to the left. They nest here every year and should be active now. Please be very quiet and make no sudden moves."

Potter was obviously very excited at the prospect of seeing the tits, but his party of pensioners were really only on the guided walk for a bit of a change from their otherwise uneventful lives. The walk was also free of charge, sponsored by the council, with the promise of free cake and a cuppa at the end. They followed him quietly off the track and turned the corner.

"Oh great!" shouted Potter, "That's all we need, a flipping film crew."

He could see men dressed in coveralls carrying boxes down the track from the central car park. Others were setting up lights. One man was holding a video camera, taking shots of the long-tailed tits' nesting sites. This was twitching taken to the absolute blinking limit!

Potter marched over to the coveralled man who seemed to be in charge and shouted, "What the hell do you think you're doing? Is nothing sacred?"

The SOCO sergeant turned to Potter and said, "Stop where you are. This is a police investigation crime scene."

"What?" said Potter, "You mean you're *not* a natural history unit? What do you mean a crime scene?"

The SOCO calmly explained, "There's been a body found, sir. We're setting up an exclusion zone around it. Now you'll have to keep well back, sir."

Then the SOCO, a little less calmly, screamed at the group of pensioners who were trying to get a glimpse of the tits' nests in the gorse, "Get the hell out of my crime scene, you bloody, bloody … people!".

"I've stood in something," said one old man.

"Who left that there?" shouted another as he tripped over something in the undergrowth, looked down and apologised. "Sorry, didn't see you there."

There was then a blood curdling squeal as one of the old ladies screamed, "He's dead! He's dead! Aaah! Call the rozzers!"

This was the starting gun for a veritable stampede of geriatrics, heading up the path towards the car park. Potter followed them shouting, "It's okay. Let's find a phone and get the bus to pick us up. Don't try to run." Then in a quieter voice, "Oh my God, I hope they've all got their pads on."

The hobbling stampede reached the top of the hill and were confronted by a police tape. They all stopped short of the tape, allowing Potter to catch up.

"Is everybody alright?" he asked.

A mumble of voices agreed that they were all still alive, if not all kicking.

"Well come on, let's get going"

A fragile voice piped up, "It says DO NOT CROSS."

"I'm sure the young lady won't mind," said Potter, lifting the tape for the group to pass under.

As they walked across the car park a large black car arrived and two men got out. One was a tall, well-built man, in an overcoat, wearing a trilby. He stared at the guided walk party as they trudged away, looking for a phone box. The second man was a little shorter, round faced, wearing a creased, well-worn grey suit.

＊＊＊＊

After a twenty-minute drive through slow traffic, Latimer arrived at the middle entrance to the wood. A small crowd of on-lookers was being held back by an attractive young woman PC, Donna Bell. Her uniform top seemed to be too small by a size or two and her dark blue skirt had obviously shrunk in the wash. She was struggling to persuade the more inquisitive in the crowd to keep behind the tape across the track to the woods. To one side, away from the throng, a middle-aged man sat on a shooting stick. He was writing in a notebook at such a rate that could only be sustained as shorthand.

Two police vans and various unmarked cars had taken over the small car park near the pathway leading into the wood. In front of a row of traffic cones stood a smaller, black van, a private ambulance, with two burly men in dark overcoats, smoking as they joked about easy overtime.

Latimer parked up, got out of his patrol car and hurried down the track, acknowledging Donna, but not stopping. He made a small diversion to the top of the cliff. Worried that he might slip on the muddy ground, he didn't go too near the edge. He couldn't make out the scene at the bottom of the sheer drop, so decided to return to the track. Ahead of him the path was steep and muddy, with heavy wooden sleepers, acting as steps every six feet, to save walkers from sliding down the hill.

He followed the path for two hundred yards and then caught sight of the CID team who were at the base of "Lover's Leap", a well-known, local, geological feature. About twenty metres away from the CID men, in the scrub, a small area was cordoned off with tarpaulins lashed to the tree branches. Some way beyond the corner of the makeshift tent, a SOCO, dressed in disposable protective clothing, was photographing something on the ground. Another SOCO emerged from the tent and walked off briskly in the direction of the river, around the corner from where Potter's party had come.

Latimer approached the well-built man in the heavy overcoat and asked, "Is it a man, sir? Was he murdered?"

DCI Richards turned to Latimer, ignored his dumb questions and shouted, "Take your size twelves and plod back up there to give Donna a hand, you dick!"

As Latimer clambered back up the path towards the wood's entrance, he muttered under his breath, "Elevens."

Richards turned to his sergeant, Willoughby, and said, "Fucking prick! Does he think we need his help or something? Jesus, what a bloody farce. Public all over the scene. Footprints everywhere. Probably enough fibres to knit a sweater! What's the delay? Is it accidental or what?"

Willoughby clasped his hands together, took a deep breath and in his almost imperceptible Scottish accent said, "There's a bit of a problem with time of death, sir. Doctor Smith says that the arse temperature indicates at least three days ago, but the SOCOs found ice under the body, so he must have fallen after 11 o'clock on Saturday night, when the snow started. We've recovered a wallet with a credit card. His name's Malcolm Burke. We've also found a stash of skunk in a pouch and an empty bottle of something in the coat pocket. We don't know what's been in the bottle yet, but it looks like he was a dealer. Oh, and he's got no thumbs."

"What? Was he born thumb-less? Was he a leper, or did he just have a very extreme nail-biting habit?" said Richards.

Willoughby was quite immune to the inspector's sarcastic streak. He replied, "Well, sir. It looks like one thumb, the left, was amputated at the last joint. It's an old wound and it's been healed for years. The end of the right thumb looks like it was chopped off recently and has left a messy wound, which hasn't healed. Doctor Smith says he'll be able to tell us more when he gets the body on the slab."

"Gangland murder, then," said Richards, "Mutilating bodies. Typical drug dealing stuff. He was probably killed after being tortured and then dumped here. Explains the time of death dilemma. I thought I might get an Easter break, but no. We've got to have a bloody murder. Let's leave them to it and get back to the station. And tell that prick Latimer he stays here until he's relieved at six."

As Richards and Willoughby walked back up the path the sergeant said, "Oh sorry sir, I forgot. His flies were open and his todger was out."

They stopped walking and Richards said, "Oh it just gets better. Okay, he was walking in the woods, felt the need for a jimmy and, trying to beat the record for Lover's Leap long distance pissing, stood right at the edge, lost his footing and rapidly descended to his death. Oh no! I forgot; he'd been dead 24 hours by then. I hope you've got all this written down, sergeant."

Richards shook his head and asked, "By the way, did we find any piss holes in the snow?"

"No sir, only a patch of vomit at the bottom, close to the body."

As the two detectives reached the small car park, Latimer and Bell were still struggling to hold back the curious. The woman PC lifted the tape. Richards gave her a smile and thanked her as he ducked beneath. Rising to his full height, he was confronted by a little old lady, grey with curling but well-cared-for hair. She was holding a large handbag with both hands and could have been anybody's granny. She smiled and politely said, "Excuse me, I think I might be able to help you, young man. I remember a long time ago, in our village there was a very naughty boy called Tommy Jones. Well, one day Tommy came home and told his mother that he'd seen a murder. Well, his mother…"

Richards stopped the old woman in her tracks. "Okay, Miss Marple. That's enough. When we need your help, we'll get in touch. Thank you!"

With that the DCI made his way to the car and changed into his shoes, putting his muddy wellies in a bag in the boot. The shorthand man rose from his seat and hurried over to the DCI, who said, "Nothing for the press, yet. There'll be a statement later this evening."

"Is it murder, Chief Inspector?" asked the man.

"Sorry. No comment."

As the detective's car drove off, the little old lady walked slowly away, saying, "Well, screw you, Kojak. Nobody loves *you*, baby. I'll not bother telling you about the couple I saw dumping the body, then bonking for all they were worth. And if you want their reg. number you can just pucker up and kiss my arse, you cocky twat!"

Back at the police station, Richards summoned Willoughby to his office. Moments later the sergeant arrived carrying two mugs of tea.

"Sit down," said Richards, "Right, before we go any further, let's see what we've got in the wood. First can we rule out accidental death?"

"Not totally, sir," Willoughby said, "He could have slipped in the dark or just walked over the edge while blinded by the snow. It was pretty heavy overnight. If he stopped for a pee and he aimed it over the edge, it would have dispersed before it hit the bottom, so there would be no sign of it in the snow. Besides that, it's all started melting."

There was a knock on the glass panel of the open door and a young PC entered the room, saying, "Sorry to interrupt, sir. I've got the address."

Richards replied, "Thanks lad. Do we know if he was married?"

"No sir, that's to say, we know he wasn't married. He lived alone. His sister reported him missing yesterday," added the constable.

"Really? How long had he been missing?" asked Richards.

"Just overnight, sir, but er … he was going on holiday, due to fly out yesterday morning? So, she was worried about him when he didn't return from a do in the city. I can get the sheet if you like, sir"

"Do that, lad, quick as you can. And well done. It's good to have somebody around here who can do his job properly," said Richards, smiling.

Five minutes later the PC returned, accompanied by a uniformed sergeant.

"What's the story, Jim?" asked Richards.

The sergeant replied, "The sister, Angela, reported him missing at 14:00 hours yesterday. Her brother had gone to a school reunion at the Kings Head on Saturday night and didn't return. He was due to pick her up at the airport at 10 o'clock Sunday morning. She'd been away on holiday."

Richards turned to Willoughby and said, "We'd better get someone down to the King's Head to do some digging. We need to know who organised the reunion and talk to them. Then we need details of all the people at the event. When did this berk leave and who was he with?"

The uniformed sergeant interrupted. "We've already sent a man to make enquiries at the hotel, sir."

"What? Have you got so many spare bodies that you can follow up missing persons after less than a week? You'll be getting your budget cut," said Richards.

The sergeant sent the young PC away then leaned over Richards and whispered, "The sister's a friend of the wife of a certain ACC, if you get my drift, sir"

Richards slowly shook his head then asked, "So what did your man find out?"

"Well, he ran into Peter Green who just happened to be staying at the hotel."

Richards said, "What? Sergeant Green? I thought he moved back down south when he retired?"

"Yes sir, that's right. But Peter's wife, Teri, was at the same school as this Burke fellow, so they were all at the reunion. Peter said that about a dozen of them went out to a party afterwards, in some old farmhouse. Burke was amongst them. They went there in a minibus but Burke wasn't on the bus when it returned. Oh, and he said that he could smell weed some time during the party."

"I knew it was linked to drugs. Call it instinct, but I've just got a sixth sense when it comes to these things. Sounds like we need to get out to the farmhouse, where's it at?" said Richards.

"Well, I'm not sure sir, the officer I sent to the King's Head radioed in from the hotel and said he was going to look for the place, but he hasn't returned yet. He was called in for crowd control at the woods. I'll get him in for debriefing," said the sergeant.

"Not Latimer? Don't tell me you sent Latimer," said Richards.

"I'll get him to come in and report, sir," said the sergeant, leaving the room.

102

Inspector Richards' intense antipathy towards Latimer was common knowledge throughout the station. Opinion was polarised. With one notable exception, CID declared their support for Richards' view that Latimer was overly pedantic and should stick to the plodding side of police work, instead of trying to show off his so-called superior deductive skills. Most of the uniformed officers, whilst sympathising with Latimer, didn't dare to make their feelings public.

While they waited for Latimer's return, the two detectives discussed developments.

"If Burke was at the party on Saturday night, Dr. Smith must have got it wrong. Maybe he mis-read the temperature or something," said Willoughby.

"Well, you know my opinion of Smith," Richards said, "Most people have their off days, but he seems to have more than most. Let's forget about that for now and concentrate on how he died. We can't rule out accidental death and we'd better not rule out suicide yet. But why did he have no thumbs? Did we find any blood spots at the scene?"

"None, and no sign of the right thumb either, sir," replied Willoughby, "Could someone have chopped it off to avoid fingerprint evidence being found?"

"Why stop at the thumbs? If you wanted to prevent him being identified you'd take off all the fingers and remove his teeth. Then probably smash his skull in for good measure. And you don't leave his wallet on the body. No. The thumb job was just to inflict pain. Probably done with bolt croppers. Typical gang stuff. All to do with drugs."

"Do you want the incident room here, sir, or should we get the mobile?" asked Willoughby.

"Open it up here. Let's treat it as suspicious for now. Get the teams organised."

When Latimer arrived in DCI Richards' office, the natural daylight outside was beginning to fade. The harsh, cold fluorescent light filled the office as the constable stood to attention, with a drop on the end of his red nose. He held his helmet under his left arm. A white band on his face showed where the strap had been. Above the red ears, his damp, sweaty hair was still moulded to a hemisphere.

"PC Latimer, reporting, sir."

"Okay Latimer," said Richards, "Starting with this morning, tell us what's in your notebook. Nothing more, nothing less."

Latimer placed his helmet on the desk in front of him and took out his notebook. The drop fell from his nose onto the cover. He sniffed and wiped the notebook with his cuff.

"I attended the King's Head hotel at 08:15 this morning and asked to speak with the manager, a Mr. Braithwaite. As I was waiting to interview Mr. Braithwaite, I recognised an ex-colleague, a Mr. Peter Green, in the foyer. Oh, sir. Sergeant Green didn't look too well but he …"

"Just what's in the notebook, Latimer," Richards said.

Latimer flipped a page and started to read.

"Braithwaite manager. Peter Green and Teri in foyer. Green said Burke at reunion Sat night. Green said party at farmhouse. Hosts Sam Black and it looks like Alan somebody. It could be Murphy, sir. Green said he smelt wee. Green very sick stomach on Sunday …"

"Get to the point, constable," said Richards.

Latimer continued reading. "… said it was murder. Braithwaite said George Wilson booked reunion room. I have since ascertained that Sam Black…"

"Just your contemporaneous notes, constable," said Richards, cutting Latimer short.

"But I went to…"

"Thank you, Latimer," said Richards, raising his voice, "Go and do your paperwork."

"Sir," said the tall, skinny copper, replacing his notebook in his breast pocket and picking up his helmet.

Latimer left the room as Richards turned to Willoughby and asked, "Get all that?"

"Every fascinating little bit, sir"

* * * *

Samantha Black was late getting home from work. Unusually, there had been traffic problems, which delayed her by fifteen minutes. Alan had the computer monitor switched to CCTV and watched his partner park up and approach the front door. He pressed the remote release button for the front door lock, then left the plant room and headed up the cellar steps.

They met in the hall as Sam discarded her outdoor clothes on the small coat rack.

"Nice day at the office, dear?" asked Alan.

"Not really. They're talking about stopping the trial. Some problem with rat genetics, and the dog results are poor."

"What does that mean?" asked Alan.

"It might not work in humans at low doses and they think that higher doses might cause horrific side effects before the tumours are affected. They're even looking at the vet medicine market, for Christ's sake. Can you imagine, all that effort and money just to develop a cure for cancer in rats? Or maybe curing pussies of their brain tumours? I need a bloody drink. They're going to close us down, for sure."

"Might not be such a bad idea, given recent events." Alan held out his open palm to reveal two white pills.

"Oh, I forgot it was Monday. Good idea," smiled Sam, taking one of the pills, "What's for tea?"

Ten minutes later, neither Sam nor Alan could really give a stuff what they were going to have to eat. The question had been entirely rhetorical. Their Monday evening meal would be as they had enjoyed for years, drug fuelled sex, followed by beans on toast as they came back down to Earth.

By seven o'clock, their ritual over, with heads starting to clear, they sat in the kitchen ready to discuss more serious matters over a yoghurt for dessert.

Sam asked, "Did you fit the new battery?"

Alan said, "Oh I forgot about it. We had a copper round this morning. Wanted to know about Burke, seemed like a bit of a thicko. He asked about the quickest way to walk back to town, so I told him about the river path. Then he asked about Whitehouse Wood."

"Oh, shit! They weren't supposed to start looking there for at least a week. Never mind. I'd better work from home tomorrow, just in case they come back." Sam was not very confident in her partner's abilities as a liar and much less so, when it came to thinking quickly. His redeeming quality was his unselfish staying power in bed, or on the sofa, or wherever they happened to be when the urge overtook them.

"They know that Burke was here, but I told him that he left early," said Alan.

"How did they find out about the party? I wonder if George told them. That's it! Somehow they found out that Burke was at the reunion."

"Yes. Maybe his wife told them. She must have reported him missing when he didn't get home," Alan said.

"Who'd marry him? She'd have to be some sort of bloody masochist. No. If he was married, he'd bring his wife to the reunion, wouldn't he? Maybe he lived with his mother and she told them. Anyway, they got George's name out of the King's Head people and then George coughed up about the party here." Sam's logic was undiminished by the residual amount of the drug tickling her brain cells.

As Alan scraped the last of his yoghurt from the sides of the pot, the front door alarm sounded.

"Oh, the copper said they would be back tonight."

"Okay, I'll get it," said Sam, rising from her chair. "Let me do the talking."

She opened the door and in walked George Wilson. He said, "Have you seen the North-East news? They've found Burke. They're treating it as a suspicious death. They haven't released the name, but it's got to be him."

Sam said, "Okay, calm down. They had to find him some time. Now, what did you tell the police?"

"Eh? What do you mean? I haven't talked to the police," said George.

"Well, we've had them round here," said Sam, "And they knew he was here on Saturday night. Somebody must have told them about it … It must have been someone at the party who told them."

"Well let's see," said George. He started counting on his fingers. "We dropped Rat off near his house. Dixie and Wendy were staying at the Royal and left yesterday morning. Lesley Connor and her girlfriend stayed at the King's Head, and so did Teri and Peter."

"The coppers wouldn't know to go to Rat's house or the Royal, so it must have been Lesley or the Greens who blabbed," said Sam, "Whoever reported him missing told the pigs he was going to the King's Head reunion."

George pulled out his mobile phone, extended the aerial, and said, "I'll call Johnny Braithwaite and see if the cops talked to him. He's the boss at the King's Head."

"Hello Johnny. Yes, it's me, mate. Listen, have you had the police round asking about one of my reunion guests going missing? … You have? Well, guess what, he's turned up dead in Whitehouse Wood. It was on the telly tonight. That is, it sounds like it's him, they didn't actually name him but … Oh yeah … I see …

Lucky for them he was there then. Just wondered if you'd heard anything. Cheers, mate."

George put his phone back into his pocket and said, "The police called at the King's Head but before they could talk to Johnny about the reunion, one of his guests recognised the copper and they had a long conversation. It was Teri's husband, Peter Green. He must have told them about the party and God knows what else."

"I knew he was trouble, poking his nose into every little corner," said Sam.

George thought for a moment, then said, "It's alright. If they suspected that Burke died here, they'd be round like a shot with their forensics people. But they haven't turned up here, so they mustn't suspect."

"You're right," said Alan, "And even if they do come round, I've got rid of the blood-stained carpet from the back stairs, and all the overclothes. We're spotless. I burnt it all in the stove this afternoon."

George stared at Sam. "The only thing that's bothering me is the thumb. Did you say that you spat it out? I wonder what happened to it."

She said, "Don't look at me. I haven't turned cannibal. I definitely spat it out in the attic. It was just the end part."

Alan said, "I wouldn't worry too much about it. I hoovered the attic floor and burnt the dust bag. Chances are that it picked up the thumb as well. Coffee, George? Or maybe something stronger?"

"No thanks, I must get back." George was still apprehensive about the fact that he was the only witness to the real circumstances of Burke's departure from this Earth. He didn't want to risk imbibing any concoctions which his ex-girlfriend might have learnt about in her long biochemical career.

The shivers which ran down George's spine were no ordinary ones. These were the elite of shiver society – Olympic triathlete shivers. They hurdled the 24 vertebrae, starting at the brain stem with the finishing line at the sacrum. Then came the long jump into the pit of his stomach, and finally the marathon swim down the alimentary canal, to the rectum, where the medal ceremony would take place before an open anal sphincter. Gold went to the thought of coffee flavoured wild mushrooms, capable of causing an agonising death in minutes. The silver medal was won by the possibility that Sam had a vivarium full of small, colourful, South American frogs of the genus Dendrobates, all wanting to show their affection for George by wiping their slimy skins on the rim of his tea cup.

"I think he was feeling a bit stressed," said Sam, as George's car pulled away.

"Can't imagine why," said Alan, "Everything's covered. Cocoa time?"

"Yes, why not?"

Chapter 5

Tuesday 4th April

"Sorry to disturb you Mr. Wilson, but there's a lady in reception asking to see you. She's very emotional," said the receptionist.

"Yes! I'm emotional! You'd be emotional if your man was on a slab in the hospital!" screamed the emotional lady.

"I'll be down in a minute," said George, who had just been woken by the phone in his apartment. He thought, *What time is it? What day is it?*

He looked at the clock. It was just after nine. *Why had he overslept?* Then he remembered – six codeine tablets. His head was still banging, but not quite as badly as when he'd arrived home the night before.

He walked over to the bathroom, splashed some water on his face, brushed his teeth, took another two tablets and wearily dressed. The shower would have to wait. The emotional woman would just have to cope with the slightly sweaty smell. He yawned his way to the lift, and wondered if he had dreamed about a man on a hospital slab.

Reaching the ground floor, the lift opened its doors. George stepped out and saw ahead of him, the back of a woman, dressed in a lemon-yellow coat, with a large suitcase at her side, still verbally abusing the receptionist. George loved his job, but it didn't normally consist of the day to day running of any individual hotel. He couldn't understand why the receptionist had called him rather than the duty manager. Moreover, he didn't understand why he had to deal with an emotional customer when his own head was giving him all the grief he needed for the time being.

"I'm not staying there. They killed my husband. I'm going to sue them for all they're worth," the emotional lady repeated for the hundredth time.

"Please, madam, try to stay calm. It'll be alright," said the receptionist for what seemed like the hundred and first time.

Then George recognised the voice of the woman

"Teri? Are you okay?" he asked.

She turned and threw herself at him, bursting into tears as she collapsed. George caught her and guided the dead weight to an armchair.

He pulled a handkerchief from his pocket, then thought better and took the pack of tissues the receptionist was offering.

As Teri gathered her composure George asked, "What's happened?"

"It's Peter. He's dead." She could hardly utter the words. "I've been with him all night at the hospital. They said it was a heart attack, but it started just after dinner. I know he'd had a bit of trouble with his heart, but he was on tablets for that, and it hadn't flared up again for ages."

At this point her speech changed from a whimper to an accusative shout. "They poisoned him! He was perfectly okay until he had the seafood. Just you wait and see. I'm going to sue the bleeding arse off them!"

Teri was no longer crying, and her shouting moderated to a normal voice level.

"I need a room for the night. I'm not stopping in that dump any longer. I thought I'd get a room here for a few nights. But George, do you know how much they charge here? It's ridiculous. You couldn't be a love and get me a bit of discount, could you?"

She gave him a sad smile and a couple of mascara flashes.

"Of course, no problem. The group has a policy of giving staff discount for friends and family. As far as I recall, it would be ten percent off," said George.

"Ten percent? I was thinking more like fifty."

George was in no mood for haggling. His headache seemed to be getting worse with every vibration of his eardrums. *Ten percent, ten o'clock, ten percent, ten o'clock, tick, tock, tick tock.* Suddenly he remembered that he had an appointment with his consultant at ten o'clock. "Okay. Half price. Sorry but I've got to go." Then turning to the receptionist, he said, "Frank, can you put her in the Van Mildert wing, if you've got one vacant. Otherwise, just sort it out, can you?"

As he hurried back to the lift George shouted, "Sorry to hear about Peter."

Fifteen minutes later, George stepped out of the lift into the foyer. The headache was starting to wear off. He'd had a long hot shower and a cup of weak, instant coffee. As he passed the desk, he smiled at the receptionist and asked, "Did you get her sorted, Frank?"

The receptionist replied, "Yes, Mr Wilson. She's in the Van Mildert with a riverside view. She seemed to settle down after you talked to her. Oh, and she left you a message. Could you join her for a drink this evening in the bar? Seven o'clock."

"Thanks, Frank. I'm off out for a couple of hours. Could you let Doris know, please? Should be back in the office by about eleven."

"Will do, sir."

George left the hotel and walked to the car park, mentally going over his agenda for the consultant. Firstly, he wanted palliative chemotherapy. Ostensibly for pain relief, but really to explain away the miraculous shrinking of the tumour when the Meth 4 took effect. Next, he wanted some better pain relief in the short term, as the codeine tablets sometimes just weren't touching it.

* * * *

At ten thirty DS Willoughby went for gold. His record for cautioning a suspect was 5.9 seconds. He took a deep breath and said, "John Foster, I'm arresting you on suspicion of murder. You do not have to say anything, but it may harm your defence if you do not mention when questioned something which you later rely on in court. Anything you do say may be given in evidence." Willoughby glanced at his digital wristwatch. A disappointing 6.2 seconds. He needed more practice.

Still dressed in his pyjamas, Rat said, "Bloody idiots. What are you on about?"

"Get dressed. DCI Richards wants a word with you down at the nick," said the sergeant.

The uniformed PC, who accompanied Willoughby, escorted Rat upstairs and waited as he dressed.

114

When they arrived at the police station, Rat was taken to an interview room and left to stew for a short while. He'd seen better interview rooms – warmer ones with at least a little bit of padding on the chairs, rooms that didn't smell quite so badly of stale cigarette smoke. He stared at the uniformed PC standing guard near the door. Maybe this plod could arrange a transfer to a no-smoking room. Why not? They have no-smoking train carriages, don't they? The door opened and two men entered. Rat recognised the arresting officer. The taller man dismissed the uniform with a flick of his head, sat down opposite Rat and gave him a steely stare. This was the precursor to DCI Richards' usual third degree.

"We've got evidence linking you to the death of Malcolm Burke. What have you got to say? Admit it, you pushed him off Lover's Leap after you argued with him, didn't you?"

"I want to speak to my lawyer," said Rat. His tone was calm and quiet.

"What size shoes do you take?" said Richards.

"Lawyer," said Rat, singing almost as sweetly as a cathedral choirboy.

"I'm going to crush you; break you like the little hippie bastard you are!" shouted Richards.

Willoughby, sitting next to the inspector, gestured towards the tape recorder and coughed. He then looked under the table and as he emerged, he said, "Size eight, sir."

Richards calmed down slightly and said, "Okay, Mr. Foster, we know that your accomplice has big feet. What's his name?"

Rat burst out laughing. "You really are a scream, man. Now, I'm not saying anything without a lawyer. I know my rights, man."

Richards clenched his fist and banged it on the table. "Okay, let's do it the hard way." He turned to Willoughby. "Get the duty solicitor."

Rat looked Richards in the eye and said, "I'll call my own brief, thank you." Suddenly, Rat was no longer playing the part of the downtrodden hippie with the squalid little business, dealing drugs, but was acting the part of a much more powerful, upstanding member of society.

As Richards left the room, Rat said to Willoughby, "Could I please have my mobile phone back? Oh, and a cup of tea please, and maybe a biscuit or two, as you dragged me here before breakfast?" His manner was that of a stockbroker, ordering tiffin at his club in the city.

Willoughby did the honours with the tape machine and suspended the interview at 11:30.

DCI Richards and Willoughby returned to the incident room and approached DI Peter James, who was running the show.

Around the room were three inquiry teams crowded around six desks, with not even enough chairs for half of the officers present. Richards, Willoughby and James stood at the front of the room where two large whiteboards were covered in various bits of barely legible scribble.

As Richards began to speak, the room went quiet. "Let's have reports. First, house to house. Anything?"

A young DS stood up from his desk and said, "Nothing significant yet, sir. We've covered the streets nearest the wood around the Whitehouse estate, but nobody saw anything suspicious. A couple of residents reported cars going down the lane towards the wood on Sunday evening, but they couldn't even say what colour or make they were. There's always a bit of traffic down there on a night."

"And what would that traffic be doing there?" asked Richards.

"Well, I suppose it'd be courting couples, sir"

"Have we been down there at night yet?" Richards asked.

This drew a blank from the assembled teams, so Richards turned to James and said, "Make a note. We need to interview any courting couples who turn up at night, starting tonight. We need to know if they saw or heard anybody arguing or fighting near Lover's Leap on Saturday night or early Sunday morning."

Richards then addressed the gathering with, "Okay. Statements. Any progress?"

"Nothing yet, sir," said a voice from the back.

"Right. Willoughby, let's have an update."

Willoughby took out his notebook and said, "Coroner's office has been informed. A post mortem's been ordered. We should have the results today. Preliminary indications are that death was caused by severance of the spinal cord in the neck. Consistent with a fall. There was no bruising around the neck to indicate any form of ligature. The victim appears to have fallen or been pushed from Lover's Leap. SOCOs found ice under the body, indicating that

117

death occurred Saturday night or Sunday morning. This is consistent with reports that he was at a reunion and party on Saturday night. Dr Smith initially estimated time of death at least 24 hours before this. He has since said that if the overnight temperature was lower, time of death could be later."

The assembled CID officers showed their collective opinion of the pathologist's prevarication with hoots, laughter and foot stamping.

"Quiet!" yelled Richards.

Willoughby continued, "The skunk pouch found in the pocket had prints belonging to John Foster, a local drug dealer, currently in custody. The bottle in the pocket contained a small quantity of tetra-hydro-cannabinol in a solvent. This is a class B drug derived from cannabis. If it had been full, the quantity of THC in the bottle would be enough to keep a hundred dope heads going for a year. It's very concentrated. The bottle itself has several unidentified prints on it. None of them's Burke's. We've checked the database, but there's no match. Whoever gave Burke the bottle of dope hasn't got a record. SOCOs haven't had much success with footprints. Most of them would have been in snow, and the general public have disturbed the scene. We've got good casts of size eleven prints at the top of the cliff. They could be from the accomplice, helping to push the victim over the edge."

"Thanks John," said Richards. Then, addressing the whole room, he gave his pep talk. "This is a murder; of that I am convinced. This Foster bloke, we have in custody, pushed Burke over the cliff. Both him and Burke, they were drug dealers by the look of it. Maybe it's the start of a drug war. Maybe Burke strayed onto Foster's patch, or *vice versa*, we don't know yet. There's obviously an accomplice, whose prints are on the bottle. The accomplice held Burke down while Foster used the bolt croppers on his thumb or *vice versa,* we don't know yet. We need to break this Foster and get a confession out of him. He's also going to tell us the name of his big foot partner. Meanwhile, we need hard evidence collected by you. Look out for blood stained bolt croppers and the like. Farley, take your team to do house to house around Foster's neighbours. Anything they can tell you. Who he hangs about with, especially people with big feet. His movements over the weekend. You know the drill. SOCOs are turning his house over right now. I'd bet my pension they find a pair of bolt croppers, covered in blood. Go to it."

This monologue impressed the audience in much the same way that Richards' previous serious crime investigation fiascos had done. He could turn a fight in an infants' school playground into a hunt for a serial killer. To paraphrase the Mounties motto, '*Richards always gets it wrong.*'

Richards and Willoughby returned to the office, while they waited for John Foster's lawyer to arrive.

"Has anyone talked to this Wilson bloke yet?" Richards asked.

"Not yet, sir," Willoughby replied.

"We'll go and see him after we've finished with Foster."

Willoughby knew damned well that his boss never worked late on a Tuesday. Personal commitments, that Richards couldn't get out of, meant that the sergeant would end up interviewing the Wilson bloke on his own.

"Where's the lawyer coming from?" said Richards.

"Well, the firm's based in London, sir, but they're sending an associate from Newcastle. He should be here before lunch."

＊＊＊＊

Edward Littlefield of Thorley, Littlefield and Green arrived at the desk of the custody sergeant at 12:45, presented his card and asked to see his client, a Mr John Foster. Littlefield was a very well-built man of sixty years, over six feet three tall with a really stern look about him. His thinning, grey hair was combed flat and held in place by old-fashioned, greasy hair cream. The custody sergeant didn't know Littlefield personally, but he was familiar with his type. This was a man not to be crossed.

A uniformed PC escorted the big lawyer to the cells and showed him into number three, the temporary abode of John Foster. As Littlefield shook hands with Rat and introduced himself, the door was shut behind him.

The lawyer took out a large handkerchief and dusted off the chair before sitting down next to Rat. He asked, "First of all, how have they been treating you? Are they respectful? Have you had a meal?"

Rat replied that he had no complaints regarding their treatment of him, apart from the overbearing attitude of the DCI, the tasteless, weak, vending-machine tea and the cheap biscuits which were starting to go soggy and had a smell of peeling wallpaper about them. Littlefield then went through the arrest procedure, which Rat agreed had been conducted correctly. As he read from the sheet of paper he was holding, Littlefield confirmed that the arrest was on suspicion of the murder of one Malcolm Burke on either Saturday night or Sunday morning.

Littlefield looked at Rat and said, "Did you do it? Not that it matters, really."

Rat said, "No. Of course not. Burke was a bit of an arsehole, but I've met a lot worse and never felt the need to top them."

"Okay, I had to ask. Need to know lie of the land, you might say. Now, have they presented their evidence for detaining you?" asked the lawyer.

"No. I don't know what they've got on me. I was at a party on Saturday night into the early hours and …"

"So, you've got an alibi? With lots of witnesses," Littlefield interrupted.

"Well Burke was at the party until well after one, I think. I stayed until the end. About three, I think. It's a bit hazy, if you know what I mean."

"Precisely what do you mean?"

"Well, I'd done a bit of weed and booze, so you know, I wasn't looking at my watch. … I suppose I could have been wearing a watch. … Anyway, I got home about four. The minibus dropped me off. I went straight to bed and then I was out like a light."

"Can anyone verify that?"

"I live with my mum, but she was asleep in bed when I got home. Listen, the pigs are at my house right now. Mum will be upset. She's not very well. Can you get them to take it easy?"

"Leave it to me," said the big man, obviously spoiling for a fight. At this the lawyer rose from the chair. As he crossed the cell he turned and asked, "You are aware of our firm's rates?"

"Oh yes," replied Rat, "I've been paying Charlie's rates for years."

"Oh, you know Charlie, then?" Littlefield smiled.

"From long ago," Rat nodded.

"Oh well, there should be no problem, then," said Littlefield as he banged loudly on the door.

A constable released Littlefield and locked the door before escorting him back to the custody desk.

"I'd like to speak with the Senior Investigating Officer, please," Littlefield said.

Five minutes later Littlefield sat across the table from Richards and Willoughby in a small interview room.

Littlefield fired a salvo. "I want you to release my client from custody forthwith and desist from your search of his property. Failing this I shall be advising my client to sue the constabulary and the arresting officer for false arrest."

"On what grounds?" asked Richards, smirking at the lawyer.

"On the grounds that you arrested him without giving any reason and that you instigated the search without a warrant."

"We don't need a warrant if we've arrested him."

"But you arrested him unfairly, without any evidence, so your privilege of searching his property without a warrant is totally void, rendering the search illegal and any evidence obtained from it inadmissible."

DCI Richards went quiet, thinking for a minute, then said, "His prints are on a tobacco pouch, found in Burke's pocket, so he had contact with the dead man. He's a known drug dealer. It's a drugs war. We're going to hold him for the duration and we're going to complete the search."

"I would strongly recommend that you do not follow that path. I will now consult again with my client."

Richards said, "We'll be interviewing Foster shortly in the room next door. You can talk in here for now."

Richards and Willoughby left the room and a few minutes later Rat was led in to talk with Littlefield. The lawyer held his index finger to his lips to silence Rat, then smiled as he switched off the tape recorder on the desk.

"They claim that your fingerprints were found on a tobacco pouch in Burke's pocket," said Littlefield, breakimg the silence.

"Oh, that's where it got to!" said Rat, "I must have put it in the wrong coat. We were both wearing sheepskins."

"Please, start again. How did you come to put it in the wrong coat?"

Rat explained to the lawyer that, at the party, the music was rubbish and that he had gone out for a smoke. When he came back, he went to the kitchen to put his stash back into his coat pocket. The coats were piled up and he must have put the stash into Burke's pocket by mistake, even though Burke's coat was a little more worn and grubby compared to his own. He would never have made the mistake if he'd not been a little bit hazy.

"Well, if you give them that account, they will have no case against you apart from possession of a small quantity of class B drug."

"It might not be quite as simple as that. The amount in the pouch could be construed as a dealer's stock, not that I've been dealing, you see. But they might be able to convince a court. I've got a bit of previous. It was a long time ago and they couldn't prove it, but mud sticks, yeah?"

The quick-thinking lawyer suggested, "So what you're telling me is that you went to the kitchen, sometime during the party, to get your *cigarettes* from your coat, stuck your hand in the coat pocket, pulled out a tobacco pouch and put it back after realising the coat wasn't yours. An easy mistake to make, especially when you were under the influence of alcohol, a perfectly legal drug."

"Sounds good to me," said Rat, "Except I don't smoke fags. Terrible habit. Early grave and all that."

"Right," said Littlefield, "You've just started. Ask for a cigarette first thing in the interview. You've left yours at home and you're desperate. Alright?"

"Yeah."

"Okay. Remember, fags in coat pocket. Tobacco pouch. *Oh, what's this? Better put it back.* We'll have to work on your alibi for the time when you got home. It would be nice to have a reliable witness who could vouch for the fact that you never left home after four o'clock. Ready?"

The two men rose from their seats to leave the room. As Littlefield opened the door, the PC, who had been standing guard outside, lost his footing and fell towards the big lawyer.

There was a disturbance in the corridor with a female voice shouting, "Pigs!" followed by a male voice saying, "Get her down to the cells!"

When it seemed safe to leave the room, the PC took Rat by the arm and led him into the corridor. Rat escaped the policeman's grip and ran down the corridor towards the fracas, shouting, "Leave her alone, you bastards!"

The little old lady with grey, curling, well cared for hair, turned around and smiled as Littlefield won the race against the PC to get to Rat. Littlefield tried to calm him, saying, "Leave it. It's nothing to do with you."

Rat turned to the lawyer and replied, "Yes, it is. That's my mother! What are they doing to her?"

DCI Richards arrived on the scene. The PC had Rat in an armlock on the floor. A female voice shouted from far away, "I'm alright, Johnny."

At 13:20 Willoughby announced, "Interview resumed at 13:21 – Present, DCI Richards, DS Willoughby, John Foster and counsel, Mr. Edward Littlefield."

Rat was still seething. "What've you got my mother here for? Have you taken to beating up old women?"

Richards replied, "Your mother has been arrested for assaulting a police officer in the execution of his duty. Now can we get on with the interview?"

"No. I'm saying nothing till you let her go. She's seventy-two for fuck's sake, leave her alone."

"May I have a word with you, inspector?" asked Littlefield.

"No, you may not!" said Richards.

"Then I would like you to know that I shall be acting on behalf of my client, here, Mr John Foster and also for his mother, whom you have in custody." The lawyer turned to Rat, raising his eyebrows in a query. Rat replied with a nod.

"What?" exclaimed Richards, "You can't do that."

"Oh yes I can," Littlefield replied calmly, "Now, I'd like to consult with my other client, Mrs. Foster, please"

Willoughby, fed up with all the fuss, conversed with his old friend, the tape recorder. "Interview suspended, *again* at 13:24. Mr. Littlefield has left the room. And now DCI Richards has also left the room. I'm now going to leave the room, 'cos I need a slash. Over and out." With this, he turned to Rat, shrugged his shoulders and rose to leave the room.

Before Willoughby reached the door, Rat called to him, "Can I get a fag, mate?"

Willoughby turned and said, "Sorry, I don't smoke but I'll get you a pack from the machine. What do you want?"

"Any. Can you get me a light as well? Left mine at home."

"Okay. But you can't take it to the cell."

"Cheers. Appreciate it," said Rat as Willoughby left.

As Littlefield was escorted into the small room where Mrs. Foster was being held, she stood up and shouted at him, "You the chief pig, then? Why have you picked on my little Johnny? He's not done nothing wrong. He's a good boy. Might do a little bit of dope

126

now and again, but he'd never hurt nobody. In fact, most of the time he's too far out of it to hurt anybody. Except himself, maybe. When he falls down."

The lawyer smiled at her as the door closed behind him. He said, "I'm not one of the pigs, Mrs. Foster. I'm John's lawyer. John needs you to tell the police what time he came home in the early hours of Sunday morning, you know, the night of the party."

"What? How would I know? I was asleep in bed. He's got a key, you know. They said he murdered somebody. He'd never do that. Who's he supposed to have bumped off?"

"The dead man was called Burke. They found him in the woods, not far from your house."

"Oh yes, I remember. I saw them dumping the body on Sunday night."

Littlefield thought to himself, *How can I train this silly old bat to give an alibi. She's away with the show folks. The murder was the night before.* He decided to give it a try and started to speak very slowly. "Listen to me. Your little Johnny needs you to tell police that you waited up for him until quarter to four on Sunday morning. Then he went to bed and never left the house. Do you understand, dear? It's very important. Little Johnny could go to prison for a long time if you don't get it right."

"I'm not stupid, you dickhead! You want me to alibi him for Sunday morning. Why didn't you just say? Get the pigs in here and I'll give them my frail, little old lady act."

"Sorry," said Littlefield, "I thought you might have been hard of hearing. I'll get the pigs later, but for now

I've got to go in with John. Don't worry, I'll have you both out of here in a couple of shakes."

Ten minutes later Richards entered the interview room. The air was thick with an acrid atmosphere which attacked his eyes and assaulted the lining of his lungs. At the other side of the table sat Foster next to Littlefield, who was advising his client, in a whisper, "Don't overdo it. I'd really appreciate not dying of lung cancer from secondary smoking."

Rat dumped his sixth fag end in the ashtray and started to cough. His face was turning pale. Holding back the vomit, he said, "That's better."

Littlefield continued in a whisper to Rat, "She's alright. They've arrested her for assaulting one of the scene of crime officers when he opened her diary. Called him a pervert, then kneed him in the knackers. That's a legal term, you understand? I'll get her off, no trouble. Let's get started and get you and mummy out of here. Remember, mummy was awake when you got home."

"Can we get going then?" asked Richards.

"Go ahead, inspector," Littlefield said, smiling.

Richards leaned forward, looking Rat in the eyes. "Where were you in the late evening of Saturday last? After ten o'clock?"

"I was in the King's Head. Lots of witnesses," said Rat after glancing for approval from Littlefield.

"At what time did you leave?"

"Around eleven o'clock."

"Where did you go then? Was it Whitehouse Wood to meet another dealer?"

"No. I went to a party. Sort of surprise do, at Alan Murray's place. I was there until three in the morning."

"Alan Murray, you say? Would that be the same party that Malcolm Burke was at?"

"Yes," replied Rat, "But I think he must have left early, 'cos I didn't see him by the end of the night."

"So, you left at three and followed Burke? Met him in the woods to do a deal and killed him after you argued about the price? Is that the way it happened?"

"No. I didn't see him after the party. He'd gone. He wasn't on the minibus home."

"How do you explain the fact that we found your prints on a tobacco pouch in Mr. Burke's coat pocket?"

"Eh?" Rat tried his best to look surprised. "Oh. Now I remember. I left the party to go for a smoke outside. My fags were in my coat pocket, so I fished around but pulled out a tobacco pouch. It must have been Burke's coat. He had a sheepskin as well, you see. All the coats were just piled up on the kitchen table, you see. Anyway, I put the pouch back, then I found my own coat, got my fags out and went outside to light up."

Richards frowned in disbelief at Rat's version of how the prints got there, and pressed him with, "What time was it when you went out for a smoke?"

"About twelve."

"So, you were at the party after that until the end?"

"That's right."

"And you got the bus back to the centre of Durham with the others?"

"No. I got dropped off at home."

"What time would that be?"

"Can't remember. Must have been around four. Ask my mum, you've got her banged up downstairs. She always waits up for me when I'm out for the night. Worries about me."

Half an hour later Richards and Willoughby entered the room and sat down, across the table from Mrs. Foster and Littlefield. She instantly recognised Richards, but refrained from jumping on the table, dropping her knickers and mooning at the DCI, shouting, "Kiss this, Kojak!"

Instead, realising that Richards hadn't a clue about their previous meeting, she aged herself by fifteen years and thought back to the untimely death of her favourite pussy cat, until a tear welled up in the corner of her eye. She whimpered, "What's he done? Why have you got him here?"

Willoughby beckoned to the attractive woman PC behind Richards. She came forward and gave Mrs. Foster a tissue. The old lady blew her nose and returned the tissue to the woman PC before continuing, "He's a good boy."

Richards, unmoved by the performance, asked, "Can you confirm what time your son returned home last Sunday morning?"

"Well, I waited up for him. He was very late. It must have been after three. No. It was later, 'cos I heard the clock strike the half hour. Must have been about quarter to four. Yes, that was it. About quarter to four. The little tinker. He comes home at all hours after he's been out with his friends. He must have been very tired, because he went straight to bed after he gave his old mother a kiss. Slept like a log till quite late."

Littlefield smiled at Richards and held out his hand. Richards refused the offer to shake hands, at which Littlefield said, "I think you could release both of my clients now, inspector. You have a corroborated alibi for Mr. Foster. He was at the party, with a great many witnesses, after which he returned home and never left the house until the next day. Your search of the house was illegal, so my second client was perfectly within her rights to use reasonable force to prevent interference from your officers."

The frustration of being outwitted by a bent lawyer showed on Richards' face as he said, "I'll release Mrs. Foster for now, but your other client stays here for the full thirty-six hours, while we check witness statements from the partygoers."

Littlefield took Richards to one side and offered once again to shake hands. When Richards refused, the solicitor quietly said, "You haven't got thirty-six hours; your superintendent won't be authorising more than twenty-four. He knows the score. You have no concrete evidence, just circumstantial stuff which my associates will shoot down. Let's put it this way, the man you have in custody has some very influential friends. Your job and pension are very much at risk. Have a word with your CS. I'll be with the old lady in the front waiting room."

Chapter 6

George Wilson had suffered a terrible morning. The appointment with his consultant, due at ten o'clock, had been delayed due to an emergency. Rather than re-schedule he had decided to wait, even though the pain in his head was building up again. At twelve o'clock he had finally got to talk with his surgeon just as his headache was reaching its peak intensity. George asked for palliative chemotherapy. The surgeon reiterated his opinion that surgery was the best option. He couldn't understand why George had dismissed this course of treatment.

"Mr. Wilson. It's operable. With the position of the tumour being as it is, there's every possibility that we can remove all or most of it without any damage to surrounding tissue. As I have said before, whilst it's not immediately life-threatening, your symptoms would be reduced dramatically. The benefits far outweigh the risks. Please let me help you."

George wasn't listening. In his mind, the risk was overwhelming. He could be left a cabbage if the surgeon coughed while the scalpel was near his brain. *The surgeon coughed his brain* … Pain was taking over. He couldn't think. Pain. *Outweigh the risks. Let me help you.* His eyes were screwed up and he was moaning as his head throbbed. Then suddenly, a moment's clarity.

A male nurse, in a dark blue uniform said, "George are you alright? Here, this should help."

A scratch on his arm, then within seconds, a pure relief. The pain had gone, replaced for a few seconds by giddiness.

The nurse was still leaning over George, taking his pulse.

"Is that better, George?"

"Oh. Thank you," he said with a smile, "That's great stuff. Can I take some home?"

The consultant asked again, "Won't you reconsider surgery. It's really the only way. Palliative chemotherapy is really just to make you a bit more comfortable towards the end. And that's not likely to be for some time yet."

"I'll think about it," George said, thinking that his best chance of a cure was still the Methyphenax 4.

"Okay. You've got my number. Take some time, discuss it with your nearest and dearest, then call me in the next few days. We can arrange for the procedure at very short notice, say a couple of weeks. Meanwhile here's a prescription for some morphine tablets and an even stronger laxative. You're likely to need these for a long time if you don't have surgery."

George drove back to the Royal feeling very light-headed. Maybe he shouldn't be driving with the powerful drug in his bloodstream, but it reminded him of happy times at the fairground on the dodgems. Fortunately, the traffic was light and he made it home with only a few minor traffic law violations. He parked with three wheels on the tarmac, more or less slap bang in the middle of his reserved space, then tottered his way to the staff entrance. He arrived at his desk just as the phone started to ring. Fumbling with the receiver he managed to get it to his ear. The voice at the other end said, "George. I've been trying to call you all morning. It's George Mahler. I took those pills over to the pharmacology lab tech and he ran them this morning."

George said, "Who? Oh, yes. How are you? … Pills? … Oh yes, those pills. That was quick. I thought it would take weeks. What's in them?"

"Well, they're basically a high dose paracetamol. About four times the normal strength."

"Nothing else in them, then?"

"Not really. There are traces of some stuff which we couldn't identify. Not enough to be pharmacologically active. Oh, and very small traces of tetra-hydro-cannabinol, the active compound in pot. Again, very unlikely to be enough for any effect. Where did you get them?"

"It was a friend … A friend gave me them; said they were very good for headaches, but I've found something even better."

"Well if you do use them, just be careful how many you take. They're well above the normal dose and you could end up doing yourself a lot of harm."

"Thanks George. Owe you one, mate" said Wilson and he replaced the receiver.

He sat at his desk and thought for a while. His head was getting a bit clearer. Why would Sam and Alan give him paracetamol instead of Methyphenax 4? If it was an attempt to poison him, they would surely use something more lethal. Maybe they were just putting him off until they could get the real thing, or maybe they can't get the real thing. If they couldn't or wouldn't get Methyphenax 4 for him, his only option would be surgery. He called the surgeon's secretary and arranged another appointment for the following week.

* * * *

At five o'clock, PC Latimer turned off the main road into the lane leading to the old farmhouse and made his way to the bottom of the hill in his wreck of a Land Rover. He enjoyed driving his own vehicle for the fact that he was much higher up than when driving the police patrol car. He could appreciate the view and felt so much more in control. With every pothole, the assorted junk in the back jumped and rattled under the canvas cover. As he reached the gravelled parking area, he braked too hard and skidded into a large plant pot near the front door. Grinding gears as he found reverse, he pulled back, parked and then got out. The plant pot wasn't damaged, so he approached the door. He heard a bell ringing and then the door was opened by a slim, middle-aged woman with short blonde hair. She walked past Latimer and inspected the plant pot, then turned to him and said, "No harm done. What can I do for you, officer?

"Sorry about that, madam. Must have been a patch of ice. I'm here about the missing …"

"Oh, come in," said Sam, "Let's see if we can't get you somewhere a bit more comfortable. I've got a nice cosy place to put your hat."

Sam's laboured attempt at sexual innuendo went soaring majestically, high above the helmeted head of the dumbfounded bobby.

They both entered the hall and Sam showed him to the kitchen. He sat down at the table and took out his notebook.

"I'm making enquiries about the …"

135

Again, Sam interrupted. "Would you like a drink, officer?"

"No thank you, madam. I …"

"Oh, I forgot, policemen don't drink while they're on duty, do they?" she laughed.

"Well, actually, I'm not technically speaking, on duty, but I don't partake of alcohol."

"Okay. How about a cup of coffee? I've just made some. It's arabica."

"That would be very nice, madam," said Latimer and then, trying to regain control of the interview, "As I was saying, I'm making enquiries into …"

Sam turned to the policeman, as she poured the coffee, and once again interrupted. "Black or white?"

"White please."

"Sugar?"

"Yes please, two. I'm enquiring into the disappearance …"

"Oh, dear, we're out of brown. I'm afraid it'll have to be white granulated. Is that okay?"

"Eh? Oh, yes. I don't usually have brown sugar in coffee, anyway."

Sam leant over the policeman and pushed her cleavage into his face as she reached up into a cupboard above his head. She took out a plastic jar, opened it and spooned the sugar into his cup, stirred the drink and handed it to him.

This time Latimer wasn't going to be interrupted. He swallowed a mouthful of coffee, pulled a face, then spoke quickly. "I'm enquiring into the disappearance

136

and subsequent murder of Malcolm Burke. I believe that Mr. Burke was at a party here on Saturday night. Is that correct?"

"Murder?" said the sham shocked Sam, "But who would want to kill Burke? Where was he killed? And *how* was he killed? Was he bludgeoned with a blunt instrument in the boudoir, or stabbed through the sternum in the study, or stricken with strychnine in the kitchen?"

Latimer took another sip of the strong coffee and grimaced, "He was …"

This time Sam interrupted with more fun in mind. Maybe the copper had picked up on the reference to strychnine. "Is the coffee a little bitter? More sugar, perhaps?"

"Yes please. It's a bit stronger than I normally take it."

Sam went to the cupboard again and took out the plastic jar. She filled another spoonful and held it over the coffee saying, "Did you know that one spoonful of strychnine is enough to kill about fifty people?"

Sam stirred the white crystals into the coffee and replaced the jar in the cupboard, next to the jar labelled *POTASSIUM CYANIDE*.

She said, "It must be quite difficult to get hold of strychnine or any other lethal poison nowadays. Your average poisoner must have a devil of a time finding it. Not like the old days when you could kill rats with any chemical known to man, or even kill men with any chemical known to rats."

Latimer spat out his mouthful of coffee back into the cup as Sam tittered. "Of course, if you work in a pharmacy research lab, all you need to do is go to the poisons cupboard and take it."

Latimer hammered his cup down on the table and jumped to his feet. He thought, *How long does strychnine take to act?* He vaguely remembered that it was very fast. There was no time to waste. He could make it to A & E in ten minutes if he broke the speed limit through the middle of Durham City. Running to the front door, he passed Alan, emerging from the cellar. Alan tried to say hello but the policeman was out of the house, revving his Land Rover and grinding gears before Alan's vocal chords could start vibrating.

In the kitchen, Sam was still holding the strychnine jar. Alan reached into the cupboard for the potassium cyanide jar, took a teabag from it and went over to the stove to get a cupful of hot water.

"Wasn't that the copper who came around yesterday?" asked Alan.

"Yes," said Sam, "He's a bit strange. We were just talking and he leapt up and ran out. Said he wasn't on duty. Are they allowed to interview people when they're off duty?"

"Hmm! Never cared for coppers," said Alan as he reached in the fridge for the milk.

Meanwhile, Latimer was indeed breaking the speed limit through the middle of Durham City. He managed to get his battered old Land Rover up to 35 miles per hour on his way to the hospital's A & E department. Having parked in the ambulance unloading bay, he ran through the open doors and barged people out of his way to the reception desk, where he jumped the queue and shouted, "I'm dying. Help me!"

The receptionist suggested he take a deep, calming breath and join the end of the queue, at which Latimer repeated, "Dying! Poisoned with strychnine!"

This attracted the attention of a nearby nurse who took him aside and said, "Can you please keep the noise down, officer. There are sick people in here."

A second, older nurse came over and took Latimer by the arm. "Here, love. Come this way. I'll check you out."

She led the copper into a treatment cubicle, sat him on the bed and then proceeded to check his pulse and blood pressure. She looked at his pupils and asked, "How long ago did you take it?"

Latimer was shaking as he looked at his watch. "Nineteen minutes and twenty-five seconds."

"What religion are you, dear? Would it be Roman Catholic by any chance?"

"Why do you ask?" said Latimer, quite annoyed that they were more concerned about getting his personal information, than giving him urgent medical treatment.

"I just thought you might want the Chaplain to come and talk to you."

"Talk about what?"

"Well they usually talk about sin or sins and absolving you and stuff."

"Well I'm Independent Methodist, if you must know, and I'd rather you just got on with my treatment. Strychnine poisoning can be very serious, you know."

"Hmm. Look on the bright side, pet. You're still alive. Should be nearly dead by now. Sure you don't want the Chaplain? Haven't had any spasms, have you?"

"No."

"Well that's a bit strange. No tightness of your chest? No trouble breathing yet?"

Latimer coughed. "No."

"How much did you take?"

"About a teaspoonful."

She said, "A spoonful? Wow! That would probably be enough to kill …"

"… about fifty people," Latimer interrupted.

"Oh, I was going to say a whole station full of coppers … You're sure it was strychnine?"

"Yes, I'm quite sure! Now can you please hurry up and give me the antidote. It's over twenty minutes, now."

"Oh, there's no antidote, love. But we'll see what we can do to get it out of your system, if it's not too late. Now just relax while we try to put you right. Maybe it hasn't got into your bloodstream yet."

Two more nurses were summoned to help. They then set to work on the patient. A spray, with a disgusting taste, was directed at the back of his throat. Following this, one of the nurses grabbed a handful of hair and yanked his head back, as the other fed a length of semi-flexible pipe down his gullet. The young nurses seemed to delight in filling his stomach with saline from a large jug and then siphoning. PC Latimer wasn't enjoying the experience one bit. Then, when the stomach pumping was done, he was given a foul black, gritty drink.

The two younger nurses left the cubicle, giggling like a pair of milk maids with their bucket of contaminated saline and stomach pump. The older nurse then announced that they'd done everything they could and he appeared to be physically fine. She checked his pulse and blood pressure again, then left him to finish his drink.

The psyche nurse arrived and interviewed him at length. She asked if he had family problems, how much strychnine had he taken, where had he obtained it, and informed him that all cases of attempted suicide had to be reported to the police.

Finally, Latimer snapped and said, "I *am* the police. What do you think this uniform is? I was poisoned. I didn't try to top myself."

He rose from the armchair and pulled on his overcoat, just as a doctor entered the cubicle.

Latimer was out of earshot as the doctor said, "Good news, officer. You're not going to die – yet."

Latimer left the department, fuming. By his quick thinking and decisive action, he had saved his own life. The fact that he was still alive meant that the treatment had been successful and the poison hadn't entered his bloodstream. He made his way to the ambulance bay and found that his beloved Land Rover had gone, even though he had left his bobby's helmet exposed in plain sight. He walked over to the car park, thinking that it might have been moved there, but could see no sign of it. Returning to the ambulance bay, he found a notice on the wall. *Oh, marvellous!* he thought, *Impounded with a £50 release fee.*

141

Thirty minutes later Latimer arrived at the private parking company's yard, having walked about one mile and taken a bus ride of three more. Fortunately, the pound was open until late. He grudgingly paid his £50 and drove off. The light of day had faded to reveal a bright red sunset as he took the bypass around the city. He was determined to finish his interview with the woman he now regarded as a suspect, in what was probably a double murder case. The toxicology report on Burke was due sometime the next day. Latimer was certain that strychnine or a similar poison would be involved. Peter Green had been looking unwell when they had met on Monday morning and had been admitted to hospital with gastric problems. It all added up to poisoning, and as most poisonings were carried out by females, the obvious suspect had to be the woman who'd had the opportunity to administer her deadly mixture to both victims. And that woman was Samuel Black!

* * * *

John Foster, his mother and Mr. Littlefield walked into the public bar of the Royal Hotel and sat at a small table, near the window. Outside, the natural light was fading to a beautiful sunset. Clouds glowed pink and purple against a light blue sky. The streetlamps were gradually brightening as their discharge changed from a dull red to orange. Littlefield ordered drinks and asked if he could have a dinner table for three. Presently the waiter brought a tray, placed a petite doily, embossed with the hotel name, on the polished table in front of each of the seated guests, and left the drinks.

Littlefield proposed a toast. "Here's to Durham's finest. Long may they chase their tails."

They had a little laugh, then Littlefield asked Rat, "So, John, how do you know Charlie?"

Rat explained that he'd worked in London during the early seventies and had to use Charlie's services to keep him out of jail a few times. Charlie had been recommended to him by one of Rat's showbiz clients.

"Oh, you had theatrical clients. What was your business?" said Littlefield.

Mrs. Foster answered on her son's behalf. "He was a chauffeur. Drove all the pop stars and politicals around. Made a fortune, but left his old mum up here all alone, after his good-for-nothing father left."

Rat corrected her. "I was a gopher. Supplied them with all the stuff they couldn't be seen buying for themselves, if you get my drift. They paid top whack, and they used stuff by the ton. I took my little cut and that's how I could afford Charlie's rates. He was brilliant. Said he reckoned he could always get anybody off with just a kind word and a simple handshake. Anyway, by the mid-eighties the trade dropped off, so I retired here and came back to mum. Sorry, but I really must go for a jimmy."

Rat left the table and walked over towards the foyer. At the doorway, he met George Wilson and Teri Green, coming into the bar. They stopped for a short chat.

Back at their table, Mrs. Foster said to Littlefield, "He dumped the body on Sunday night. I saw him."

Littlefield, thinking that she was wandering again, said, "No. You've got it wrong, dear. It was Sunday morning, in the early hours when he died. Nobody dumped him on Sunday night. Your little Johnny didn't do it."

The old lady gave him a stern look and then went silent. She wasn't going to say any more to him if he was going to treat her like a dotty old spinster.

When Rat returned from the toilet, his mother said, "I saw him dumping the body on Sunday night."

Rat shook his head and said, "What? Have I missed something? Who did you see, mum?"

"That ginger man you were talking to. Him. Sat down at that table with another woman."

"George? What do you mean with *another* woman?" asked Rat, intrigued.

"Well, when he was dumping the body, he was with a blonde. Then they took off their clothes and got in the car and started bonking away. Is it time for dinner? I could eat a horse."

Littlefield caught the waiter's attention and asked if their table was ready. The waiter then showed them to the dining room and took an order for more drinks.

From their table in the bar, Teri and George had a good view of the room and through the doorway to the foyer. Teri had been quizzing George about how long he'd worked for the Royal group. George didn't seem to be interested in talking much, and suppressed a yawn.

Teri went quiet for a minute, then said, "You know, Peter wasn't a bad man. I know that people didn't like him much, but he was always kind to me. Maybe he liked his beer a bit too much, but we never went short and we've got a nice house, nice car, no mortgage. Ideal really. I'm really going to miss him. Of course, I'll get half his pension, so I won't have to go out to work or anything like that. Oh, I didn't tell you, did I? The hospital are saying now that he might have taken too many of his heart pills. Mistaken them for antacids and that could have caused the heart attack. Bloody cheek! What a load of rubbish. I called the environmental health people. Said that Peter's heart attack was brought on by the stress of being taken to hospital with food poisoning. Told them to get off their arses and go and swab the kitchens in that dump. Anyway, they're going to pay them a visit. I'll be putting in a claim for compensation. They won't get away with it."

George was a little distant. The morphine tablet was working, perfectly controlling his pain, but making him a little drowsy. He took a small sip of his tonic water and asked, "So how long will you be staying? Don't you need to get back to, er …?"

"Godalming," she said, helping him. "We've got open returns, and not really anything to get back for. I'll stay for a few days and sort out the undertakers to get him home."

Saying this, Teri looked past George, towards the foyer. She screwed up her eyes and said, "That's Martin Richards. I wonder what he's doing here. … Oh, I see. He's got dirty Belladonna in tow. The slut! Now I know what he's up to."

George turned around and saw the couple approaching the desk.

"Don't stare," whispered Teri.

"Who's Martin Richards?"

"He's DCI Richards, and she's PC Donna Bell. He's a married man and she's working her way through most of the senior officers in the county."

"Really?" said George, "Would you care for another?"

George summoned the waiter and said, "Same again, please, Carl."

He rose from his seat and said, "Won't be a minute, Teri."

George left the bar and went behind the desk in the foyer. He acknowledged the desk clerk and then looked at the last entry in the register. Flipping the page to the previous week, he noted the same entry at the same time and day.

"Sorry about that, just a little bit of business to take care of," he said, as he took his seat next to Teri. "How about dinner? My treat."

* * * *

At seven thirty, PC Latimer turned off the main road into the lane leading to the old farmhouse and bumped his way to the bottom of the hill in his trusty Land Rover. This time he approached slowly and missed the large plant pot by six inches. He quietly closed the cab door behind him as he prepared to sneak over to have peep in at the window. He would then surprise the couple by bursting through the front door and catch them off their guard.

He took a sneaky step and was immediately blinded by two high power security lights. A bell sounded in the house. He walked over to the oak door and was greeted by Sam.

"Constable Latimer, what a pleasure. Please, do come in. You left in such a hurry; I hope you weren't called out to some emergency."

They crossed the dimly lit hall and entered the kitchen.

"Please, have a seat. Can I get you a drink? Oh, no. You said you don't. What about a coffee, then? Or tea?"

"I'd rather stand, madam," said the constable, "And if it's all the same, I'll not have anything. Thank you. I have some questions to put to you regarding the deaths of Mr. Malcolm Burke and Sergeant Peter Green, retired."

"Peter Green?" said Sam, "Teri's husband? He's dead? How?"

"I believe he was poisoned," said Latimer.

"Poisoned? That's terrible. But when did he die?" said Sam.

"Sergeant Green died in hospital yesterday evening. Both Mr. Burke and Sergeant Green attended a party here on Saturday night. Is that true?" The policeman's facial expression was one of determination. He quickly scribbled the gist of the interview in his notebook.

"Yes, but they were both quite healthy when they left," said Sam, "By the way, did you know you've got something black on your chin? Here, let me clean it off."

Sam took out a tissue and wiped the constable's chin and said, "There, that's better."

"No. Stop that!" said Latimer, raising his voice, "I'm here on official police business."

"But I thought you were off duty?"

"I'm never off duty. Now, you work in a chemist's, is that correct?"

"Not quite. I'm a research biochemist."

"You have access to poisons, like strychnine. Is that true?"

"Well, I could get it if I needed to, but ..."

"So, you can get strychnine," interrupted Latimer, "And you had the opportunity to lace the drinks of Burke and Sergeant Green on Saturday night."

Latimer was getting more excited. His interrogation was going really well.

Unfortunately, Sam spoilt his accusative flow. "But I don't have any strychnine in the house. Why would I have it? Besides, I haven't seen Burke for years, and I'd never even met Peter before Saturday. What possible motive would I have to harm them?"

Latimer crossed the kitchen to the spot where he'd been sitting earlier and said, "Right now, I don't know why you did it, but I know that you've got the stuff in here!"

He flung open the door of the wall cupboard and took out the jar labelled, *STRYCHNINE*.

Sam laughed and said, "That's sugar. You had some in your coffee earlier." Then as the smile fell from her face she continued, "Oh my God. Activated carbon. You've been to hospital. That's why you left in such a hurry. Oh, you poor thing! Thinking you'd been poisoned with strychnine. It must have been awful. I'm so sorry. All that silly talk about the stuff. That label. It's our little joke, we use old chemical jars for our food. It keeps the insects out. We used to have terrible trouble with ants and moths getting into the packets of sugar, flour and cereals. Then we decided to use empty jars from work. Of course, we give them a good wash out, but we leave the labels on, just as a joke. Oh, how awful, thinking that you were about to die. I'm so sorry."

Latimer, still suspicious, opened the jar and sniffed at the contents. He hadn't a clue what strychnine smelled like, but he thought it might look as if he knew what he was doing. Sam grabbed the jar off him and poured out a spoonful of the crystals on her hand. Then she licked the sugar up and swallowed it.

Sam returned the jar to him and said, "Here, try some."

Latimer looked at the white crystals in the jar and thought to himself that she might have taken the antidote before eating the poison, so he declined. "I'll take this for analysis. Meanwhile, let's finish the interview, unless you'd rather go down the station. What time did the minibus get here on Saturday night?"

"About half eleven."

"And when did Mr. Burke leave?"

"I don't know, around half twelve? I didn't see him leave, but I can't recall seeing him after half past. He must have been bored and decided to walk home. I'm afraid we're not very good at throwing parties."

Oblivious to the presence of the PC, Alan entered the room saying, "Definitely the wrong terminals. I'll have to take it back and change it. Oh hello. Are you back again? What are you doing with the sugar?"

Sam turned to Alan and explained, "Constable Latimer has had a very nasty experience tonight. He thought he'd been poisoned with strychnine. I was just trying to tell him about our little bit of fun with the labels."

"Oh, the old reagent jars. I suppose it might look a bit suspicious." Alan then asked Latimer, "Could you pass the sodium hydroxide, please. It's about cocoa time. Would you like a mug or do you have to get away?"

Latimer put the sugar down on the table and took the sodium hydroxide jar out of the cupboard. Unscrewing the lid, he got a small cloud of cocoa powder on his hands. Again, he sniffed the contents, not knowing if sodium hydroxide had a distinctive bouquet. What he smelt was the inviting aroma of chocolate. Suppressing a sneeze and feeling a little embarrassed, Latimer held the jar for Alan, who snatched it out of his hand.

Latimer looked on silently as Alan took the cocoa and sugar over to the worktop near the range, where he mixed three mugs of cocoa. Before giving the drinks a final stir, Alan added a pinch of salt from the salt cellar to each mug.

Latimer's suspicions were once again aroused and he asked, "What's that you're putting in?"

"It's salt, my secret ingredient for the perfect cup of drinking chocolate. Brings out the flavour perfectly. We're having crumpets, constable. Suppose you'll be wanting some as well?"

As the three of them sat around the table drinking their cocoa and eating crumpets, Sam noticed a black stain on Latimer's shirt collar.

"That stuff gets everywhere," she said, "Let me see if I can get it off. Can't have you going back to the station like that, can we?"

"I'll be going straight home."

"Well, would you like to finish interviewing me before you go?"

Latimer took out his notebook. Sam handed him a piece of kitchen roll to wipe the butter from his fingers.

"Mr. Burke left early. Did anyone else leave early?"

"No," said Sam, turning to Alan, who agreed by shaking his head.

"And you both stayed in after the bus left?"

"Yes, we had no reason to go out. We just went to bed. It really had been a very long day," said Sam.

"Finally, do you know anyone who might want to do Mr. Burke harm? Did anyone argue with him at the party?"

Sam and Alan both shook their heads and murmured, "No. Can't think of anybody."

"That's it," said Latimer, "No more questions."

"So how did Burke die?" asked Sam.

"I shouldn't really tell you, because it hasn't been released, but you'll find out sooner or later. He either fell or was pushed off the cliff in Whitehouse Wood. Broke his neck. The DCI reckons it's murder, but there's no forensics. The crime scene was a mess. Members of the public had been all over it. They reckon it's some sort of drugs war. He'd had his thumb chopped off, probably using bolt croppers. The DCI arrested a local drug dealer but had to release him 'cos he's got a watertight alibi. The only evidence against him was his fingerprints found at the scene, but he had an explanation for that."

151

Latimer's tongue had been loosened more effectively, with a kind word and a mug of cocoa, than a skinful of alcohol could ever do. He went on to disclose the details of the tobacco pouch, full of weed, the bottle and the discrepancy about the time of death.

Sam decided to risk putting a different scenario to the officer. "What if he was killed somewhere else and then dumped in the woods?"

"Ah well, the pathologist has a test which tells whether the body has been moved. But it hadn't. Or if it had been moved, it must have been kept in the exact same position as it was found. Something to do with how the blood settles in the body when a person dies."

"How fascinating," said Sam, "He definitely died in the woods?"

Latimer nodded and said, "I'll have to be going. Thank you for the cocoa and crumpets. I must remember, salt. It really does make it nicer, more chocolatey."

Sam and Alan showed him to the front door and when he'd gone, they each gave a great sigh of relief.

"Nice lad. When he stops being a copper," said Sam, "I felt so sorry for him. He took it all in. Strychnine and all that. He didn't realise I was joking. He thought I'd poisoned him. Poor beggar."

Alan said, "I still wouldn't trust him. Once a copper, always a pig."

Sam said, "Behave. Did you see the charcoal on his shirt? Just like our first aid drills at Falmer's, except we didn't have to actually drink the stuff."

Alan disappeared back down to the cellar for a final check before bedtime. Sam returned to the kitchen to wash up the cocoa cups.

The telephone rang but stopped before Sam could dry her hands and get to the cordless handset on the kitchen table. She finished the washing up, turned out the light and joined Alan in the hall.

"Everything alright? asked Sam.

"I'll swap the battery first thing in the morning. I can't believe I got the wrong one."

Chapter 7

The next morning Sam answered the front door to find two men in overcoats, waiting to be allowed in the house. The taller man was wearing a trilby.

"DCI Richards, and this is DS Willoughby," said Richards as he flashed his warrant card, "We're here to talk to Mr Alan Murray and Mr Samuel Black. Are they at home?"

Sam toyed with the idea of stringing the pompous plod along, but thought better of it. "Alan's not here at the moment, but I'm Samantha Black. There is no Samuel Black."

"Oh, sorry Madam. We've obviously been misinformed. Do you mind if we come in?"

Sam showed them into the living room. Her rationale for choosing the cold room was to make them as uncomfortable as possible, so that they would be more keen to leave. The same logic demanded that they would not be offered any refreshments. Instead she simply asked, "How can I help you, inspector?"

"We're inquiring into the suspicious death of a Mr. Malcolm Burke. We are led to believe that he attended a party here last Saturday night. Is that true?"

"Yes. He was here," said Sam.

"Tell me, at what time did he leave the party?"

"I'm not sure. He was here at about twelve, but I can't recall seeing him after that."

"Who else was at the party?"

"Well, there was myself and Alan, Teri Green and her husband, Lesley Connor and her friend, George Wilson, Rat Foster, Wendy Simpson and Dixie. That's John Dixon."

"Rat Foster, madam?" said Richards.

"Sorry, John Foster. We always called him Rat at school. We'd been to a reunion at the King's Head before the party. Oh, and a young couple, called Bob and Catherine, arrived at the door towards the end of the party. Poor things had been stuck in the snow."

Richards waited a few seconds while Willoughby finished writing all the names in his notebook. "Can you vouch for Mr Foster being here throughout the party? He didn't disappear for any length of time, did he?"

"As far as I can remember he was in this room all night. He became the resident DJ. Oh, wait, he did go out for a smoke some time."

"How long was he away."

"Just a few minutes. Is it important?"

"It could well be," said Richards, "We're just trying to build up a picture of everyone's whereabouts at the moment. Did anyone else leave the party early? Was anyone else missing for any length of time?"

"No, they all stayed until the bus came, apart from Burke. I didn't notice anybody going out of this room except for bathroom visits. The weather was pretty bad outside."

"Can you think of anyone who might have wished Mr. Burke harm?" said Richards.

"Well, I don't think he was a very popular man. He wasn't liked at school, but I can't really say that anyone would wish him harm. Excuse me for asking, inspector, but do you think he was murdered?"

"Oh yes, madam. He was definitely illegally killed. Whether it was murder or manslaughter is open to debate, but somebody pushed him over the edge in Whitehouse Wood. No doubt about it."

"Really?" said Sam, "How awful."

"Would you mind if I used your bathroom, please Miss Black?" asked Richards, employing his usual ploy to have a nose around the house.

"Of course, inspector. I'll show you where," replied Sam, equally determined not to let him poke around too much.

She escorted Richards upstairs to the toilet next to the bathroom, then stood guard at the top of the stairs, trying to listen to see if Willoughby was nosing about in the living room. She heard the flush and the basin tap running. Richards appeared from the toilet, turned along the corridor towards the back stairs and was approaching the rear landing door when Sam said, "This way, inspector. The stairs are down here."

"Oh sorry, I must have lost my bearings," said Richards.

Sam smiled and said, "Yes," then under her breath, "I know your game, mate. I wasn't born yesterday."

They returned to the living room and Richards announced that they had all the information they came for and that they might need to get back later. He picked up his hat and left the room with Willoughby in tow. As the three of them crossed the hall, the bell

156

rang. Sam opened the door and found George Wilson standing on the doorstep.

"Come in," she said, "These men are from the police. They're just leaving."

George entered the hall and said, "Sergeant Willoughby, how nice to see you again, and you must be Detective Chief Inspector Smith. Pleased to meet you."

Richards turned and gave Willoughby an enquiring look. The sergeant said, "This is Mr. George Wilson, sir."

"It's DCI Richards, actually," said the inspector.

George frowned and said, "Oh, I thought I knew you from somewhere."

Sam said to George, "The inspector came to ask about Malcolm Burke and the party the other night."

"Yes, isn't it terrible," said George, "Burke having such a nasty accident. Poor fellow."

Richards said, "It wasn't an accident."

"Are you sure?" said George with the slightest of smiles.

"Oh yes, sir"

George said, "Who would want to kill Burke? Was it a mugging gone wrong?"

"He wasn't robbed. Whoever did it, killed him over drugs. He was a dealer," said the inspector.

"Never," said George, "Burke, a drug dealer? You're kidding."

"I'm sorry but we have to get back to the station. Goodbye Miss Black, Mr. Wilson," said Richards.

As the two policemen made for the door, George said to Richards, "Tell you what, I'll give you odds of two to one that it was an accident. If I'm right and it was accidental, you buy me dinner. If you're right and it was murder, I buy you and Mrs. Smith dinner at the Royal. What do you say?"

Richards didn't say anything. He simply walked with Willoughby to the car and left.

After the police had gone, Sam turned to George and asked, "Why did you come here? It might arouse their suspicions."

"I was coming to warn you that the coppers would probably be coming to see you today. That sergeant was round the Royal yesterday, wanting to know about the party. I had to tell him your address. He seemed to be very interested in Rat. Then he asked about where the coats were put during the party. I can't think why."

"Where the coats were? They were on the kitchen table."

"That's what I told him. Oh, he asked what kind of coats Rat and Burke were wearing. I told him Burke had a sheepskin, but I couldn't remember what Rat was wearing."

"Well, he had a sheepskin as well. A woman notices that sort of thing. Men are useless at it. You don't think that the coats got mixed up, do you. We didn't put Rat's coat on Burke, did we?"

George thought for a while then said, "No. There was only one coat left on the table, so if it was Rat's, he must have taken Burke's by mistake. I don't think he was that far out of it. What's more worrying is that Burke's coat was still on the table at the end of the night. Anybody could have noticed it and told the police."

In the kitchen, as Sam prepared coffees, George said, "Where's Al?"

"He had to go into Durham. Should be back soon."

"I've got a bone to pick with him. Those pills are nothing but paracetamol. I had them analysed."

"You did what!" said Sam, "This project is top secret. You can't just give any old Tom, Dick and Harry samples of Meth 4."

"There wasn't any Methyphenax in them," said George, slightly heated, "Just paracetamol and a tiny bit of THC."

"George. They were the genuine article. I can assure you. Where did you get them analysed?"

"A friend of mine at the university."

"And what instruments did they use?

"What? How the hell would I know?"

"Okay. If they used a standard analysis using chromatography and mass spectrometry, they would probably mistake the Meth 4 molecule for THC. They have extremely similar signatures. Which is hardly surprising because they're virtually isomers and produce very similar fragments. They'd have to use a Murray-Black Fraction to be able to separate the two compounds – and the process isn't widely available yet."

"A merry black what? Never mind – consider me lost," George said. Chemistry wasn't his strongest subject.

"Well just take my word for it. THC and Methyphenax 4 are extremely similar compounds, but with very different properties. THC more or less directly affects receptors in the brain, whereas Meth 4 acts on the immune system. It only takes a tiny amount of it to activate the body's defence against cancerous cells, which is why it appeared as only a trace of THC. Understand?"

"Just about." George shrugged.

"Now for the bad news. We've just heard that the trial has been stopped. There's some doubt about whether it's effective against human cancers. I'm so sorry, George, but you're really going to have to get a second opinion on surgery."

George sat down at the table and took a mouthful of coffee.

He said, "As it happens, when I found out that the pills were duff, I went and signed up for surgery. I knew it was too good to be true. I'm just waiting for them to get back with a date for the operation."

"Oh, I'm so glad to hear that," said Sam, gripping his hand across the table, "You'll be fine."

"I bloody hope so. Scares the shit out of me."

"By the way, what was all that about with Richards? Betting him that Burke's death was accidental?"

"Oh, just a little blackmail," said George. He went on to explain how he'd discovered the DCI's little secret affair with the woman PC and that they had a regular date at the Royal every Tuesday evening as Mr.

and Mrs. Smith. "By making the bet, I was telling him that I know about his secret and if he continues to treat Burke's death as suspicious, it won't be a secret much longer."

"Oh, you naughty boy. But, don't you think it was a bit too subtle. He might not get it."

"Possibly, but it's only an insurance policy anyway. I don't think they've got much evidence of foul play."

* * * *

By the time that the two detectives arrived back at the station and entered Richards' office, DS Willoughby had heard enough of his superior officer's rants about the ginger bastard and Wilson's disrespect for the forces of law and order.

George's blackmail attempt had been far too subtle for the great detective, who definitely hadn't got the message.

"I mean, who the hell does he think he's talking to?" said Richards, "Making a bet? And what was all that about DCI Smith? Do you know a DCI Smith?"

"No, sir. I've no idea – never heard of any DCI Smith," said Willoughby, handing an A4 envelope to his boss. "The pathology report, sir."

Richards took the envelope but delayed opening it. He said nothing for a minute as he slapped the large envelope against his left hand. Then, giving a final flap of the envelope, he said, "DCI Smith. No, I don't get it." He tore at the seal and said, "Never mind. Let's see what *Doctor* Smith has to say, shall we?"

The pathologist's report formed a stapled pile of about a dozen A4 sheets. Willoughby sighed as he looked at the sheaf and said, "I think the executive summary's usually on the front sheet, sir."

"It's alright, sergeant," said Richards, "We'll go through it and I can explain any technical stuff for you. I've seen quite a few of these in my time. Medical jargon holds no mystery for me."

Willoughby looked away and had a furtive glance at his watch.

Richards turned to the second page of the report and started to read. "*Broken neck, severing spinal cord, consistent with a fall. Fractured rib consistent with blow to chest or result of fall. No sign of post-mortem relocation. Time of death estimated midnight to 2 a.m. on Sunday morning. Core temperature inconclusive due to location in frost hollow and exposure of penis to ambient.* Hah! He's backed down. Found himself an excuse for his cock up. The SOCOs got it right and he got it wrong. Oh, here we are. *Toxicology. Small amount of alcohol in bloodstream. Drugs and toxins undetectable. Stomach contents normal for omnivorous human. Sample of co-located vomit shows presence of surfactants and high bacterial load. Not consistent with deceased's stomach contents. Old wound to end of left thumb. Recent wound to right thumb shows teeth marks in flesh and on bone surface, consistent with fox scavenging. No other significant bruising or ligature marks. Conclusions. Death caused by fall from cliff in Whitehouse Wood superior to body location. No third-party involvement can be either shown or disproven.* Oh, wait a minute. I missed this bit. *Cowper's fluid present in urethral tract. Seminal fluid absent. Sperm absent from vesicles. Evidence of vasectomy. Gland surface free from foreign secretions.* What's that mean?"

Willoughby said, "He'd had a hard on, but hadn't finished his hand job."

"So, he wasn't having a piss in the woods, then?"

162

"Maybe not."

"Dirty beggar."

"Shall I call off the search for blood-stained bolt croppers, sir?"

Before Richards could reprimand his sergeant for the cheeky little dig, the phone rang. He picked up the receiver and listened for a few seconds, waved Willoughby away and started his telephone conversation with, "Yes, sir. I've got it in my hand."

"No sir, but …"

The one-way conversation continued for a minute, with Richards meekly acknowledging his superior on the other end of the line. At the end of the call he said, "Yes sir. Straight away, sir."

Richards replaced the receiver and shouted for his sergeant.

When Willoughby returned to the office Richards said, "I've decided to scale down the murder enquiry with immediate effect. We don't have any evidence to suggest that it was anything other than an accident. Ask DI James to close down the room and tidy up the paperwork. Let the coroner's office know."

"But, sir. He could have been pushed."

"Without a witness or other evidence, I can't justify the overtime. Our only suspect has an alibi and a lawyer who'd tear us to shreds in court. It's just a case of one more drug dealer off the streets for good."

As Willoughby was leaving the office to break the news to the teams in the incident room, Richards called to him, "Tell Latimer I want to see him."

* * * *

The following day the police station was slowly returning to its normal routine. By the afternoon the officers who had been drafted in from other divisions were no longer cluttering up the corridors and hogging the hot drinks. Reports were completed and notebooks collected. By four o'clock the incident room was empty. DI James switched off the lights and closed the door behind him.

Upstairs DCI Richards sat at his desk, drinking a cup of tea. Willoughby appeared at the doorway and said "The coroner's office have set the date for re-opening the Burke inquest. Week next Wednesday at ten."

"Right," said Richards, "It'll be a formality. Death by misadventure, probably. It would have been nice to pin it on that Foster, but never mind. We can keep a special eye on him and see what he gets up to on the drugs front. He'll put a foot wrong sometime. His type always do."

"So, you'll be paying out on the bet then, sir?"

"What bet?"

"With Wilson. He said that if …"

"I know what he said, but I didn't agree to his stupid bet. Anyway, what I'm more interested in is whether the cocky bastard had inside information about the cause of death. Check him out. Previous convictions, anything on PNC, and see if he has contacts in pathology or the coroner's office."

Chapter 8

Thursday 13th April

Sam was in the plant room. As she lifted open the glass door to the access chamber, the draught from the extractor fluttered the material around the wrist of her coverall. She carefully opened the plastic jar and decanted the contents into the feeder. The empty jar bubbled as it sank into the sinkful of neutralising solution. She washed her gloves in the sink and closed the access chamber door. After giving the gloves a final wash, she removed them and discarded them in a plastic bin bag.

The red battery warning light was still flashing on the computer monitor screen. An orange light stood out among the green ones. Sam double clicked on the orange light and a box appeared on the screen, stating 'STRYCHNINE FEED LOW'. She clicked the refresh icon and the warning box disappeared as the orange light turned green. She switched the monitor over to CCTV and left the room. As she closed the plant room PVC door, the cellar door above creaked as footsteps clacked on the hall floor. Sam said, "Always gives me the willies, that stuff. Are you making coffee, sweetie?"

Looking round, there was nobody there. She left the cellar and locked the door.

"Alan? Is that you?" she shouted, "Coffee?"

Sam made her way to the kitchen, washed her hands, and put the kettle on.

"Where's Al?" said a voice behind her.

Sam turned in surprise and gasped. "Rat! Bloody hell. What are you doing here? I nearly had a heart attack."

Rat was sweating and breathing heavily as he repeated, "Where's Al? I need to see him."

"Okay. He's just outside feeding the hens. He'll be back soon," said Sam, wondering what Rat was after.

"Where's he at?" said Rat, getting more agitated.

"Calm down. He won't be long."

"I know all about you," said Rat, as he tried to hold his left leg to stop its involuntary spasm.

Sam tried to settle him. "Okay, breathe slowly, deep breaths."

This seemed to calm him down, so she asked, "How about a nice drink?"

"Yeah, why not? A nice drink. That's what I need."

"Tea or coffee? Milk and sugar?"

Rat reverted to panic mode with, "I'm going through the big C …" He coughed and curled up with his arms around his chest. He tried to continue. "Big C.T." Another bout of chest pain as he coughed again. "Yeah, milk and sugar. That's gonna sort me out. Get me the stuff."

"Oh my God. I'm so sorry, Rat," said Sam as Alan walked into the room.

Rat turned his attention to Alan, and said, "I've got to have the stuff. It hurts fuck and my head's going to burst."

"What did the doctor say? Is it operable?" asked Sam

"Operable? Don't be fucking stupid. Doctors can't do anything for this," said Rat.

Sam beckoned to Alan and said out of earshot of the sweating Rat, "He's got cancer as well, and he says he knows all about the Meth 4."

Rat said, "I know you're talking about me. I'm not deaf."

Sam offered him a cup and said, "Here's your tea. White with sugar. Now what's this about?"

Rat pushed the cup away and said, "I know your little secret. I need the stuff and if I don't get it, I'm going to the police."

"What secret?" asked Sam.

Foster's right shoulder rose involuntarily and his neck twitched as he replied, "Burke died here in this house. His coat was still on the table when the bus came. He wouldn't have left in the snow without it. Now, give me the stuff or I go to the cops."

Sam said, "I don't know what you're on about, but the stuff only works on rats. It's no good for human use."

"Are you taking the piss? The name's John and I want a hundred tabs for starters. And I never did like that nickname."

Sam looked at Alan, who shrugged and said, "I'll go and press some pills."

"Make them five milligrams," said Sam.

"Five? Are you sure?" said Alan.

Sam nodded. "Best to be on the safe side."

With Alan out of the room, Rat made himself more comfortable in a chair near the range. He was still sweating and twitching as he said, "I know your other little secret."

"What other little secret?"

"You and George Wilson." said Rat, with a laugh which seemed to cause him a great deal of pain. "Dumping ... dumping Burke's body then having it off in the car."

"Who's been telling you that?" she laughed.

"Somebody who saw you," said Rat, with a smile, not daring to risk another laugh.

"You can't believe everything that people tell you."

"Oh, I think I can believe her. She even got the car number plate. All I have to do is tell the coppers anonymously. They look up the number and then come calling."

"You wouldn't do that, would you?"

"Try me. If you don't play ball with me, the coppers will be swarming all over here. And, I don't believe that gear in your cellar's a home brewery. That's where you make the stuff, isn't it? You'll get done for that as well as murder."

"Our operation here is completely legal," said Sam, ignoring the fact that they had a massive stockpile of THC in the cellar.

"There you go again. Thinking that they're going to legalise it. It's not going to happen."

"What?"

Rat continued, "There's far too much at stake. The government's run by brewers and distillers. They'd lose a fortune if it was legalised. That Commission which recommended decriminalisation got shot down when the bloody Ministry of Health published the lies about addiction and lowering sperm counts. They'll never legalise it."

Sam went quiet as she tried to understand his ranting.

When Alan returned with a bottle of pills, Foster was still threatening. "I know you're making the stuff here and if you don't want the cops round here, you'll keep me supplied." He then took one of the pills.

Sam said, "You'll only need them for about a month, one every eight hours, then everything should be sorted."

"A month? I'm going into it big time. Wholesale."

"You can't do that, there's a patent on it," said Sam.

"You've got to be joking," said Rat as he left.

When Rat had gone Sam turned to Alan and said, "He looked in a really bad way. I don't know what sort of dose he's going to need."

"It's okay, I put five milligrams in them. That's pretty strong. I ran out of the pure stuff and had to make it up with raw."

Sam said, "The only trouble is that if he takes too much, he might get some really bad side effects."

"Well, with that amount of THC in the mix, he'll definitely get one side effect. But then he'll be too stoned to worry about any of the others."

Sam said, "I don't think he's going to last long enough for the Meth 4 to work. His doctor must have told him it's terminal. He was in terrible pain. The only other time I've seen anybody like that was when you overdosed on THC. Do you remember? You had the twitches, the shakes and you were sweating buckets."

"Yes. I don't want to go through that again. It was awful. It wasn't so much the overdose, more the withdrawal. It was like going through cold turkey. Aches and pains. Bloody awful. When I coughed, it hurt like mad. The only thing that helped was more of the same. I can see how people can get addicted to cannabis if they take too much."

Alan realised that Sam was not listening to him. She seemed to be daydreaming.

She said, "What was it he said? *Going through the big C. Tea with milk and sugar?* He didn't even drink it."

As John Foster walked by the river, he popped another pill and thought that if these were as good as the ones Alan had given him before, he could make a real killing supplying the Durham students. Within a couple of minutes, he could feel the effect coming over him. The muscular pain was retreating and he no longer had the shakes. He laughed and it didn't hurt.

* * * *

At six thirty a battered old Land Rover parked next to the large plant pot outside the farmhouse. Alan walked over to have a look at the clapped-out heap. He seemed to be particularly interested in the interior of the vehicle. "Nice motor," he said as Latimer got out. The two men crunched over the gravel to the front door and crossed the hall into the kitchen, where Sam was making a pot of tea.

170

Latimer explained that his visit was strictly a social call, and that he was off duty. He was calling in to thank Sam and Alan for their kindness to him on Tuesday.

The young PC said, "I don't get to talk to many people outside of work. It can get very lonely, being an off-duty policeman."

Sam asked, "You're not married, then?"

"No, not yet. I've been going out with someone for two months, now. She's very pretty with her turned up nose. A bit older than me, but she's got a sort of mental block about men since she was abused by her brother when she was young. Right now, I live alone in a pokey little flat. Costs a fortune in rent. Maybe I should move out of Durham. Get out of the student area. Most nights I just sit in and watch television, except when I take Angie to the pictures."

Sam said, "So where exactly is your pokey little flat, then?"

Latimer said, "The top end of Bishop Street."

"Well that's quite a nice area," said Sam.

"No, it's not. It's awful. In term-time the noise overnight is terrible. I can't sleep when I'm on days. I really look forward to night shift," said the policeman.

Alan said, "Well, maybe you should join in the student parties. Could be fun. Have a few drinks, maybe do a bit of cannabis, you know."

"I don't drink," said Latimer, "And cannabis is illegal." He sniffed the air in the room and continued, "You don't use it, do you?"

171

"Of course not," said Alan, "Whatever gives you that idea?"

"Well, you always seem to be so relaxed, — happy even," said Latimer, "Maybe I'll take some when it's legalised."

"Yes, I think you might enjoy that," said Alan. He turned away from the copper and muttered, "Might stop you crying in your cocoa."

Sam felt such pity for the depressed young man that she nearly gave him an open invitation to come for a chat any time. However, she realised that this could well be disastrous if Latimer wandered into the house as easily as Rat Foster had done earlier.

She said, "If you ever fancy a chat, just give us a call and we can meet up for a coffee in Durham somewhere. Tea?"

"I'd like that," said Latimer, accepting the cup. He continued, "It's good to have someone nice to talk to for a change – especially when you've had the DCI threatening you with the sack."

"Oh, that's awful," said Sam, "Why would he want to do that?"

"He said that it was me that started the murder hunt. But all I said was that Sergeant Green, or ex-Sergeant Green, or now the *late* ex-Sergeant Green, had complained about feeling unwell and he said it was murder. I never said that Malcolm Burke was murdered. So now the DCI says that I was responsible for wasting a lot of time and effort and overtime, chasing a murderer when it was accidental death. And he says I should resign or he'll get me sacked."

"Well I think that's terrible," said Sam.

"Can he really do that?" asked Alan.

"Well, I don't think he can do it straight away, but he could get me a written warning and then stitch me up later. He as good as said so. I could kill him." Latimer was close to tears as he continued, "Police work's all I've got. Left school with 'O' levels, but I can't do anything else. I hate him. Wish he was dead."

"That's a bit strong, isn't it?" said Alan

"You wouldn't be talking about DCI Richards, by any chance, would you?" asked Sam.

"Yes, why?" said Latimer.

"Well I don't think you should worry too much. He's got a dirty little secret," said Sam.

"What little secret?"

Sam then told Latimer about DCI Richards' Tuesday nights with dirty Donna at the Royal. She suggested that if Richards approached Latimer again, he should threaten to spill the beans and that would keep Richards off his case. The young PC perked up and said that he would need to get proof, to substantiate the story, and he knew exactly how to get it.

Latimer smiled and said, "He even accused me of making a fool of him, 'cos I didn't tell him that Sam was short for Samantha. He said he'd asked about Samuel Black when he came to see you."

"Well, he'd have to be a right idiot to assume that Sam could only be short for Samuel," said Alan.

After a short silence Latimer said, "I tried to tell him it wasn't Samuel at the debriefing, but he just went on. *Just the contents of the notebook, Latimer.*" He tried to do his impression of his senior's pompous delivery, but broke down in laughter.

"Thank you for tonight," said Latimer, rising to leave.

"Thanks for calling," said Sam, leaning forward to give him a peck on the cheek before escorting him out of the house.

As she returned to the warmth of the kitchen, Sam asked Alan, "I thought you put the new battery on?"

"I did."

"Well the warning light's back on again," said Sam.

"Must be the charger circuit. I'll have a look at it in the morning."

Sam took the tea cups to the sink and emptied the dregs out. "Didn't you say that you burnt all the blood-stained stuff from the back stairs?"

Alan replied, "Yes I did, why?"

"There's still a cloth near the sink downstairs, and it's got blood on it. Best get it in the fire, straight away."

"Oh, it's not Malcolm Burke's blood. I had one of my nose bleeds. I'll chuck it out tomorrow."

Sam broke off her washing up and turned to Alan. "You've started getting them again?"

He gave a half shrug and said, "Maybe my blood pressure's up again with all the stress."

* * * *

At five thirty on the following Tuesday evening, a man sat reading a tabloid newspaper in the lobby of the Royal Hotel. He was seated at a small table, directly across the room from the reception desk. All that the receptionist could see of him was the man's fingers holding the newspaper up. Occasionally, as the front door opened, the top of the man's head would appear above the newspaper. He was wearing a flat cap and sunglasses. A waiter approached the table and asked if he could get him anything. Without dropping his newspaper, the man ordered a mug of drinking chocolate, with a small pinch of salt in it.

With his wife safely on her way to her weekly keep-fit session on the exercise cycle at the gym in Chester-Le-Street, DCI Richards arrived at the Royal with the delectable Donna, eagerly looking forward to his own bike ride. He didn't need to say much to the evening receptionist who handed him a room key after asking him to sign the register. Mr. Smith was becoming a bit of a regular, along with the young Mrs. Smith.

Flat cap man changed his grip on the newspaper such that he could hold it up with one hand. With his other hand, he held his disposable camera up above the newspaper and pressed the shutter release, hoping to get a covert shot. "Bugger," he said, as he realised that the flash had operated.

For a second, Richards was taken aback, then as he spotted the would-be paparazzo, he strode purposefully towards the man with the camera. The man stood up, dropped his newspaper and spilt the cocoa as he ran like a frightened bunny for the door.

Having seen all of the action, a red-haired man, sitting at a vantage point in the residents' lounge, laughed as he watched Richards and Donna take the lift. He felt a headache coming on and reached into his pocket for another Morphine Sulphate pill. He read

175

the letter again for the third time. It informed him that his appointment on Thursday had been cancelled as the consultant did not need to see him to arrange the date for his operation. Instead, the patient was asked to attend a pre-operative check-up at the hospital in preparation for the procedure, which would take place in four weeks' time.

He then pulled a leaflet, *Brain Tumour Surgery – The Facts*, from the large envelope on the table. Reading through it, he found that he would need a total of four hospital visits in the next month before the operation. No matter how much reassurance the leaflet offered, George knew that there was still a chance that he might die on the operating table, wake up paralysed or never wake up at all and spend the rest of his life in a coma. He pushed his fingers through his hair and felt the scar in the scalp on the top of his head where they had drilled for the biopsy and thought about how they were going to peel back the skin and saw a piece out of his skull. He shivered. There was still time to cancel the operation.

Chapter 9

Wednesday 19th April

DCI Richards arrived early for work on Wednesday morning. Before he reached his office, he shouted for Willoughby to get Latimer.

Before Latimer could say anything, Richards slammed the door behind him and demanded, "What the hell were you playing at last night? Were you stalking me, you little pervert? I'll shove your fucking balls down your throat. Just keep the fuck out of my private life. Understand?"

Latimer stood to attention, but winced as the big man shouted the words in his ear. Then, as Richards stopped to take a breath, Latimer said nervously, "I've got a picture of you, sir. And I'll use it."

"You'll do what!" shouted Richards. His fist was clenched ready to strike, until he looked through the office glass partition and realised that the lower ranks were watching, enthralled.

"Get out! I'll expect your resignation within the hour," said Richards, dropping his fist from Latimer's face.

"I'll not resign, sir," said Latimer, "And if you keep victimising me, I'll go public, sir"

With that, Latimer hurriedly left the room.

Willoughby entered, to be greeted by, "What now!" from Richards.

"We've just got a report from the General, sir. That drug dealer, Foster – he was admitted last night and died in the early hours."

Richards took a calming breath and said, "That's all I need. A drug war. How was he killed? Drive by shooting? Or was he thrown off a cliff as well?"

"The report says it was an auto-immune condition."

"AIDS?"

"No sir," The sergeant read from the sheet of paper he was holding. "It was a Myasthenic Crisis? Cause of death, respiratory failure. He was admitted yesterday and his condition deteriorated very quickly."

"So, they're saying it was a sudden death?"

"They say it's caused by the body's immune system going wrong. It starts to attack the body itself. They reckon that people can live with it for some time without too many symptoms, but then if they get stressed or some sort of trauma it can trigger an attack. Apparently in Foster's case he got worse and it progressed very quickly at the end. They couldn't save him even on life support. There were other complications. Liver and kidney damage."

"Any indication of a poison being administered?"

"No sir. Not yet. There's toxicology results outstanding, but the hospital's path lab hasn't found any sign yet."

"Hang on," said Richards, "There's something fishy here. First, we get one drug dealer, Burke, falling or being pushed off Lover's Leap, then Peter Green dies of what looks like a heart attack, and now we've got the other dealer, Foster, dying of some sort of super

AIDS. There's one common denominator. They were all at that party."

"That's right, sir. But there's no sign of foul play. And no evidence to link the three deaths to the party. Surely it's just a coincidence."

Richards lectured his sergeant. "As someone once said – *In our profession there's no such thing as coincidence, just work to be done.* There's definitely something dodgy about that Black woman. She was on edge all the time we were in the house and she wouldn't let me out of her sight. They've just got to be hiding something, and I'm going to find out what. That farmhouse is far too big for just two people. No kids or live-in relations. Why would they need such a place as that? Answer – because they're growing cannabis. It's ideal for them. A nice big attic. In the middle of nowhere. Peter Green smelled weed alright. It was probably permeating the whole house. "

"Well I couldn't smell it, sir."

Richards continued, "It's there alright. And I'm going to find it. Get a search warrant and we'll surprise them this afternoon."

Willoughby exhaled and shook his head slightly. "Do you think that's wise, sir?"

"What do you mean?"

"Well, we haven't any firm evidence, just hearsay. The beak wasn't very happy last time, especially when we didn't find any arms cache and your dealer turned out to be a friend of a friend of his."

"Okay, sergeant. No need to drag up ancient history. Here's what we'll do. You're going to invite Alan Murphy and Samantha Black to come to the

179

station to help with enquiries into the Foster death. You know – *Did he look ill at the party? What did he have to eat? Did he seem stressed or traumatised?* Improvise. See if they know what could have triggered this myasthingy crisis. I'm going to have a look around that farmhouse. Keep them here for a good hour or so. When I've found the skunk farm, I'll call you on my mobile and you can detain them here."

"Are you sure, sir? Wouldn't it be better to wait until we can gather more evidence against them and then get a warrant?"

"Trust me. We've got to strike while the iron's hot. Give them a call right now."

"You might want to let the iron cool down a little, sir. You've got that inquest at ten."

"Damn, I forgot about that. Okay, as soon as the inquest's done, we go."

The inquest was for the most part a formality. Two witness statements delayed matters for a short while. Doctor Smith's uncertainty about time of death threatened to derail the whole process until the coroner was satisfied that the estimate was indeed subject to a large possible error due to the unseasonably cold night. Following this, DCI Richards' begrudging acceptance of the lack of evidence of a criminal act put a doubt in the coroner's mind. He repeatedly asked Richards to give a definitive answer as to whether any evidence had been found to suggest third party involvement in the fall. Eventually the coroner decided that enough time had been wasted and thanked Richards, telling him to stand down.

The coroner summed up the findings, saying that Mr. Burke's death was caused by severe damage to the spinal cord due to a fall from the top of Lover's Leap while the deceased's mind was distracted. As a comfort to any relatives in court, he reiterated Doctor Smith's opinion that death would have been instantaneous and that the deceased would not have suffered. The verdict was then announced – death by misadventure.

Richards drove to his rendezvous with Willoughby in a lay-by on the main road near the turn-off for the farmhouse. He signalled to his sergeant to go and pick up the couple for questioning and waited in his car until he saw Willoughby driving them away up the main road. He pulled on a pair of latex gloves, checked his watch, and strode off in the direction of the farmhouse.

As the detective approached the front door, he heard a bell ringing inside the house. He decided that it wasn't loud enough to attract attention from anyone passing by on the main road. Sizing up the solid oak door, he didn't fancy his chances of being able to force the lock with his small jemmy.

Around the side of the house he found the kitchen door, half glazed with Georgian style frosted panes. This was more like it – a flimsy old excuse for a rear entrance. He shoved the jemmy into the gap between the door and the frame next to the lock and levered the tool. Nothing gave. This was no ordinary back door, he decided. Maybe the key was in the lock. He tried to smash the double-glazed unit nearest the lock. Taking the jemmy back like a golfer on a tee shot, he whacked the frame between two of the glazing units. As the jemmy hit the sash, a pain shot up his arm as hard metal met even harder metal.

"Shit!" he cried as the pain hit him.

The blow from the jemmy caused a glazing unit to crack and as a fragment of glass fell away, he noticed the metal foil, stuck to the surface, peel and shear. After a delay of two seconds a deafening siren started sounding.

His curses were drowned out by the 130 decibel sounder. He looked up to see where the noise was coming from. It was directly above him, under the eaves, at a height of about five metres. In desperation, he hurled the jemmy at the sounder. To his amazement the siren stopped. Then he looked up, much as Sir Isaac Newton had done, observing an apple as it fell to the ground. Unfortunately for Richards his Granny Smith bore a worrying resemblance to a hardened steel bar with a nasty sharp end. During its descent, the jemmy broke its journey to Earth with a short visit to Richards' temple.

A little while later, Richards felt the unpleasant sensation of soil in his mouth. He tried to open his eyes and tears flowed involuntarily as grit ground between eyeballs and lids. He could taste blood and spat out some sort of rotten vegetation. For a moment, he wondered why he was unable to focus his eyes. Then he realised that immediately in front of his face was a terracotta plant pot on its side. He reached out his hand to steady himself as he rose to a sitting position. Through the thin gloves he could feel that there was something slimy under his palm. As he sat up, he lifted his hand, revealing a large black slug. Next to the slug was a mortise lock key. At last his luck was changing!

He took out a handkerchief and cleaned as much of the soil away from his eyes as he could. Then he wiped the slug slime off his hand and took the key, thinking how stupid some people were, leaving keys beneath plant pots. He laughed to himself as he contemplated asking the crime prevention officer to call around. Rising to his feet, he dusted off the damp soil from his trousers and offered the key up to the lock. Unfortunately, the lock refused to admit the key. He rattled it about a little, then decided that it was the wrong lock.

Looking at his watch, he calculated that he had only lost five minutes when he was out. He ran to the front door and found that the key didn't fit. At the other side of the house he found a set of steps leading down to a door below ground level. The door looked old and dirty, with cobwebs covering the panels. This was obviously the cellar door and it just had to be a fit for the key. He pushed the key into the lock. This time, it fully engaged and the stiff levers of the lock begrudgingly allowed the key to turn. He was in, at last.

By the door, Richards found a light switch and turned it on. As he entered the room his foot kicked an empty, green, ribbed glass bottle, which skidded noisily across the floor. The hand-written label read 'Tinc D. Purpurea'. In a corner stood the heavy metal chassis of a diesel generator set, bolted to a concrete plinth. Next to the set, a jerrycan lay on its side. Looking around the small room, it became immediately obvious that this was being used as a garden tool shed. In front of him was a very sturdy looking steel door, with neither handle nor keyhole. A label was stuck to the galvanised steel surface – Emergency Exit, Keep Clear.

Realising that this was not going to be the easy way into the house, he left the room and continued his search outside.

Richards had run out of doors, so he looked up at the windows of the farmhouse. He decided to shin up a drainpipe and try his luck with the first-floor French windows. Standing on the balcony, he checked the windows for adhesive foil before bashing the glass with his jemmy. As the pane shattered there was no sound of a burglar alarm, so he climbed through the frame. A quick look around the upstairs sitting room didn't seem to reveal anything of interest. Scientific text books lay open on the table. Nothing related to cultivation of indoor plants, so he made his way to the door and then out into the corridor. Richards recognised the bathroom and toilet from his previous visit and made his way along the corridor towards the back stairs. The door was locked but succumbed easily to the jemmy. He opened the door and was at first disappointed to find the staircase. Then he realised that the upward flight would lead to the attic, the usual place to hide a cannabis farm. He quickly climbed the stairs and arrived at a corridor with a low ceiling.

Opening the first door off the corridor he found nothing but a few stalks of straw on an otherwise clean floor. He left the room and opened another door, causing clouds of dust to fill the air. Long abandoned spider silk wafted into his face and stuck to his hair. Again, there was no sign of a cannabis farm. He felt the urge to sneeze, but managed to hold it back, sniffing. As he walked towards the next door, he realised that the floor boards further down the corridor were covered in a layer of grime which had not been disturbed for years. Richards retraced his steps and descended the flight to the first floor. Suddenly he noticed that the bare wooden boards of the landing had spots of something red on them. It was blood! He touched the red spot with his finger. The blood was fresh and still wet. He looked around and listened for any sign of someone else being in the house. There was murder afoot, and he didn't intend to be the next victim. Taking the jemmy from his coat pocket, he looked down the staircase towards the kitchen. Nobody there. He pushed the door open to reveal the upstairs corridor. It was quiet. With the jemmy raised and ready for action, Richards silently walked along the corridor in the direction of the main stairs, following the trail of blood spots. He pushed open a bedroom door and looked in – no skunk farm and no potential attacker. The trail of blood stopped at the upstairs sitting room. Quietly he pushed on the door and looked in the room – nobody. For a moment, he debated whether to abandon the search and leave by the broken French window. The blood trail showed that the injured person must have gone out to the balcony and left the scene. The attacker could still be in the house. With his heart beating hard and fast, the inspector decided to carry on. He could handle himself. Any attacker would feel the hardened steel truncheon across their heads. Looking both ways down the corridor, he left the sitting room door open and proceeded in a Southerly direction, past the top of the stairs and into a darker passageway. More rooms led off. He looked into the first room. It smelled unpleasantly musty and damp. The only furniture was a double bed. The walls were covered in scruffy old wallpaper, peeling and showing signs of a black mould. In the next room, he found nothing but a filthy mess of cobwebs and a dirty carpet. The remaining rooms all showed the same lack of house pride, and still no sign of a cannabis farm.

Richards returned to the wide staircase and looked down. As he listened for signs of life downstairs, he physically jumped, as a loud beeping noise started. He pushed the alarm cancel button on his watch, just as a red spot appeared on the back of his hand. His head was throbbing and starting to ache. Another red spot appeared, this time, on his watch strap. For a few seconds, he looked at the blood, relieved that he wasn't going to have to face an attacker, bigger, taller and stronger than himself. Taking out his handkerchief, he mopped the wound above his eye. Only ten minutes left to get out of the house and back to the lay-by before Willoughby brought the couple back.

With the jemmy back in his poacher's pocket, he raced down to the kitchen. Richards wasn't too sure about exactly what he expected to find, maybe a stash of skunk. He started on the bottom drawer of a kitchen unit near the door. Working his way up to the top drawer of the set, he found nothing but kitchenware, cutlery and an old cardboard box full of photographs. Closing the drawers, he turned his attention to the wall cupboards near the table. *Hello*, he thought, as he opened the cupboard door, *What have we here?*

He took out the jar marked STRYCHNINE and wondered why anyone would keep something so poisonous in their kitchen cupboard. It wasn't a branded product like rat poison or ant's nest killer, but was simply labelled as chemically pure strychnine. None of the three deaths looked remotely like strychnine poisoning. He knew that this particular substance was very quick acting. For a minute, he tried to think of how he could get a conviction, but then a far more lucrative plan started to crystallise in his mind. Laughing to himself, he took a plastic sample bag from his pocket and decanted a few teaspoonfuls of the white crystals into it, then replaced the jar in the cupboard. Exactly how he was going to frame Sam and

Alan for Latimer's murder was still to be worked out, but he was confident that it could be done. This would get rid of the blackmailing runt and put the blame onto the Mrs. Big of the Northern drug scene, who thought she could evade justice at the hands of the soon-to-be Detective Chief Superintendent Richards. He looked at his watch. Oh God, three minutes! He took out another sample bag and picked up a dirty teaspoon from near the drainer, taking care not to smudge any possible prints on the handle.

Richards left the kitchen, ran upstairs, then dropped back down the drainpipe and hurried up the lane to the main road, just in time to be out of sight as Willoughby returned with Sam and Alan. He made his way to the lay-by and sat in his car, catching his breath and thinking for a few minutes before starting back to the station.

Willoughby followed Richards into the staff door of the nick and asked, "Any joy, sir?"

"No. Nothing really. Clean as a whistle."

"How did you get that, sir?" Willoughby was pointing at the cut above the inspector's right eye.

"Oh, I tripped over. Caught the wing mirror on my car."

"Best get it cleaned up, sir. Looks a bit deep. Could get infected with all that muck about it."

＊＊＊＊

It wasn't immediately apparent to Sam and Alan that their house had been broken into. As they entered the hall, Alan silenced the alarm warning tone without noticing the extra light on the panel. They sat in the kitchen and over a cup of tea, they discussed why they had been taken to the police station.

Sam said, "What the hell was that all about? First, he tells us how they think Rat died. Then he needs to ask us some questions just to clear up a few points. In the end, he hardly asked anything. It sounded really urgent when he called, but we could just as easily have done it here or on the phone. A complete waste of time. What a dickhead!"

Alan took a sip of tea and put forward his theory. "I think he was just trying to scare us into saying something we shouldn't. Police are sneaky like that. They take us to the station so they're on their home territory?"

He looked at Sam as if asking permission to proceed. She nodded. He went on, "I mean, they know damned well what Rat died of. The poor beggar's been suffering all these years with that Myasthenia thing and now that it's killed him, they're trying to make out that we've caused this crisis somehow. The pigs think they can pin it on us."

"You should stick to the mechy engineering, dear. Do you really believe that Rat died of *that Myasthenia thing*? It was the Meth 4 that got him. He must have taken too much. It supercharged his immune system until it started eating away at his vital organs and his nerves. That's how it works, except in this case it wasn't cancerous growth that it did battle with, it was the all of the healthy tissue in his body. And his body lost the fight."

"Blimey," said Alan, "I didn't realise it was so dangerous. Maybe five milligrams was a bit too strong. Maybe we should have warned him not to exceed the correct dose."

Sam said, "Well it might be nice to know exactly what the correct dose is. There's a lot more work to be done on it."

"And that's why the trial's been stopped?" Alan appeared to be about to continue, but no sound emerged from his open mouth.

"Yes," said Sam, "It works fine in rats because something in their genetic makeup stops their immune system from going into overload. In dogs and humans there's some magical dose, above which everything seems to go crazy. Just below the trigger point, the immune system wipes out all the body's cancer cells, but we think that the safe dosage varies wildly in different individuals."

"Can't you test for this trigger point in each individual patient?"

"Look, I've had to simplify it for you, but basically, to test for the safe dose, you have to administer the drug. If you get it wrong by a molecule, the patient goes into autoimmune suicide. They're working on Meth Five now. Hopefully in a few decades they'll have it cracked."

"Decades?" said Alan.

"How long do you think pharm companies have been working on this?"

"Bloody hell!"

"Looks like we're going to have to shut down, but we've still got the early termination clause, so we should be okay. Falmer's will have to bear all the cost. Meanwhile sweetie, it's your turn to check on the babies."

189

"Suppose so," said Alan as he finished his cold cup of tea and left the kitchen.

A minute later Sam was looking at the calendar on the kitchen wall as Alan returned. "We've been burgled!" he said.

"What?"

"The system's showing a tamper on the sounder box."

"Oh, it's probably just the wind or something."

"You should stick to biochemistry, dear. I'm telling you; we've been burgled. Come on. Let's have a look."

A burglary of a semi in town would leave the owners feeling a bit sick, but they would have the consolation of knowing that their insurance would pay up and put things right. For Sam and Alan, a burglary could never have any such mitigation. They had no insurance. Keeping their secret was far more important than having the reassurance that they could claim compensation for such losses.

When they reached the side door it was obvious that someone had been trying to break in. The sounder box, above their heads, had been knocked off the wall and was dangling precariously by a single wire. At their feet, the plant pot was on its side, having disgorged its spring bulbs and soil over the paving. Alan noticed the cracked pane in the door as Sam said, "The decoy key's gone."

They both ran to the outside cellar door and found it open.

"Well at least they didn't get in the house," said Sam, "Let's have a look at the tape, shall we? Not

190

much we can do. We can hardly call the police, but it might be interesting to see which little tow rags did it."

After reviewing the tape and seeing Richards they decided upon a more rigorous search of the house and found the broken window in the upstairs sitting room. They couldn't see any sign of Richards' having been in the cellar, and nothing of importance seemed to have been disturbed.

Chapter 10

Thursday 20th April

At nine o'clock on Thursday morning Richards set his plan in motion. It would require some tricky timing. He asked Willoughby to check that there were two free interview rooms that morning from 11 o'clock, and to reserve them for himself and Latimer.

With Willoughby out of the room, Richards spoke to Sam on the telephone and asked if she and Alan could attend the station once again. He apologised for the inconvenience but suggested that 11 o'clock would be a good time to go through some photographs of local villains. He explained that he thought that the couple, calling themselves Bob and Catherine, had been at their house to 'case the joint'. If they could identify the couple, the police could detain them and prevent their house being broken into. As he replaced the receiver, he congratulated himself on his excellent nose for sniffing out a villain. Any law-abiding citizen would have mentioned, at some time during the conversation, that their house had been broken into, the day before. The only reason not to mention it was if they had something to hide. In the event of Miss Black mentioning the break-in, he could have used that as a reason for them to look at the mugshots. As they say in chess circles, he had forked them. Or had he skewered them? He couldn't remember the exact term from his days in the school chess club. It was a long time ago. Anyway, it didn't matter. What was more important was that he could now declare checkmate in two.

Latimer was told to bring in Mrs. Foster at 11 o'clock, to look through the mugshots of local drug dealers and users. If Mrs. Foster could identify any of them, they would be questioned in connection with her son's death. Donna Bell would sit in on the interview.

At 11 o'clock Willoughby escorted Sam and Alan to Interview Room 1, where Richards was waiting. The DCI dismissed Willoughby.

Sam noticed the plaster on the inspector's temple. "Have you had an accident?"

Richards said, "Just a scratch. Bumped my head on the garage door. Anyway, thank you for coming. My sergeant should have gone through this yesterday. My apologies. Can I take your coats?"

As he hung up the coats he said, "Please sit down. I'm going to show you some photographs of people with a history of housebreaking and burglary. If you recognise any of them let me know. Take your time. Oh, before we start would you like a coffee?"

Richards left the room and returned carrying two cups of coffee, which he placed on the table in front of his guests. He picked up his own coffee and said, "I'll leave you to it. I'll be back in ten minutes to see how you're getting on."

In the corridor, Mrs. Foster sneered at DCI Richards as Donna showed her into Interview Room 2. Richards caught Latimer by the arm and took him aside.

"Look here, Latimer. I'm not an unreasonable man. Why don't we forget all about your resignation and maybe I'll see if we can't get you a transfer to CID."

Latimer smiled and thanked Richards for his change of heart.

Richards handed Latimer the coffee, saying, "Here you can have this, I must have pressed the wrong button. I wanted black."

Latimer accepted the cup, thanked the inspector again and entered Interview Room 2, where he sat down opposite Mrs. Foster. At the back of the room, Donna was sitting reading a magazine, completely engrossed. She was the nominal chaperon, there to make sure that the sex fiend, Latimer, kept his hands off the old lady.

"I haven't been feeling so good lately," Mrs. Foster whimpered, "What with that business in the wood and now my poor Johnny going like that. The old ticker's not what it used to be, you know."

"I'm sorry to put you through this, Mrs. Foster, but it might help to throw some light on how your son died. The doctors think that some kind of trauma might have triggered the fatal attack. We think that one of his friends or associates, might be able to explain what caused it."

"Well I'll give it a try, but he never used to bring any of his friends home, so I didn't really know any of them. Oh, wait a minute. I tell a lie. I did see one of his friends in the Royal, last week. Oh, I feel a bit dizzy!"

"Can I get you a drink of water?" said Latimer.

"No thanks. Maybe a coffee. Wake me up a bit."

"Here you can have mine. I haven't touched it."

She sipped at the drink, then gulped the whole cupful down in one. "It's a bit cold, but nice and sweet, just how I like it. Now, where was I?"

"You saw his friend in the Royal."

"Oh yes. Johnny was talking to him for a few minutes, but I didn't hear what they said. I'd seen them bonking in the car park."

Latimer said, "Wait a minute. You saw your son talking to his friend in the Royal Hotel, and they'd had relations in the car park?"

"Yes. Johnny said he works at the Royal. He's not a waiter. Somebody higher up. Maybe the night porter or something."

"You saw the night porter and your son having sex in the hotel car park?"

"No! Whitehouse Wood car park. They were at it after they dumped the body."

"Which body?"

"That bloke they found at Lover's Leap. They dumped him there on the Sunday night."

"Malcolm Burke?"

"Yes, that's him. Nobody would listen to me, so I just thought, *Stuff it!*"

"So, your son and his friend disposed of Burke's body?"

"No! My Johnny had nothing to do with it. It was the night porter and a woman who dumped the body."

Latimer crossed out the last few lines in his notebook, then started writing again as he said, "Your son was talking to the night porter, who you recognised as the man who, with a woman, dumped Malcolm Burke's body in Whitehouse Wood. Are you sure it was the same man?"

"Oh yes. The man was ginger, mid-forties. The woman was blonde. Not bad looking"

Latimer rose from his chair and said, "I'll not be a minute. I need to tell the inspector about this. It could be very important. He'll probably want to talk to you."

"I'm not talking to that pig! He's horrible!" said Mrs. Foster, standing up. "Forget it! I'm going home. Oh! I feel all dizzy."

"Please don't upset yourself, madam. The inspector will just want a statement from you."

Donna looked up from her magazine. The old lady was rubbing the middle of her chest with a lightly clenched fist. Donna thought of offering some mint chewing gum for her indigestion, but decided that *Ten Top Turn-Offs on a First Date* was far more deserving of her attention.

Mrs. Foster said "Oh, that really hurts. Could I have a drink of water, please?"

Richards was sitting in his office, biting the nails of his left hand and drumming the fingers of his right, waiting for the news of Latimer's demise. Willoughby rushed into the room and said, "There's been a fatality in Room 2, sir."

Trying hard not to smile, the inspector gave the sergeant his shocked look. "What? How did he die?"

"I never said it was a man, sir"

"Don't give me that, who do you think you are, Latimer?"

"Sorry sir, but we're not sure how *she* died."

"*She?* Not Donna? Oh, no! Please tell me that sweet young thing's not dead." He paused and smiled. "Oh no, couldn't be her. She doesn't drink coffee."

"No sir. It's the old woman, Mrs. Foster. What's that about coffee, sir?"

"What's got into you, man. Coffee at a time like this? Let's get down to the crime scene."

"Crime scene, sir?"

"Okay. *Potential* crime scene."

In Room 1, Sam and Alan were making no progress identifying Bob and Catherine from the hundreds of photographs. They were convinced that the whole exercise was nothing to do with Bob and Catherine, but some more of the inspector's skulduggery. Sam had agreed to attend out of sheer curiosity and to determine exactly how much rope the inspector needed to hang himself.

The door opened and a uniformed constable entered as a familiar voice outside said, "Keep an eye on them. Nobody leaves, nothing is to be disturbed till the SOCOs get here."

The door closed and the policeman took up his station at the table opposite Sam and Alan. The commotion outside of the room grew louder. Sam asked, "What's happening?"

The constable checked that the tape machine was switched off and said, "Shouldn't tell you, but there's been a death in the interview room next door."

Sam said, "Oh dear, that's terrible. What happens now?"

"I'm not sure. It's the first time we've had somebody die in here. Could take a long time to sort out, though. They're waiting for the doctor now. Then the SOCOs will get started. Then I think they'll have to report it to complaints."

"Well why do *we* have to stay? It's nothing to do with us."

"Don't know. The DCI says you've got to stay for now. If the doctor says it's natural then I'd think you should be able to go pretty soon."

In Room 2 the doctor was examining the deceased old lady, with DCI Richards hovering. The doctor said, "I'd say it was a heart attack, possibly brought on by some kind of mental trauma. You really should be very careful when interviewing ladies of this age. You can't just go giving them the third degree, you know. You need to be more mindful of their fragility. Mrs. Foster has been quite poorly of late."

Richards said, "Heart attack? Are you sure? I think I got a slight whiff of bitter almonds and her lips look a bit blue. Doesn't that suggest strychnine poisoning or something?"

"No. It suggests that you know nothing whatsoever about medicine."

"Well Doctor, I don't like to tell you how to do your job."

"Good. Maybe I should tell you how to do yours. First, inform the coroner's office and then get a pathologist in attendance. If you need my fingerprints for elimination, you've got them on file somewhere. That's if you can find them. I'm off. There's nothing more I can do for her now."

The inspector said, "You've been treating her recently, have you?"

"Yes, she was on my list."

"On your list, what list?"

The doctor rolled his eyes and replied, "I was her G.P."

Richards said, "Oh, right. So how did you get here so quickly?"

"I happened to be here to show my driving licence and insurance to your traffic officer. A complete coincidence."

Willoughby chipped in, "As we always say in our profession – there's no such thing as coincidence, just work to do."

The doctor headed for the door and, with a shake of his head, said, "No wonder they have to resort to using speeding fines to improve the clear up rate."

Richards turned to Willoughby and said, "Nobody touches anything in here, especially not that coffee cup. I'm going to talk to Latimer and Bell. You go to Room 1 and get them to turn out their pockets. There's something fishy here. I think it's a poisoning. Now, why would they want to kill her?"

"Who, sir?"

"Mrs. Foster, of course."

"No, sir. I meant who would want to do the killing?"

"Those two next-door. Isn't it obvious? Somehow, they spiked her coffee. Get to it. Bag everything you find. Oh, and don't forget to check their overcoat pockets. I'll see you back in my office."

At two o'clock DCI Richards sat in the canteen, toying with his chicken salad and chips, wondering how his plan had gone so wrong. Latimer was still alive and capable of finishing the inspector's career. For now, this wasn't a problem as Latimer hadn't linked the old lady's death with the coffee. Richards was confident that complaints would sort it out, finding the strychnine in the coffee and the poison in Murray's pocket. When their house was searched the couple would be unable to explain why they had a supply of a restricted substance. How did the old woman come to drink Latimer's coffee? Of course, it was obvious. Latimer gave it to her. He could still fit up the couple for attempted murder. They had spiked his coffee, not knowing that he would give it to Latimer, who then gave it to the old woman. There could also be a charge of manslaughter against them.

Willoughby approached and sat down. "We're in the clear, sir. The local pathologist agrees that it was a heart attack. Bell confirms that Latimer was treating the old woman perfectly calmly and that she just got up from her chair and then collapsed. Complaints said they don't need to be involved and there's no need to get the Home Office man in. The couple in Room 1 have been taken home. They couldn't recognise any of the mugshots."

"Did you search them? What about the coffee cup?"

"Well, that Murray bloke's a bit of a strange one. He had a little bag of sugar and a teaspoon in his coat pocket. Denied all knowledge. Wonder why he carries that around."

"Sugar? Are they sure? How did they know it was sugar? They can't have got the analysis back yet."

"Oh no, sir. SOCOs didn't need to send it off. I had a taste. Thought it might be some sort of drug. Just touched it on the end of my tongue – like they always do in the films. But it was definitely sugar, sir. I'd say that it was from BSC's plant in Bury St. Edmunds, probably from beet grown just to the south of Diss."

"Okay, Sherlock, how the hell could you possibly know that?"

"Simple, sir. I was brought up in the area. My dad worked at the plant, so I learnt the subtleties of the process when I was a boy. The Bury plant's evaporators always produce a very slight caramel flavour, only detectable with years of practice."

"Rubbish! Sugar tastes of sugar, nothing more. You're having me on … aren't you?"

Richards looked Willoughby in the eye, waiting for him to blink. When it became apparent that the sergeant was going to hold his poker face longer than Richards could, the inspector pushed the sugar bowl over and said, "Okay, where's this from?"

"I'm not tasting that. Look at the state of it. It's full of bits of tea and coffee. Could completely ruin my palate, or at the very least give me typhoid."

"It was definitely sugar?"

"Yes, sir."

"What about the cup?"

"Don't know, sir. I think it went in the bin. Was it important?"

"No, no."

Willoughby snapped his fingers. "Sir, I think I've worked it out."

"Worked what out?"

"Why Murray had the sugar in his pocket. It's in case he ever has to get a cup of tea in a place like a police canteen. Look at the state of that. It's disgusting. He's not so daft as he looks. I think I'll start carrying a little bag myself."

"Have you quite finished?"

"Yes, sir … Oh, *and* they never wash the spoons properly. Might start carrying my own clean one as well."

＊ ＊ ＊ ＊

Alan Murray watched as Sam held the dessert spoon over the gas blowlamp. The white crystals melted into a brown liquid and started to bubble then smoulder as dense smoke rose. She wafted the smoke and smelled it.

"Caramel," said Sam.

"Stinks," said Alan.

"So, it dissolves readily in water, melts to a brown viscous liquid, then burns with a smell of caramel. It must be sugar. Are you sure you didn't have it when we left here? And where did the tea spoon come from?"

"It wasn't in my pocket earlier. The spoon's definitely one of ours. It matches the others."

Sam held the blackened dessert spoon under the cold water tap and scratched at the carbon with a knife before throwing the mess into the washing up bowl to soak.

"Let's try it again with a sample of sugar. Pass me the jar."

As Alan held the open jar, Sam put a clean dessert spoon into the white crystals, but withdrew the empty spoon. She pointed at the label on the jar. "The bastard! It was Richards. He planted it in your pocket to incriminate you. That's what the whole thing was about. The photos and all that. Just a smoke screen. He tried to poison somebody with it and put the blame on you. He's a very dangerous man."

Alan laughed and said, "He can't be that dangerous if he tries to poison somebody with sugar."

"Oh, you silly bonobo! He pinched it from here when he broke in. He thought it was …"

Looking at the label, Alan said, "Strychnine!"

"I think we'll have to do something about the inspector before he goes too far. It looks as though he might have it in for us," said Sam.

"What can we do?"

"Well, we could encourage PC Latimer to expose his indiscretions. He said he was going to get some evidence, didn't he? It might be enough to get Richards demoted or sacked. I don't know how seriously the police force take that sort of thing, but it's worth a try."

Alan smiled and said, "And if Latimer does the work for us, Richards won't come after us if it all goes breasts up."

"Tits up, dear," she corrected him.

"Yes. Shall I give Latimer a call at the station?"

"Yes. Ask him if he could come out to see us. By the way, did you notice a smell of something burning?"

"It was the sugar. It really stunk the place out," said Alan.

"No. I mean down in the cellar. I caught a whiff of something overheating. Can you have a look at it after you call Latimer, sweetie?"

Alan left the kitchen to get the handset from the charger in the hall. Sam took a pizza from the fridge and placed it on a baking tray. She sighed and started to pick off the anchovies, before dropping them in the bin. She washed her hands and sniffed at her fingers before washing them again. As she placed the tray in the oven, Alan returned, saying, "He's off duty till Monday. They wouldn't give me a contact number."

"Okay. We'll just have to wait. You've just got time to check out that burning smell before dinner. Oh, by the way, you got the wrong pizza again, you careless colobus! Don't let it happen again or I'll have to sort you out."

She waved a clenched fist at him. He replied with a face fit to win a gurning contest as he beat a rapid retreat down to the cellar.

Ten minutes later, the pizza was divided into segments on a large plate on the kitchen table. Sam was about to call for Alan when he appeared, attracted by the smell.

"I can't smell anything burning," he said.

"Are you sure? No alarms?"

"Nothing. It's all going perfectly smoothly."

"Oh well, maybe I was mistaken, but I could have sworn it was a sort of electrical smell, like you get when insulation's about to fail. Reminds me of fish, somehow."

"Well, I had a look at all the controllers and there was no sign of anything wrong. Eat your pizza and stop worrying about it. It's all under control. Since I increased the current, the battery seems to be charging just fine."

Sam said, "Maybe I'm just getting paranoid. Anyway, we'll probably be starting the shutdown in a week or two. I've got to see Steve again next week. He's working out some sort of new deal for me. At a guess, I'd say he'll want to close the Meth 4 project and then give me some work on the next generation. It might mean that I'll have to work in their lab, 'cos they won't have any need for pilot production for a while."

"What about me?"

"Once you've shut down the plant, you can either go back to being a kept man, or sell the patent and live off the proceeds. You could retire quite rich. Or, you could try to get some work from one of your mates. Doesn't Georges need anything building?"

"Oh, don't make me go over there again. I'd rather be a kept man. All cuckoo clocks and cow bells. Very pretty, but nothing to do. Besides, I told you. Last time his lab tech took a shine to me."

"Yes, but it might broaden your outlook to have a new friend."

"It wasn't my outlook I was worried about. He was after broadening a part of my anatomy."

"You'll be alright. It was more than five years ago. He's probably moved on years ago. I'll give Georges a call tomorrow. See if he's got anything for you. Meanwhile, *I've* got something for you."

Sam took a high ball glass from the cupboard and brought a bottle of beer from the fridge. She opened the bottle and poured out the dark brown ale, then gave Alan the glass and showed him the label.

She said, "Edinburgh's finest Export Heavy. Just like my great uncle Angus used to drink."

"Why?"

"Well, he was Scottish and he liked a beer."

"No. What I meant was… What do you mean, he was Scottish? You never had any Scottish uncles."

"He was my *great* uncle. My grandmother's brother."

"But you never mentioned him before."

"Oh, he died before I was born. I've got a photo of him somewhere. It's in with those old bits of stuff my mother left me. You drink up and I'll go and find it."

"So why have you got me a bottle of beer. I don't usually drink the stuff in the house."

"Well I thought you might want to give the other stuff a break for a while. It's not good for you if you take it every day. Anyway, I got you a crate full of the Heavy, so you'll have to drink it now."

"What do you mean. It's not good for me? I'm fine."

"I'm a little bit worried about you. You might be getting addicted to it, and your sperm count could be suffering. Drink your beer."

Sam opened a drawer, took out a grubby old cardboard box and placed it on the table. She opened the lid and took out a bundle of photographs bound with a large rubber band. Taking the first picture, she laid it on the table to flatten out the curling caused by the band.

"There, that's uncle Angus."

Alan wasn't looking at the photograph. He was staring at Sam's face. As he put down the beer, he said, "You don't have to put yourself through all that stress again, not for me. I've accepted it now. We just can't have kids. I couldn't stand to see you like that again. It's nobody's fault. Not yours or mine. It's just nature."

He took the photo out of her hand and placed it on the table. Then he stood up and gently caressed her. He had a frown on his face and his eyes were starting to fill. She was smiling slightly.

She said, "You know, I was just thinking how wonderful it is to have such a beautiful life partner as you. You sweet, sweet man, always thinking of me. But really, I'm okay. You've given me so much over the years, and now I just want another chance to give you what you've always wanted. You know what? I'm feeling lucky. Now, if we can purge your system of cannabis derivatives for a couple of weeks, we might stand a chance."

He sniffed and took a deep breath. "Well, if that's what you want, I'll lay off it for as long as necessary."

"Right. Oh, and don't worry. This time we won't have all the charts and thermometers. No waking up at four o'clock and definitely no headstands. I'm getting too old for that."

His hands slowly dropped from her shoulder blades and reached her waist on their journey South. She grabbed both arms and freed herself. "Not until you've built up your count. Maybe tomorrow or the weekend."

She handed him the photo. "He was a big fellow. A few pints of Heavy didn't do him any harm, eh?"

Alan looked at the heavy Heavy drinker, admiring his physique. The muscular Scotsman sported a full head of bright red hair and a huge bushy beard. He appeared to be looking to his right. His right arm was cropped at the edge of the frame. Uncle Angus was wearing a plain white singlet with a thistle logo and a blue tartan kilt with a broad leather belt. The background was out of focus, but seemed to show a crowd in a field. Alan turned the photo to read the writing on the back.

"I thought you said he died before you were born?"

"Yes, he did. I never knew him," she said.

"That's strange. It says *Braemar – August 73* on the back."

"Let me see."

Alan handed back the photo.

"Oh, you silly Sassenach! That's *Angus 73*. He died shortly after, just before his 74th birthday."

Alan leaned over to have another look at the picture. "He looks pretty fit for a pensioner. Look at those muscles. Wouldn't like to meet him on a braw night in Glasgow."

"Well that just goes to show what a regular dose of Edinburgh Heavy can do for you. Drink up, Tiger."

* * * *

The next day Sam called their friend and associate, Georges. "Bonjour, Georges. Ça va?" She started the conversation, using her limited schoolgirl French, but was soon forced to admit defeat. He was deliberately speaking far too fast for her to understand. His vocabulary also included many words which had never featured in the 'O' level syllabus. Having revealed her deficiency in modern languages, her old friend switched to English and reaffirmed his offer of French lessons at their previous price, an evening of blissful passion. Once again, she declined and called him *un vieux pervers*. The light-hearted chat continued for a few minutes and then they got down to the serious business of pharmaceutical research consultancy.

After ten minutes Sam hung up. Alan had got the gist of the conversation but she filled in the blanks. "He still wants to buy the patent outright. I told him it was out of the question, but he's still very keen. I think we should keep him waiting. He'll up the price. Could always play him off against Falmer's. That's if they can afford to keep up with him. Then if you decide to sell, you'll be able to retire. Anyway, they're going to put a plant together in Basel, starting later in the year. Should be a very lucrative job, if you can keep your hands off Thomas."

"That was his name, *Thomas*. I don't think I could work with him again. It would be embarrassing."

"Don't panic. Georges says that he's got a steady boyfriend now. You should be quite safe, sweetie. Sounds like it would be right up your street. We could license the process to them and make a bit more."

Chapter 11

Tuesday 25th April

The following Tuesday evening, PC Latimer visited the farmhouse. He removed his muddy shoes and left them near the front door. With one big toe poking through a hole in his sock, he followed Sam to the kitchen.

The constable said, "Been searching down by the river, near Chester-Le-Street, all day. A body's been found in the Wear. Well, not exactly a whole body. It's been in the water for a long time. Looks like a suicide. He weighed himself down with a plastic sack full of stones."

"What an awful way to go," said Sam.

"Yes. There's not much left of him. Mostly just bones. The fishes have been at him. All of his clothes have disintegrated. Just his walking boots and a plastic map pouch around his neck. They reckon he'd never have been found except for the river being in flood with all the melt water. He was washed to the bank and when the water subsided a couple of kids found him."

Alan walked in, carrying a softback folder of electrical diagrams, which he closed and put on a shelf away from Latimer. "I can't see what's wrong with it," he said as he unloaded a small collection of tools from the pockets of his overall.

Sam said, "Just get a new one. You know you're not very good at the electrical bits."

She turned to Latimer and said, "The central heating's on the blink."

Latimer said, "Oh I'm no good at that sort of thing, either. Why don't you just get a heating engineer in?"

"Good idea," said Alan, "Would you like a coffee?" He looked down at Latimer's feet as he filled the kettle.

"Oh, I was just telling Miss Black. We've been down by the Wear all day, looking for clues. A body's been found."

Alan said, "You can tell us all about it over coffee."

Sam said, "It's all a bit gruesome. Can we just skip it and talk about why we wanted to see you? We were wondering what you've been doing – whether you've shown your latest evidence to the inspector?"

"Well, I had a bit of excitement the other day, but I didn't get any evidence. You need to be able to prove it to call it evidence. It's what we would call intelligence. If I'd had the tape running, it could be called evidence, but it's just intelligence because I'm the only one who heard it. Donna was busy reading her magazine. So, it's really only hearsay. My word against the night porter's."

Latimer paused. Sam, who had been looking slightly confused, asked, "You were going to tape the conversation? That was your plan?"

"Oh no. It was just a photo session. It never even got properly started. Donna was in the room with me, but she was gone before I got everything down."

"You and Donna were in the room? Where was the inspector? Wasn't he in the room with Donna?" said Sam.

"No. He was in the room next door with someone else. I don't know what he was doing."

"What happened?" said Sam.

"Well, one minute she was telling me about the night porter and the blonde. Then, when I told her I would have to get the inspector involved, she went crazy. She said she hated him, and the next thing she was gone. That was that."

Sam said, "So how was the night porter involved?"

"He'd been hiding the stiff with the blonde woman."

Trying not to laugh, Alan turned to Sam and asked, "*Hiding the stiff?* Does that mean what I think it means?"

Sam said, "I think we've heard enough of this."

Alan was still standing with the kettle in his hand. He took a deep breath to control his mirth and asked Latimer, "So you didn't get any evidence to confront Inspector Richards with?"

"What?"

"You said you were going to gather evidence, to keep him from getting you sacked."

"Oh that. No. I tried to get a picture of him but I lost my grip on the Mirror. Then it all went wrong. I didn't mean to, but I flashed and he chased me out of the hotel. I don't think it'll come out very good."

Alan nodded and said, "Right. Okay."

Latimer said, "As it happens, I didn't need the picture because he got all friendly before I went in the room with Donna. He even said I might get a transfer to CID."

Over coffee, Latimer announced that he was now going steady with his girlfriend, Angie. He'd told her about his job and she didn't seem to mind going out with a police officer, as it made her feel safer. For the next half hour, he proceeded to give details of all of their dates, trips to the cinema, draughty Land Rover rides in the countryside, shopping trips, romantic walks by the river in Durham and museum visits. Angie had introduced him to classical music and they had even been to Newcastle for a live performance of Swan Lake. Sam said nothing as Latimer rambled on. She yawned and looked around the room, then at the wall clock. She inspected her fingernails with great interest as the policeman continued to describe the minutiae of his newly enriched relationship.

Alan's palm cradled his chin, supporting his head as his cranial cogs turned at speed. His eyes stared at nothing in particular, but in a direction beyond Latimer towards the pile of tools on the table. He feigned a yawn and picked up the three empty mugs. The policeman either took the hint, or ran out of interesting snippets about his new-found love.

He said, "Well, must go. I'm meeting Angie in an hour."

"Pass me the 20-millimetre spanner, would you. I'm going to have another look at that boiler. I've just had another idea, which could just possibly work," said Alan.

Latimer picked up the large spanner and offered it to Alan. "This one?"

"Yes, thank you. That's just what I need. See you later." Alan put the mugs down, then took the spanner by the business end and left for the cellar.

After Latimer had gone, Alan returned to the kitchen and sat at the table. He took up his electrical file, laid it on the table and started thumbing through the pages to find the diagram of the battery charger. With his index finger, he traced the line from the battery back to another circuit symbol marked "*FS2 6.3A*". Again, he supported his head with his elbow and began to scratch. Sam came and stood behind him.

She said, "Fuse number two. Six point three amperes."

He turned to her and said, "I know that. I did electrical at college, you know. What I can't understand is why *Fuse number two – Six point three amperes* has blown. All I did was to tweak a few of those little control thingies to turn up the charger current a bit. Then what happens? Something starts to burn and the fuse blows. If I can just work out what all these little fiddly bits do, I'll have it fixed in no time."

Sam left him to his diagrams and started washing the coffee mugs. She said, "I think he's been got at."

Alan looked up from the file and said, "What do you mean?"

Sam said, "Richards has found Latimer's weak spot – Sex. Latimer went to the Royal to get some evidence to use against Richards, and ended up in a sex orgy. Richards even left Latimer and Donna alone for a photo session. Sounds like it wasn't just a weekly liaison between Richards and the lovely Donna, but the night porter and some filthy blonde hussy were involved."

"Maybe Latimer's new girlfriend will keep him on the straight and narrow," said Alan.

Sam dried her hands on the tea towel and threw it over the freshly washed mugs on the drainer. "She might be part of the scene at the Royal. How do we know that she's not the blonde tart? Knocking off the night porter and PC Latimer. *And* who was in the room next door with Richards? Sounds like he's tired of dirty Donna. Probably having three-in-a-bed sex with the night porter and Goldilocks. Whatever's happening, we can't rely on Police Constable Latimer to deal with Richards for us."

"What are we going to do? If we report the burglary, we'll end up with coppers plodding all over the house. They'll send in their soccer teams to scour the house for clues. Apart from the stuff down below, they might find Burke's DNA. We never did find his thumb, did we, dear?"

Sam said, "Don't worry. I'll think of something. Tomorrow you've got to go and get a new charger. I think it's going to be an early night for both of us. You've got a long drive and I've got to go and see Steve."

"An early night?"

"Yes, sweetie, but not that sort of early night. Leave a sample near the microscope and I'll check your count tomorrow; then we can decide if you've improved enough for a proper try this month. Now, let's have some of your delicious cocoa to cancel out the effect of the coffee."

* * * *

The next day Sam kept her appointment with her ex-colleague, Steve, at Falmer's. The meeting took only

215

an hour. The outcome was not exactly what she had been anticipating. The project was not going to be totally scrapped and there would still be a short-term requirement for the pilot production, with some further work for Alan.

Sam left the office and drove to the Royal Hotel in Durham. As she arrived at the desk, the receptionist finished his telephone conversation and turned to her. She asked to see the manager, Mr. Wilson. The receptionist politely corrected her, saying that Mr. Wilson was the Regional Director, and did she want to talk to the manager or Mr. Wilson. She explained that she wanted to see Mr. Wilson on a personal matter, at which point the receptionist called George's secretary.

Five minutes later George stepped out of the lift and smiled as he approached. "Hi Sam, how nice to see you. What's up?"

"Can we talk, George?"

"I've got all the time in the World. Have you had lunch?"

"No thanks. Is there somewhere private?"

What could be more private than George's own apartment? He explained that the hotel had been his home since his acrimonious divorce. The suite was in need of refurbishment, but every corner of the place was spotlessly clean. Part of his deal with the hotel chain was that his accommodation would be serviced regularly by hotel staff, even down to the provision of individual, prepacked beverages.

He said, "Like a drink? Tea, coffee or something stronger?"

She said, "Tea would be nice. I've given up alcohol temporarily."

George filled the tiny kettle and plugged it in. He took two cups from his cupboard and placed an English Breakfast teabag in each, arranging the strings and tags neatly over the brims.

He sat down next to her on the sofa and said, "Now, what can I do for you, Sam?"

"It's more what I can do for you."

"Oh? What would that be then?" He stared at her as she undid two buttons of her blouse, revealing a small glimpse of bra.

She stood up and walked over to the table and said, "I think your little kettle's nearly boiling. Mine's white, no sugar." She picked up an individual portion of UHT milk, looked at it and said, "On second thoughts. If that's the only milk you've got, don't bother."

He poured the hot water into his cup and dunked the teabag. "I thought you and Alan were happy. That time in the car was just a performance for the old lady's sake."

"Well, let's just say there's been a few complications."

"Like what?"

"It's a long story. And if I told you, I'd have to kill you. Now, do you want to play *Hide the stiff* or not?" she said as she started unbuttoning his shirt.

"Hiding a stiff?"

She said, "It's a euphemism."

"Oh, thank God. For a second, I thought you had another dead body to get rid of. I see what you mean, now."

She stopped unbuttoning and seemed to lose all interest in George. After a pause for thought, she said, "George, you wouldn't happen to know if they have sex orgies here involving the night porter, do they?"

He began to laugh uncontrollably and started coughing. Wiping his eyes, he said, "I'll be alright. Just need a drink."

He sipped his tea and gave himself a few seconds to recover from the coughing fit. "We've got two night porters, but neither of them would know where to start. They're both about sixty and not exactly rebellious types. I can't imagine two people less likely to take part in an orgy. Have you heard something?"

She said, "No, no. It's probably a complete misunderstanding. Now down to business. Just a quickie. No need to enjoy ourselves too much."

She opened her handbag and produced a condom. "Here. Use this."

"But I thought you couldn't, you know?"

"Get pregnant?"

"Yes."

"Well, it protects against diseases, as well."

His jaw dropped. "You haven't got the pox, have you? Oh shit, that night in the car."

"Do you mind? I'm not like that." She started doing up her blouse. "Maybe I should just go."

He said, "No. Don't go. I'm sorry. I didn't mean it like that. Are you alright?"

She smiled. "Come on then. Let's get on with it. But remember, not a word to anybody, or you're a dead man."

"Okay. But I still don't understand why we need to use a johnny."

"Don't you? Let's say it's for old time's sake. Remember our first time?" She got back to the task of unbuttoning his shirt. Her breathing was gradually getting more intense.

He loosened her blouse and unhooked her bra.

She said nothing as they walked over to the bedroom. As she let her skirt drop, she said, "I didn't really mean it, you know?"

"Mean what? That bit about killing me if I talked?"

"Oh no, I was quite sincere about that. It was the bit about not enjoying ourselves. I've got a couple of hours before Alan gets back. He's down Donnington, or somewhere, getting a part for the heating."

* * * *

When Sam arrived back home, she was surprised to see Alan's car parked outside the house. Carrying her handbag and a small aluminium box, she crossed the hall and approached the kitchen door. A call of "Hi sweetie!" went unanswered. Alan was not in the kitchen. She assumed that he must be in the cellar, fitting the new charger board. This was her opportunity to prepare the slide. She left the box on the kitchen table, ran upstairs and entered the upstairs sitting room. Alan was standing next to the table, looking down a large binocular microscope. The dust

219

cover was on the floor next to the table. He turned and jumped as she entered the room.

He said, "Hello. Did it go alright with Steve?"

"Yes. He wants to keep the plant running for now. They're going to replicate it and go into small scale production for the vet market. Meanwhile he wants me to look into resistance in tetanus. Whatever you do, don't open the transit box on the kitchen table."

"What's in it?"

She ignored his question and staring at the microscope, said, "How come you're back so early, and what are you doing with that?"

"Well Doncaster's not that far. I got the new board, but I haven't fitted it yet. I thought I'd have a go at doing a count," said Alan.

"You shouldn't. I need to set it up. It's not as easy as it looks. Where's your sample?"

He pointed at a plastic cup next to the instrument. "I couldn't see much. There didn't seem to be anything moving. They're supposed to swim about, aren't they? Does that mean my sperm count's down to zero?"

"You've probably fried them all with the heat from the light. It's far too powerful for this job. Needs a filter. Let me see."

Alan said, "I tried to get it focussed but it went all blurry. Then I tried a different magnification and it was all blurred as well. Now it's all just gone white."

"Come out of the way. Let me see what you've done."

Alan did as he was told and stepped back from the table. Sam inspected the stage of the delicate instrument. "Oh, you mucky gibbon! It's all over the forty times objective, and the ten times. And the plate's cracked. How did you manage that?"

Alan just looked sheepish and shook his head slightly. "Sorry. I just wanted to see them swimming. Can it be fixed?"

Sam put her arms around him, kissed him and said, "Of course it can, sweetie. It's only a piece of glass. There's plenty more in the drawer. Now you go and do the things that you're good at. Get back to the electrics in the cellar, while I prepare a slide and clean up this mess. Then you can come and see them all doing the breast stroke."

When he'd left the room, she opened her handbag and took out the condom.

＊＊＊＊

The next morning, Alan was whistling quietly to himself as he tightened the screws securing the new charger board to the rack of electronics. His count was up and he'd even seen his tadpoles rushing about in absolutely rude health. Falmer's wanted him to scale up the plant design for production and they'd be using his patent for separation of the fermentation products.

He clicked shut the rack and locked up the room. As he approached the bottom step, he heard a loud cry of pain from the hall above. Hurrying up the cellar steps, he heard Sam saying, "Oh I'm terribly sorry inspector. I thought you were the burglar, come back."

As Alan arrived at the cellar door, DCI Richards was stumbling near the front door, holding his head in one hand and his trilby in the other. Sam dropped the rolling pin and helped to support the detective.

They ushered the dazed policeman into the living room and sat him down.

Alan asked, "What happened?"

Sam said, "I heard someone opening the front door and I thought it was the burglar. I had no idea it was the inspector."

Richards said, "Well, the front door was open so I came through. I *did* call out, and I'm sure I heard you telling me to come in." His eyes watered freely as he winced at the intense pain of the re-opened head wound.

Sam said, "Oh, that looks nasty. Looks like it's opened up an old cut. Let's have a look. This plaster's a bit dirty and now it's all covered in blood." As she ripped the plaster off, Richards squealed in pain through clenched teeth. Sam applied a clean tissue to the cut. "Hold that in place while I get a fresh dressing and some disinfectant. It looks a bit infected. Might be septic."

After Sam left, Alan said, "Would you like a brandy?"

"No thank you." The inspector relaxed his pressure on the tissue momentarily, then pressed harder as the blood continued to pulse out. "You said you wanted to show me something about a break in?"

"Yes. It happened about a week ago. We weren't going to report it 'cos there was nothing missing, but now it looks as if something *was* taken."

"So, what was taken?" said Richards.

"Well it's very strange, but the thief seems to have only taken a spoon. One of a set. That's how we knew it was gone. Have you ever heard of that sort of thing?

222

It wasn't even a silver spoon, just stainless steel. No value, really."

"That does sound very peculiar. Nothing else is missing?"

Sam re-appeared carrying a shallow enamelled dish. She was wearing a pair of disposable latex gloves. Taking the tissue from Richards, she dried the wound with another, then placed both bloodied tissues in the dish. She then took a piece of damp cotton wool from the dish and dabbed the wound before applying a clean plaster. "There. All done," she said.

Sam put down the dish and said, "Nothing else was taken. Just the spoon, as far as we know. Of course, the thief could have helped themselves to our coffee, tea and sugar. We don't keep track of that sort of thing."

Richards asked, "You said on the phone that you had CCTV footage?"

Sam said, "We have, but it's not very clear. I just mentioned it to get a quicker response. I thought the police would be a bit more interested if they thought there was a chance of catching the villain. As it is, we don't really want to press charges, especially as we've recovered the stolen spoon. Of course, if we have any more trouble, we could always get the video enhanced, and who knows, we might be able to get an identification. From what we can make out, the burglar wasn't wearing his hat." She handed the inspector his trilby.

"I don't think you'll have any more trouble from him. Once he's been in here and found nothing of value, he'll probably not come back again," said Richards.

Sam smiled and said, "Thank you, inspector. It's nice to get some reassurance. Sorry you've had a bit of a wasted journey. Are you sure you're alright for driving back?" She pulled off the gloves, inside out, and placed them in the dish.

Sam showed the policeman out while Alan disposed of the dish contents in the cellar.

A few minutes later she joined Alan in the kitchen and threw the blood-stained rolling pin into the stove. "I'm not using that for pastry again."

Alan said, "But you only bought it yesterday. You haven't even used it. It would have cleaned up alright."

"It's the principle. He's touched it, so it's dirty now. Besides, I don't think I'm going to start baking, after all. Too much messing about."

"Oh well, it's just as well that you didn't buy all the other baking stuff. It would have been wasted."

Sam opened the stove fire door. The rolling pin was well alight. She said, "I don't think I was cut out to be a baker. Too hot and sweaty." Closing the door, she turned to Alan, smiled and said, "You did really well. Word perfect. If you hadn't been such a wonderful engineer, you could have been a great actor, sweetie."

Alan said, "Do you think he got the message? He didn't ask how we'd got the spoon back."

She smiled. "Well he wouldn't, would he? He knows we're on to him. I've sort of got a feeling we won't be bothered by Detective Chief Inspector Richards anymore."

"I'm going to have a look into Durham tomorrow. Just for a bit of a wander round. It's a while since I was down Bishop Street. Might have a little look down there," said Alan.

Sam said, "I'm going for a lie down. I don't feel so good. Maybe it was the sight of all that blood."

"Do you want a paracetamol?"

"No thanks. It's my stomach. Feel a bit queasy. Last time I felt like this it was a dodgy hotdog. It'll pass."

Chapter 12

Monday 1st May

Sam's stomach trouble didn't pass. It continued sporadically for more than a week. She was busy reading up the background information on the newly resistant strain of tetanus and preparing slides of the bacteria. Her week consisted of visits to the cellar to do the practical work in bio-secure conditions, long study sessions in the comfort of the upstairs sitting room and hurried trips to the toilet.

That week Alan spent most of his time collating documentation relating to the design of the pilot plant. Much of the paperwork associated with the design needed to be tidied up if the plant was to be replicated by Falmer's. He spent his days visiting the cellar to check measurements and working at the computer in the upstairs sitting room.

On Monday morning Sam and Alan were working in the sitting room, with warm sunshine streaming in through the French windows. Alan looked up from the mechanical drawing on his computer screen and rubbed his eyes. Sam walked up behind him and looked over his shoulder at the screen. She said, "That bit's wrong, isn't it?"

Alan turned to her and said, "This is the plan for the plant at Falmer's. Their bi-product output has to be pumped into the incinerator holding tank. It might look a bit suspicious if I showed it going into a THC storage tank, don't you think?"

"Oh, yes," said Sam, "I'll leave you to it."

After five minutes Alan turned in his swivel chair and wheeled himself over to look out of the window. A female blackbird was hopping along the path next to the hen pen, with a beakful of dry grass and chicken feathers. He watched as it flew off in the direction of a hawthorn tree. Leaf buds were just starting to open. He remembered from his youth, *bread and cheese*, that's what it was called. The buds were edible at this stage. As a child he'd never got a taste for them. Too bitter. Anyway, in those days he preferred a couple of slices of Mother's Pride with a quarter inch thick filling of Primula spread. Now that really had been bread and cheese! A squawk from the cock bird startled him back from memory lane.

He said, "I wonder if they time their nest building to coincide with the leaves opening."

"What?" said Sam, looking up from the ring-bound file she was reading.

"The birds. I wonder if they know that the leaves on the trees are due to open. If they built their nests too early, there would be no cover."

"It's all controlled by day length. The birds reproductive cycle begins when the days start to get lighter for longer. The trees' leaf production is essentially triggered by the same increase in day length."

"Okay, Mrs. Darwin, but I still think they're clever little beggars. Care for a coffee?"

Sam didn't answer, but jumped up and made a quick exit along the hall to the toilet.

When she returned Alan said, "I'll take that as a yes, then."

She smiled and said, "What? Oh, yes please."

He asked, "What time's your doctor's appointment again?"

"Half past two."

"Maybe you should go to the dentist instead."

As he left the room, she just looked bemused and got back to her reading.

After two pages, she looked up as Alan returned, pushing the door open with his foot. In his hands, he was carrying a tray with two mugs of coffee and a plate of biscuits. He placed the tray on the table and said, "I reckon I know what's causing it."

She put down the file and asked, "Causing what? The birds to synchronise their nesting or my tummy bug?"

"Your bad stomach. It's really your own fault. Actions have consequences, you know."

"Really? What do you mean?"

"Okay. Here's a clue. They're very small. They swim about and, not to put too fine a point on it, you've had lots of them recently."

It took Sam a moment to digest his revelation. She smiled. "How long have you known?"

"I've just worked it out, but I was a bit concerned about it more than a week ago. You can't hide that sort of thing forever, you know."

Alan took a mug from the tray and placed it in front of her, along with the plate of biscuits. He took his own coffee over to the French windows and sipped as he looked out. In the distance, the opposite bank of the river was painted emerald green by the larches, showing their spring colour. In the reedbed near the larches a heron broke cover and started flying nearer. Alan put his coffee on the table and took his binoculars from the bookshelf.

"Looks like we're going to get a visit from a very big bird." he said.

"Yes. It's quite exciting, isn't it?"

"Well, I wouldn't go as far as to say that."

Sam dunked her biscuit. She frowned. "You don't seem to be very happy about it."

"About what?" he said.

She carefully lifted the biscuit out of her coffee and leaned over to slurp the mush before it could go swimming. "Our imminent arrival."

Alan was still focussed on the heron. He said, "Well, I like to see them, but they do shit a lot." He lowered his binoculars and let them dangle from his neck, then watched as the heron landed in his wild garden pond. "I know there's only my tadpoles in there, but if it was those gingery-orange things, we'd have to get rid of it. What do you call them?"

"What! Oh My God. I can't believe you said that! I thought I knew you. But now you want to destroy a life. How could you?"

"No. It's not like you're destroying a life, just getting rid of it. You have to be realistic about these things. I mean, it could cost us a fortune."

Sam tried unsuccessfully to use her fingers to fish out her second biscuit from the coffee. Finally, she gave up and smashed down the mug of sludge onto

229

the tray, causing some of the liquified digestive to join its dry companions on the plate. "Sorry, what were you saying? You're talking about ending an innocent life, just because it's going to cost you money."

As the heron flew off, having gagged a frog into its crop, Alan turned to give Sam his full attention.

She said, "I thought you'd be happy, but now you want to kill it?"

"I didn't say I wanted to kill it. Just to make it go away."

"Same thing!" said Sam, rising from the table and quickly leaving the room. Alan followed her down to the kitchen. As he opened the kitchen door she shouted, "Get out!" and threw a plate in his direction. Alan managed to close the door on the missile.

Through the closed door he said, "What's the matter? All I said was …"

"I know what you said!" Sam cracked the door open and said, "Now go away and leave me alone!"

"But all I meant was …"

"Get lost!" The kitchen door slammed in his face.

"Koi carp. I was thinking about getting some koi carp. Then we'd definitely have to get rid of it."

Three more plates smashed into the door in quick succession. "You want fish! I'll give you fish!" From the kitchen, there was the sound of a cupboard being opened, then the unmistakable crash of a glass jar hitting a Yorkshire flag. Then another. And another.

Alan stood outside the kitchen for a minute, pondering his options. Should he risk going into the kitchen to give her a cuddle, or go and do some

230

practical work while she calmed down? She was obviously stressed by all the vomiting and having to go and see the doctor. The pragmatic engineer won the day and decided to go and do some work. He slowly climbed the stairs and made his way back to the sitting room.

Giving the mouse a shake, he woke up his computer. The screen was covered in small specks of coffee flavoured digestive. The cursor was still where he had left it, fifteen minutes before. The machine was waiting for him to type in a dimension. He looked at his notes at the side of the keyboard and typed in *25.4*, but the cursor stood still. No numbers appeared. Alan looked down at the keyboard and noticed a sticky puddle of coffee in the bottom right corner. He sniffed at the fingers of his right hand, then licked them clean of the stickiness, wiping them dry on his jumper. Unable to do any work, he rose and walked over to the French windows. The distant larches were even more luminous in the midday sunshine. A few wispy clouds were floating gently in the bluest of skies. He smiled to himself as he took in the scene of tranquillity. His beloved wild garden was a sea of green, then he noticed the large grey-white heron standing in the frog pond. He hurried to open the door onto the balcony and shouted, "Bugger off, you fish eating bastard!"

An equally loud shout of "Murderer!" came from the other side of the sitting room door. Turning, he heard footsteps on the upstairs corridor, followed by the bathroom door being slammed and locked closed. The heron gulped down its third frog and flew off.

Alan closed the balcony door and left for the bedroom. He knew exactly what he had to do. Sam was taking a shower, so he wouldn't be disturbed. From his wardrobe he took out a pair of old trousers, a worn-out shirt and his second-best gardening jacket. He looked through his clothes for an old jumper, but couldn't see anything suitable for his purpose. He listened at the door to check that Sam was still in the shower before stealing one of her jumpers. It looked fairly old and had gone all fluffy in the wash.

At four thirty Sam returned from the clinic. In the kitchen, she placed her bottle of tablets on the table and put the kettle on. She half-slipped on the olive oil, still coating the surface of the flooring flags, but grabbed the table to avoid falling on the broken glass. Alan was nowhere to be seen downstairs. She ran upstairs and looked in the bedroom. It was obvious that he'd been taking clothes from his wardrobe. The door was still open and various garments were untidily strewn over the bed. She looked out of the window. His car was still outside. None of the suitcases were missing. Maybe he hadn't left her. She could hear a noise, a burst of tapping, coming from the other side of the house. She left the bedroom for the sitting room. The tapping started again, but louder. This time she could also hear the long-time delayed echoes from the other side of the river. Looking out of the French windows, she saw Alan hammering nails into a wooden structure near the pond. Nearby stood a sorry excuse for a scarecrow with straw leaking from the limbs. She hurried downstairs and out to the garden.

Sam approached Alan with a half-smile on her face. Then, as she got within range, she launched a mighty slap at his cheek. He tried to turn away, but this just had the effect of exposing his left eye to the harder part of the open hand. He dropped the hammer and held his cheek. Tears flowed involuntarily from his left eye. "What did you do that for?"

Sam was alternating between shaking her right hand and rubbing her thumb. She said, "That's for calling me a bastard!"

"What! I never called you a bastard."

"Yes, you did."

"When?"

"You were in the sitting room when I was going to the shower. I distinctly heard you say something about a fish-eating bastard."

"I was talking to that big bird. It was a crane or a heron – I always get them mixed up."

Sam was clasping her right thumb in her left hand. "Now you've hurt my thumb! Big bird? Which big bird?"

He took his hand away from his cheek, revealing a red patch under the eye. He said, "I told you about it earlier. I said it was coming our way. It's visiting our pond to feed on the frogs. I told you."

"I thought you were talking about the stork coming."

"Don't be so daft! You don't get storks in England. It's either a heron or a crane. Now let me look at that thumb." His bloodshot left eye was closing up as the swelling started to take effect. He reached out to take her hand but she pulled away.

"So why have you made a scarecrow?"

"To frighten it off. I'm not trying to kill it, just make it go away. I tried to explain this morning that I wasn't going to kill it, just get rid of it, but you went off on one, calling me a murderer and all that. I've

233

covered the pond with chicken mesh as well, so if it gets past Wurzel it still can't get the frogs."

As Sam listened to his words, she thought back to their conversation that morning. Eventually she said, "Well I thought you wanted to kill something else. Anyway, just exactly what did you mean, this morning, when you said that you knew what was causing my tummy trouble?"

"What? Oh, I found your stash in the kitchen cupboard last week. Since then you've had six jars. That's what's making you sick. I mean, two or three on a pizza's alright. I don't mind them, but eating them by the jarful? That's just asking for trouble. Besides, I didn't think you liked them. Too salty and smelly, you said."

"Well, I've got a taste for them now. And, they're full of omega three."

"So, what did the doctor say it was?"

She inspected the scarecrow then turned to face Alan, smiled and gave him a hard kick on the shin.

Alan struggled to maintain his policy of not using strong language in front of the ladies, but two or three of the more colourful expletives very nearly escaped, only to be restrained by his clenched teeth. He reached down to massage his leg and as his right eye glazed over, said, "What was that for?"

"That was for ruining my new angora jumper, which incidentally, I haven't even worn yet. It makes a really good head for Wurzel! Oh, and by the way, it's snowmen who have carrot noses, not scarecrows."

He mopped his right eye with the back of his hand and said, "Sorry. I thought it was an old one. I've never noticed you wearing it recently."

She took a step toward him. He instinctively hopped back.

"Oh, come here," she said, as she leant forward to kiss him on the forehead. "In future, if you're threatening to kill something, or get rid of it, make sure we both know what you're talking about. And keep your grubby mitts out of my drawers! Now, let me see what you've done to that eye."

Alan stooped as she held his head in her hands. She said, "You're going to have a bit of a shiner, but the skin's not broken. Finish what you're doing out here and come in for a cup of tea in the kitchen. I've got something to tell you."

As she walked away, he wondered what she might be going to tell him. Maybe she was going to get some Tae Kwon Do lessons to improve her pathetically inadequate self-defence capabilities, or maybe she was going to appoint him to the post of Chief Crane Control Officer at her new anchovy farm on the River Wear, or maybe he was going to have to sleep in the stinky spare bedroom because she'd gone bonkers. He reached down into the long grass where he'd dropped his hammer. Picking it up, he said, "Shit!" and looked around for something to clean the heron droppings from his hand.

＊＊＊＊

Having finished fixing the chicken mesh to its wooden frame, Alan made his way to the kitchen, where Sam was pouring hot water onto the teabags.

He said, "How did it go at the doctor's? Did he tell you what it was?"

"Oh yes. Nothing to worry about."

He noticed the bottle of pills at the other side of the table. "What have you got there then, antibiotics?"

"No. It's folic acid."

"Folic acid? Isn't that the stuff they give you for some sort of woman's trouble? It's not something serious, is it?"

"Well I suppose you could say that. But let's get you sat down before we discuss it any further. And maybe a nice sweet cup of tea ready for you." She took the cushion from the chair and sat him at the table. Then she placed the cushion on the table in front of him, before walking over to the stove to take the teabags out of the mugs.

He said, "Come on, tell me. What is it? What did the doctor say it was?"

"We're going to have a baby."

At first, Alan's reaction to the bombshell was quite muted. For a minute he said nothing, principally because he had fainted. Sam turned and said, "I thought that might happen." She walked over to Alan and lifted his head off the cushion, gently slapped at his face, avoiding his left cheek, and said, "Wakey, wakey, daddy-to-be."

He came round as she landed another kiss on his forehead. "What happened? Did you say that … Bloody hell! That's great!" He stood up, steadying himself by leaning on the table as the blood rushed from his head, then held his open palm against her body, just below her breasts. She repositioned his hand lower towards her navel. He said, "It's in there. We did it."

He took the cushion from the table and, placing it on his chair, sat her down. "You've got to take it easy. No heavy lifting and get plenty of sleep. Now how about that nice cup of tea. You can't have anything stronger."

She said, "Hey, sweetie. I'm not ill. Don't fuss. Just pass me the tea."

He said, "Right. One cup of tea, coming up. When's it due? Did they tell you if it's a girl or a boy?"

"Probably just before Christmas. As I'm officially an elderly primigravida with a history of *woman's trouble*, they've offered me an early scan. They'll be able to fix the date, but they won't be able to tell the sex yet. I'm booked in for the eighteenth."

Chapter 13

Wednesday 17th May

George Wilson wondered why he had to wear an open-backed gown without any underclothes. It was his head that they were going to hack open. He could just as easily have worn a pair of jeans and a tee-shirt. Maybe it was simply to show who was in control. To reinforce the patient's submission to the surgeon's authority.

And why did he have to ride on a trolley to the theatre suite? His legs were perfectly functional! With his head tilted back, the pillow felt strange. No hair to shield his scalp from the stiff linen. How come they'd shaved his entire head, when they just needed to take out a few square centimetres of cranium? Or did they have plans for something bigger? And just what was that stuff they'd given him in the ward?

He counted the fluorescent strip lights. They were all still switched on, even though the natural light from the corridor windows was adequate. How much did this cost the NHS? And why, when George was bloody starving, did the moronic porter have to keep going on about the pies he'd stuffed himself with at half time at the match the night before?

As this could well be his last day on Earth, they could at least have allowed him a tiny taste of bacon sandwich. Or a boiled egg. Or even half a slice of toast? A spoonful of muesli? No, not muesli. Forget the bloody muesli.

The trolley bashed into a pair of doors, which swung open. "Here we are," said the moronic pieman, behind him.

A young man in Lincoln green leaned over and said, "Hello, George. Can I just confirm your name, please?"

"Jaw," was as much as George could manage.

"Okay, near enough. I just need to stick a few little patches on you, George. Is that alright?" asked Robin Hood.

George tried to reply but his tongue got in the way.

"Now you might feel a little scratch as I put a line in. Just a scratch."

George didn't feel the scratch, but thought that he should ask if the surgeon had pepper with his full English. He didn't want surgeon snot in amongst his grey matter, and the knife could slip if he sneezed. Again, no sound emerged. The tongue was swelling and getting drier by the minute. His eyelids were feeling heavy.

"Okay, George. You might feel a cold sensation for a second or …"

* * * *

The morning after George's operation, Sam called the hospital. "I'm not sure which ward he's on. He had an operation yesterday. Yes. It's George. Yes, I *am* a relative. He's my brother. Ward 13? Thank you."

She blocked the mouthpiece with her hand and turned to Alan "He's on ward 13. They're putting me through."

"Hello. I'm calling about George Wilson … Yes. I'm his sister …What do you mean? It was just a routine operation … Always a risk? Elderly? But he's not old … What! Oh no! Okay. Thank you. Oh, wait. What time's visiting? … Right, I see. Thank you."

She struggled to focus on the phone's red button as she tried to end the call, but gave up, and in frustration, dropped the handset on the table. "Bad reaction to the anaesthetic. They couldn't finish the operation. He's in a coma." She put both hands up to her face and wiped her eyes, then cried, "He's not expected … to last through the night."

Alan took her in his arms as she sobbed. He kissed the back of her head and said, "You really liked him, didn't you?"

She sniffed and stopped crying. In a voice, muffled by his jumper she said, "Course I did. He was such a nice person. My first boyfriend, not that we … you know."

"You should go and see him. What time's visiting?"

She lifted her head from his shoulder. "They said relatives can go anytime, given the circumstances. I'll go and see him after I've had the scan." She wiped her left eye again with her hand.

Alan asked, "Do you want me to drive you?"

"No. It's alright. I'll go on my own. You've got plenty to do here. Get the last of the THC into the incinerator."

"It's done. I finished it yesterday. All I need to do now is to get rid of the storage tank, then we'll be legal."

Sam arrived at the nurse's station of ward 13 at five o'clock. She said, "Hello. I'm visiting George Wilson."

The nurse ran her finger down a list of names on a sheet of paper and said, "I'm sorry, he's not on this ward."

"But I was told he was on ward 13. This is ward 13, isn't it?"

"Yes, but he might have been moved. I've just come on, so I'm not sure who's been moved where. Just a tick."

The nurse clicked the mouse and looked up the name on the computer. "There you go. He's in the HDU on ward 15. Next floor up, turn left when you get out of the lift."

"HDU?"

"High Dependency Unit."

"Right. Thank you."

The HDU nurse on ward 15 said, "George is quite poorly at the moment. He's in a coma, but we think he might still be able to hear you. So, talk to him, but don't expect any response."

Sam entered the side room. With the curtains half drawn the late afternoon sunshine was lighting up the wall on the opposite side of the room to the bed. While the overriding smell of ward 13 had been one of overcooked cabbage, this room had the chemical aroma of hospital. George lay in the bed, surrounded by instrumentation, his bandaged head supported by two pillows. Wires trailed from sensors stuck onto his body, up to a rack of monitoring equipment, measuring his pulse, breathing and oxygen saturation.

241

On the side of the bed hung a plastic bag half full of dark straw-coloured urine. Two drips, mounted on stands, were connected to his wrists.

She sat down on a plastic padded chair next to the bed. "Hello George. It's Sam. How are you feeling? Sorry. Silly question."

The video monitor was displaying a heart-beat pattern and the slowly varying ups and downs as he breathed. The heart beat display showed 85 beats per minute.

She gripped his hand and said, "I've got something to tell you. Remember when you said that you wanted kids. Well, you're going to get your wish. You're going to be a father. I'm pregnant. Not that it matters much to you now. You're not going to be around to see them."

The heart rate display jumped to 95, then slowly began to drop back.

"I know I told you I couldn't have kids. That wasn't quite true. It wasn't me. It was Alan, but I couldn't destroy his self confidence on top of his greatest disappointment – never being able to father a child."

Sam sat silently for a few minutes, wondering what life would have been like, had she stuck with her first conquest. Would they have married and settled down to a life of relative poverty with a troop of ginger-nut kids? Would George have had to take a job, well below his capabilities, to keep their family, never reaching anywhere near his true potential, missing out on the gradual progression which had taken him to such a senior post in the hotel business?

A sudden noise broke her thought train as the automatic blood pressure monitor inflated the cuff on George's arm. Once again, the heart beat jumped up for a few seconds.

She said, "Anyway, I just wanted to say thank you for what you've given me. It's going to be the best thing to happen to me and Alan. I'll never, ever forget you, George. It's such a shame. You'd have made a wonderful uncle George."

Suddenly an alarm started sounding its shrill, three-chord cacophony. She looked up at the monitor. The pulse rate display was flashing three minus signs. The oxygen saturation reading was zero. She cried, "Oh George. Oh, no!" Her face distorted, turning the attractive woman into an ugly hag as the intense emotional pain gripped her.

A nurse rushed into the room and smiled at Sam. "Let's have a look, dear." Sam stood up and got out of the way, allowing the nurse to approach the bed and start pulling back the bedclothes.

Sam turned to look at the open door, expecting to see the crash trolley racing to the scene. She peered out into the corridor. Where was it? Was it ever going to come, or had they decided to allow him to die?

Maybe George had stipulated that he should not be resuscitated. So, this was to be the last time she would be with her first conquest. Her bottom lip quivered as she came back into the room to say goodbye to him. The nurse was standing next to the bed, holding the finger clip, which Sam had inadvertently dislodged. "Found it! Happens all the time. I'll put it on his other hand."

With the alarm silenced, from the other side of the bed the nurse said, "You okay, love? Can I get you a cup of tea?"

Sam wiped her eyes. "No thanks, I'm fine. He's not in any pain, is he? Only, I'd hate to think that he was going to spend his last few hours in pain."

"No, no; your brother's quite comfortable. But don't upset yourself, love. He's not dying. It was just the oximeter sensor. He might look a bit fragile, but believe me, he just needs a bit of a rest. He's been through a major operation. It might look a bit dramatic, hooked up to all the monitors and that, but it's really just routine. Hey, it's like a production line in here, love. They're admitted, get chopped open, into HDU to recover, then onto the ward and off home, in no time at all. You'll see."

The heart beat monitor steadied at 86 beats per minute.

Sam recalled her earlier telephone conversation. "But they said he wouldn't make it through the night."

The heart beat rose to 96 per minute.

The nurse said, "What do you mean, *not make it through the night*? It's just an induced coma to help him recover from a small brain bleed. He should be fine in a few days. Mind you, we're not sure yet whether he'll make a complete recovery. Apart from the slight risk of the cancer returning, he could have a few problems with medium term memory, but he's not going to die any time soon. Where on Earth did you get that idea?"

"I called ward 13 this morning. They said he was in a coma and they didn't expect him to survive the night."

244

"Ward 13? Are you sure? He's never been on ward 13. That's geriatric male surgical. Mostly ingrown toenails and the like. Leave it with me, I'll give them a call and see what they're playing at. And don't worry! He's fine."

The jovial nurse left the room. Sam sat down again, took George's hand and squeezed hard. "Forget what I said. Alan's the father and if you ever breathe a word, it'll be the last bit of breathing you do. Do you hear?"

The heart rate jumped to 110.

Sam relaxed her grip and said, "I've got to go now. If you can hear me, just remember. Forget everything I said."

On her way out, Sam met the nurse, who said, "You'll never believe it, my love. I've spoken with the sister on ward 13. It was a complete mix-up. An elderly patient with the same name, George Wilson, was in for a hip job. Would you ever credit it? So, there was a problem with anaesthesia. Well I know who I'd prefer between Mr. Chater and Sonny Liston. Give me the right hook every time, much more reliable. Anyway, the old gent never regained consciousness and the poor soul died this afternoon. Oh, and you didn't hear it from me. Patient confidentiality and all that."

Above the noise of the late April rain shower, Alan heard the car engine as Sam pulled up outside the front door. He rose from his seat at the kitchen table and put the kettle on again.

She would need all of his support after visiting her dying friend, and what better than a nice sweet mug of cocoa to do the job.

He heard the front door slam. This was a very, very bad sign. It took a lot of effort to slam such a massive door. He must have underestimated how upset she would be at the loss of her old friend.

"Damn!" he heard as she crossed the hall. *She must be really upset*, he thought. Quite understandable if she'd just visited an old friend who's not expected to see tomorrow. Alan was going to have his work cut out, with some really serious comforting being needed.

A dripping Sam entered the kitchen. She smiled and said, "Hi sweetie. Pass the towel, please. There's a love."

He took the driest towel from the rail near the stove and walked across to hand it to her. As she patted her hair and face, he said, "Are you alright? How did it go? He's not…"

"No. He's going to be fine. It was a right cock-up. Another George Wilson was on his death bed apparently. Ginger George is going to make a full recovery, although they did say his memory might be affected." She stood with the towel draped around her shoulders and opened a cupboard door, revealing a stock of jars of anchovies. She took out a jar and walked over to the cutlery drawer to get a fork. "Oh well, we'll just have to wait and see what happens." She opened the jar and said, "Oh, and I've got some other news. Maybe you'd better sit down."

"What? Is it the scan? Something's wrong, isn't it?" he said.

Sam guided him to a chair and placed a cushion on the table in front of him.

Chapter 14

Monday 22nd May

Away from the HDU, the rest of ward 15 had the same pervasive aroma that Sam remembered from ward 13. As she walked up the wide corridor past the first bay, she wondered whether the staple food of the hospital was overcooked cabbage, or whether there was a hint of bedpan in the air. She approached the nurses' station where a large woman in a light brown uniform was wiping a damp cloth over the exposed surfaces of the desk. Without smiling, the large woman looked up from her cleaning and said, "Who are you after?"

Sam said, "George Wilson."

"Private room, second left just before the patients' toilet."

As the woman got back to her desk wiping, Sam thanked her and walked away. She wondered if the unpleasant atmosphere had somehow permeated the brains of the ward staff, destroying all neurons responsible for conversational pleasantry. The room door was open and as Sam entered, a young nurse looked up from her task and said, "Look George, your sister's here."

He lowered his newspaper and looked blankly at Sam. His chin was covered in orange stubble. The top of his head was still bandaged. The nurse smiled at Sam and said, "I'll be done in a minute. Just changing him." She stood up and raised the polythene bag of urine to head height. "Brilliant," she said, "We'll have you out of here in no time, George."

Sam wondered if human urine had bestowed immunity to the cabbage gas upon some of the nursing staff. She took a chair and sat next to the bed on the side away from the catheter drain.

She said, "Hello George. How are you? You're looking a lot better than you did last week."

He said, "I'm sorry, you're my sister. Is that right?"

"Yes. Of course. Don't you remember me?"

George didn't reply. He just looked her in the eye and shook his head. The newspaper rustled as he roughly folded it into an untidy heap and placed it on the tray by the bed, nearly knocking over an empty tumbler. His frown gave way to a strained smile. The nurse closed the door behind her.

Eventually Sam broke the silence. "Samantha. Or Sam for short."

He said, "Nice name."

She decided that now might be the time to do what she had come for. "You really don't remember anything?"

"Well, some things are clear. I work in a hotel. The Royal? I was married but now I'm divorced." George leaned over the table at the side of the bed and poured himself a glass of water.

Sam said, "How much do you remember about the reunion and what happened after it?"

George took a sip of water. "Yes. I do seem to remember organising a school reunion. I booked the function room at the King's Head. Did it go alright?"

"Yes, it was a great night. You don't remember being there?"

He shook his head and shrugged.

"Oh well, I'm sure it'll come back to you in time. Did you know you'd been in an induced coma for a few days?"

"Yes, the consultant told me. He said the operation went well, but there was a bleed, so they put me to sleep to give my brain a rest and help me to recover."

"That's right. They said you could hear what people were saying to you while you were comatose. Do you remember anything about it?"

He leaned over and picked up the tumbler, then glanced in her direction. She was staring at him as she waited for his answer. "Afraid not. It was just like having a long sleep. Dead to the world."

She said, "Maybe it's just as well. It would probably just confuse you as to what was said to you and what you'd been dreaming."

"They said it should mostly come back to me in time, but it could be a slow process," said George.

Sam thought for a moment then said, "How would you feel about coming to stay with us for a few weeks while you recuperate and get your memory back? We're both at home all day and we've got a spare bedroom. I'm working from home on theoretical stuff and Alan's just pottering on most of the day."

George picked up the tumbler and took another sip. "Who's Alan?"

"Oh, I forgot, you've lost your memory. Alan's my partner. Do you remember Minty from school?"

"Minty? That's a funny nickname. No, I'd only be intruding on the pair of you. It's okay, I'll just go home."

"Nonsense," said Sam, "It's no trouble. We'd love to have you. We could help jog your memory. Besides, they won't discharge you if you haven't got anybody to look after you. I won't take no for an answer. I'll talk to the sister."

Chapter 15

Tuesday 30th May

Two men got out of the black Audi, parked outside of the farmhouse. The driver was a tall skinny man dressed in an ill-fitting, dark blue suit. His passenger was a shorter man, wearing a dark grey overcoat and a trilby, perched precariously on the top of his head. The two men walked over the gravel to the front porch. The hot morning sunshine had dried up the worn Yorkshire flags near the door. The tall man looked among the ivy for a bell push. As he drew aside a handful of loose branches, he uncovered a tarnished brass plaque inscribed with 'Samanal Pharm Ltd. Registered office'. He said to his companion, "Huh! Spelling's atrocious."

"Good morning," said a voice behind them. A short man, dressed in khaki shorts and camouflage top, with a map pouch hanging from his neck, was approaching from the direction of the river. "My name's Potter. I'm with the Low Fell ramblers and I'm planning a route for our annual memorial river walk, next week."

"That's really interesting," said the man with the trilby.

Potter went on, "The river bank path has been washed out, and I was wondering if you would mind if I brought my party over the field and crossed over back to the footpath further along."

"Not at all. We wouldn't mind one bit," said the trilby man.

"Oh, that's very kind of you. We wouldn't do any damage to your field. We'd keep to the edges," said Potter.

Trilby man shook his head and said, "We haven't got a field."

"What? Isn't that your field?" asked Potter.

"Oh no. I think it belongs to the people who live in this house."

"Huh! You could have told me," said Potter.

"True, but then I wouldn't have had such a pleasant and interesting conversation with you. It's alright, we'll knock on the door for you."

The tall man knocked on the door. As he rubbed his knuckles he said, "Maybe they're not home, sir."

"Try again," said the trilby man.

The tall man raised his clenched fist to knock harder, but the door opened before he could make contact. Sam pulled her head back just in time.

Potter looked up at Sam, screamed, turned and ran away towards the river, his bare legs chafing against damp khaki.

Smiling, Sam said, "PC Latimer and Sergeant Willoughby. We haven't seen you in a while." She looked in the distance at Potter and said, "Oh. And you've brought a strange little man with you, but now he's run off. What was all that about?"

Willoughby shrugged his shoulders. "I think he said something about having a party in your field."

Sam said, "Oh that would never do. Like Woodstock, with all those drug crazed hippies? No thank you. Now what can I do for you, sergeant?"

Willoughby replied, "Well, actually, it's Detective Inspector Willoughby now, Miss Black. Can we come inside?"

"Yes, of course, and congratulations. Are you off duty, constable?"

"No, madam. It's DC Latimer, now," said the taller man.

"DC? Actually, I never had you down as AC or DC, to tell the truth."

"Detective Constable. I'm no longer with the uniformed division," said Latimer.

"Oh! Plain clothes! Congratulations. I'm so happy for you. Please, would you both like to come through to the kitchen." Sam was about to open the kitchen door when she heard a cough coming from within the room. "On second thoughts, why don't we go into the living room. We'll be much more comfortable in there."

The television was playing loudly as they entered the room. A goofy, bespectacled presenter was giving his opinion on the relative merits of fillies versus colts in the next race. Sam searched the sofa for the remote control, finally finding it under an untidy mess of newspapers. Willoughby seemed to be quite interested in the goofy man's opinion and looked slightly disappointed when Sam hit the power button.

Sam noticed the policeman's interest and said, "Sorry, sergeant. Were you watching that?"

"Oh, no. It just looked familiar. I was brought up in Chepstow. My father was a jockey. Rode quite a few winners on that course."

Latimer and Willoughby exchanged glances.

Sam bundled the papers and looked around for somewhere to lose them. As she stuffed the papers behind an armchair, she said, "Please, sit down."

The two policemen plonked themselves on the sofa. Willoughby reached beneath his backside and produced an empty bottle. Sam took the bottle and put it with the other three Edinburgh Heavy empties on the coffee table. She said, "What can I do for you, inspector?"

"Well, Miss Black, it's nothing to worry about. It's just a courtesy call to let you know that we are no longer treating the death of Mr. Edward Hughes as suspicious."

Sam said, "Well that's a relief. Edward Hughes? I'm sorry, but who exactly is Edward Hughes? Or rather, who *was* Edward Hughes?"

Willoughby got as far as saying, "Mr. Hughes was …" before he was interrupted by George Wilson entering the room.

"Who switched it off? I was watching that," said George.

George's shaven head was now covered in a layer of very fine orange stubble, which matched his unkempt beard perfectly. His dressing gown was half open, revealing Alan's old, striped blue and white pyjamas. In his right hand, he held a freshly opened bottle of beer. He looked at the two policemen, then turned to Sam and said, "I'm sorry, I didn't realise you had visitors. I'll go back to the kitchen."

Sam said, "I don't suppose it matters, George. You might just as well stay. These men are from the police. Inspector Willoughby and Detective Constable Latimer."

Willoughby said, "We've met before, I think. It's Mr. Wilson, isn't it?"

George stared at Willoughby. "I'm sorry. I don't remember."

Sam said, "George has a problem with his memory. He underwent brain surgery recently, and it left him with temporary partial amnesia. We invited him here to recuperate while his memory comes back."

Willoughby said, "Oh, I see. Well Mr Wilson, if it's any help, I interviewed you at the Royal Hotel some time ago concerning a missing person, a Mr. Malcolm Burke. Does that ring any bells?"

George shook his head. "No. I don't remember you, sorry." He slumped into an armchair and took a drink of beer before placing the bottle on the coffee table. He smiled at Sam, then turned to Willoughby and said, "Oh, wait a minute. I think my solicitor was called Burke. I remember writing my will before the operation, and some other stuff to be opened in the event of my death. Of course, I could be mistaken. Might not have been Burke."

Sam smiled at George then said, "Please go on, inspector. You were saying about Edward Hughes."

"Yes. We've now identified a body, recovered from the river near Chester-Le-Street, as that of Mr. Hughes. He went missing five years ago."

Alan walked in the room. "Oh, hello. It's Sergeant Welby and PC Latimer. How are you doing? Are you off duty, constable?" He sat on the arm of Sam's chair.

Sam took Alan's hand and said, "It's Detective Inspector Willoughby now dear, and PC Latimer is in plain clothes because he's a detective now."

Alan said, "But if you're an inspector, what happened to the other inspector? Richards, wasn't it? Has he been kicked upstairs and given a desk job?"

Sam said, "Inspector Richards is a *Chief* Inspector, dear. Sergeant, sorry, *Inspector* Willoughby still reports to DCI Richards. Isn't that how it works, inspector?"

Willoughby said, "I'm afraid that DCI Richards met with a tragic accident and he died a month ago."

Sam said, "How awful. Such a nice friendly man. What happened?"

"He tripped and bumped his head on his garden wall and it became infected. His head, that is. I told him he should get it cleaned up and stitched, but he just ignored me. It got worse and he was taken to hospital, but they couldn't save him. It was lockjaw."

Alan said, "Isn't that the same as tetanus?"

"Inspector Willoughby's a busy man, dear," said Sam, "Now what were you saying about this Mr. Hughes, inspector?"

Willoughby went on, "Oh, yes. The coroner is satisfied that Mr. Hughes took his own life, so our colleagues at Chester-Le-Street have now closed the case."

Having missed half of the conversation, Alan tried to catch up. "Excuse me, sergeant, but who was this Hughes character?"

The inspector said, "Edward Hughes was a rambler who went missing over five years ago near Houghton."

"Oh, I remember," said George. He looked at Sam and said, "Sorry, my mistake. I don't remember. Getting a bit confused."

The front door alarm sounded. Alan got up and went to answer it.

Sam said, "So what's this to do with me?"

Willoughby said, "Well, I don't know if you remember, but you were questioned about the disappearance because the Houghton police had evidence, suggesting that you were the last person to see Mr. Hughes alive. Apparently, he called at your house with some of his fellow walkers, to fill their water bottles. Mr. Hughes got separated from the rest of the party and was never seen again. Houghton were treating the disappearance as a suspicious death, but now it seems that he weighed himself down with a sackful of rocks and jumped off a bridge near Chester-Le-Street."

George looked at Sam, then turned to the inspector and said, "That's terrible. A sackful of rocks, you say?"

Willoughby nodded. "Yes, tied around his neck. It seems that the load on his neck acted like a hangman's noose. So thankfully he died instantly, rather than drowning."

Sam was observing George. He looked at her for a second, then turned away, picked up his bottle and took another swig.

257

Sam said, "Oh yes. Now I remember Ted. Nice man. I seem to remember our lights had fused, so I asked him if he would take a look at my box. Alan was away with his work at the time, but Ted was very obliging. Sorted me in no time at all. Then he was off to join his friends. Never saw him again. Such a waste."

Alan entered the room with a young couple. He said, "Look dear, it's …"

Sam interrupted him. "Bob and Caroline! How nice to see you again."

George said, "It's Catherine, isn't it?" He looked at Sam, who was giving him another stare. He said, "Funny the way the odd little things are starting to come back … Didn't we meet at the King's Head?"

Catherine said, "No it was here. The night of the blizzard. Don't you remember? It got really deep and we got stuck in the snow. You very kindly arranged a free room at the Royal for the night. We just wanted to say thank you in person. We asked for you at the hotel, but they said you were here, recovering from a big brain operation?" Catherine presented George with the flowers she was carrying. "These are for you, to say thanks for being so kind. I hope you get better very soon. Oh, and just look! It's such a shame they had to shave off all your lovely red hair."

Hearing this, Latimer took out his notebook and thumbed through the pages. Finally, he found the page he was looking for and said, "You work at the Royal, do you, Mr Wilson? You're not the night porter by any chance?"

"Night porter?" George frowned and laughed. "No. I'm Group Regional Director."

Latimer said, "You haven't got a blonde girlfriend, by any chance, Mr. Wilson?"

"Latimer!" said Willoughby, "I can only apologise, Mr Wilson. My colleague sometimes gets a little bit over-inquisitive. He's got a bee in his bonnet about an entirely unrelated case."

Sam laughed and said, "Sorry, constable, but you're barking up the wrong tree. George is gay, bent as a nine bob note. Wouldn't have any interest in a girlfriend, blonde or otherwise. Isn't that right, George?"

George said, "Yes, quite correct, love. I'm a right old puff." He pouted. "What time do you get off duty, constable?"

Latimer flushed and looked around the room. He leaned towards Willoughby and cuffed his hand around the inspector's ear. "Sir, I'm sure it was murder. Wilson and the young lady, Catherine. They were seen disposing of the you-know-what."

Willoughby said, "What are you on about? It was suicide. The coroner's finished with it. Case closed."

Latimer whispered, "No, sir. I mean the other case. You know, the accidental death."

Sam took the flowers from George and said, "I'll go and put these in a vase. Won't be a tick."

As Sam left the room Latimer whispered to Willoughby, "Before she died, Mrs. Foster said it was a red-haired man and a blonde who dumped the body. She recognised the man as someone who worked at the Royal. It's just too much of a coincidence, sir."

Sam reappeared and said, "Anyone for coffee? It's Colombian. A hundred percent Arabica."

Latimer said, "Thanks very much, but we have to get going."

Willoughby said, "Lighten up, man. We've got time for a quick Java. Mine's black with two sugars, please."

Sam smiled at Latimer and said, "As I remember, you'd be white with two, constable?" She turned to the young couple and said, "For you?"

Bob said, "White, no sugar, please."

Catherine said, "No thanks. We've got to go. Only called in to say thank you to Mr. Wilson. Oh, and you, of course, Miss Black."

"Oh, come on. Surely, you've got time for a coffee? Young people today. The way you rush about all the time, you'll be rush, rush, rushing into an early grave," said Sam.

George said, "Leave them alone. It's lovely to see them, even if I can't remember them very well. I'm sure they've got more interesting things to do than sit around here drinking your coffee."

Alan said, "Come on, you two. I'll see you to the door and get me and George another beer. Shall I put the kettle on, dear?"

Sam said, "Yes. Okay, but before they go, I'll just get Bob and Catherine's address, so we can keep in touch."

George said, "No need to, I've already got it. That is, I seem to remember getting it sometime in the past." He looked at Sam. "It's a bit fuzzy, but it's slowly coming back."

For a few moments, Sam looked at George and unconsciously massaged her lips with her index finger as she studied him. She smiled and then walked over to give Bob and Catherine a kiss goodbye. "Lovely to see you again, drop by and have a coffee next time you're passing. And don't leave it so long."

When Alan had left with the young couple, Sam said, "Now constable, tell us all about what's been happening to you. You must be very excited to be part of CID."

Latimer said, "Yes. I've been trying to get into CID for a long time. Since DCI Richards passed away there's been a few changes. Now I'm even allowed to do some digging into a recent fatality, which wasn't cleared up properly, in my opinion. It's a fascinating case. When he was found, the ends of both of his thumbs were missing. His sister told me that he lost one in an accident at work, ten years ago, but the other one was taken by some wild animal. I've got very good intelligence that the body was moved, but I've got no proof. It's like a deathbed statement, but I'm the only one who heard it. Now, if the body was moved, it would change the case completely. It would be *murder* rather than accidental death."

Willoughby rolled his eyes and said, "Latimer, just because you're the ACC's golden boy, doesn't make you bloody Maigret."

"Sorry, sir. May grey? What's that?"

Willoughby sighed and then took a few seconds to think. Sam got as far as saying, "Georges Simenon…" before Willoughby silenced her by holding up his hand with an outstretched index finger.

He said, "It's an old Chepstow racing tradition. The first race of the Spring meeting is always the Two-Year-Old Gelding Selling Plate. If it's won by a grey,

261

it's supposed to be a sign of good luck and foretells a bumper cider apple harvest for the local farmers that year. And for the person who buys the May grey, it means a fortune in stud fees. A very desirable piece of horse flesh."

Latimer tutted. "Do you mean to say they're so thick that they still believe all that Mumbo Jumbo down there in Suffolk? Isn't that where they go around singing to the apple trees?"

"Be careful, constable, I'm from down there," said Willoughby, "Now, all this about bodies being moved, leave it for now. We'll discuss it later, back at the station. If there's anything to it, we'll get to the bottom of it. Either way, it's nothing to do with these good people."

Sam smiled at Willoughby and said, "You learn something new every day. I'd better go and see if the kettle's boiled."

George scratched the back of his neck and said, "Suffolk?"

Alan arrived, carrying two opened bottles of Edinburgh Heavy. He said, "I was going to make the coffees but all I can find is the instant stuff, and we've run out of sugar. I'm sure there was plenty in the bowl this morning. There should be some in the cupboard, but I can't find the jar." He burped and held out one of the bottles for George.

Sam said, "Well I think George might have used the last on his cereal, this morning."

"But I had full English today," said George.

Alan said, "Yes. That's right. I remember."

262

Sam said, "No dear, he had full English *yesterday*. George had cereal this morning. Now you're losing *your* memory."

Alan hiccupped, and then swallowed another mouthful of beer. George gave Sam a puzzled look.

Sam said, "It's alright, sweetie. I think I know where there's some more sugar. I'll sort it out. Why don't you take George down the wild garden and show him your collection of baby frogs?"

Alan's face lit up. "You'll love this, Georgie. We've got hundreds of the little beauties. It's all down to Wurzel. Good old Wurzel. Come on. Bring your beer."

Sam winked at George and said, "Don't let him keep you out there for more than half an hour or so. He'll spend all day in his wild garden, if you let him. You might need another couple of beers."

Alan said to Sam, "Remember. Don't go lifting anything heavy."

She glanced at the sofa and said, "Don't worry, I'll be fine."

George's eyes darted between Sam and the two policemen as Alan dragged him out of the room. Sam turned to Willoughby and asked, "Would you like the telly on while I make the coffee?" Without waiting for a reply, she picked up the remote and switched Goofy back on.

She left the room, saying, "Won't be long. Just need to get a fresh jar of sugar from the cupboard under the stairs."

* * * *

Half an hour later, George entered the kitchen by the side door, his right cheek sporting three dirty black finger streaks. Sam was sitting at the table, drumming her fingers on the lid of an unopened jar of strychnine, with its plastic seal intact. As George closed the door, she turned to him.

"What's wrong?" he said.

"They got away ... I mean, they had to get away. Willoughby took a call. They didn't have time for coffee. Some sort of anonymous tip-off about a dead body over Sherburn. I mean, you'd think that some other coppers could sort it out. Probably just a simple case of a mugging gone wrong or something. Why do we pay our taxes?"

George stood over the sink and squirted a little washing-up liquid into his hand to clean off the greasy marks from his cheek. As he finished sluicing warm water over his face, he said, "Sherburn, eh? What's the best way to get there from here?"

"Well, you go down the main road and turn off just after the bridge. Then follow the river for a mile and then up the hill. Over the top and down the hill and you're there. Why do you ask?"

"No reason." George took the towel hanging from the rail of the stove and dried his face.

Sam said, "You could go through the city, but that's the long way round. The traffic would really slow you down at this time of day. You're not thinking of following them there, are you? You're probably over the limit, you know?"

George smiled. "No. I was just wondering when they would need to use their brakes. It's all pretty flat until you climb to the top. The first time you'd need to use your brakes would be going down that very steep hill with the sharp bend at the bottom."

Sam slowly turned and looked at him. "You haven't, have you?"

From the pocket of his dressing gown, George produced his mobile phone and waved it as he laughed. "Very handy for use in emergencies. Got to protect my genetic investment in the future. I'm not having any kid of mine being born behind bars."

"My God! You heard everything I said, that day!"

George laughed quietly, smiled and then whistled silently – obviously very pleased with himself.

Her shoulders dropped as she said, "Oh how stupid can I be? There was never anything wrong with your memory, either. It was all just an act?"

George nodded and smiled. Sam said "Listen! If a word about our little fling gets back to Alan, you're going to wish you'd got a lift to Sherburn with the coppers. Understand?"

George walked over to her and gently placed his hands on her shoulders. "Sam, darling, my lips are sealed. I'm going to be a wonderful uncle George. That's enough for me. With parents like you and Al, what more could my kids need? There's no way I'm going to spoil it for them." He kissed her brow then made for the fridge.

She smiled and said, "Yes, I think you'll make a great uncle, George."

Alan appeared at the door. He said, "Did you hear that? When I was mucking out the hens, there was an almighty bang. Sounds like there's been a smash on the main road. There's a big cloud of black smoke as well."

265

Then, with his eyes fixed on the jar, he said, "My God, what's that doing in here? I thought we had a rule about never bringing that stuff into the kitchen! It could easily get mistaken for sugar. Then someone could have a really terrible accident. Someone could get killed. Here, I'll take it downstairs."

Sam handed him the jar and said, "Sorry, sweetie. I don't know what I was thinking." When Alan had left the room, she said, "They'll be able to tell if the brakes have been tampered with, you know. It's very risky."

George said, "Yeah, but they won't be able to prove who did the tampering, will they?"

"Well, they might get a bit of a clue if there's a trail of brake fluid between here and the main road."

George took a bottle from the fridge and raked through the cutlery drawer. He said, "Okay, but the pipe could have worked loose when they drove over one of your potholes."

Sam picked up the opener from the table and handed it to him. "Even so, they'll trace the call you made as soon as they realise that it was a hoax to get them to go down the hill."

"They won't be able to trace it, 'cos I withheld my number," said George. He smiled and took a mouthful of beer.

Sam said, "I wouldn't be too sure. I reckon the police could still trace the call if they really needed to."

Neither George nor Sam had heard the front door being opened by Alan as he had been returning from the cellar. As Alan entered with his two guests, George coughed and spluttered with Edinburgh Heavy flooding out of his mouth and nostrils.

Inspector Willoughby said, "Talking about tracing calls, I wish we could find the clown who sent us on that wild goose chase. Uniform got there and checked it out. It was somebody playing silly beggars. No dead body. Nothing. We only got as far as the bypass. Then there was a big pile-up and we couldn't move in either direction. It's completely grid locked."

George said, "So were you actually involved in the accident, inspector?"

Willoughby said, "Oh, no. We were about four cars back. There was a car fire in the layby and traffic slowed down to rubber neck. Then one of those Water Board tankers had to brake hard and got hit from behind. Looks like it was full, on its way to the sewage works, because the valve at the back must have taken a knock and the contents of somebody's septic tank was spraying all over the place."

Sam said, "Sounds very unpleasant. But you didn't hit the car in front, then?"

Latimer chipped in, "No. We stopped perfectly safely. Police drivers are trained to keep control at all times and drive within the capabilities of the vehicle. There was never any danger of a collision, on our part."

Willoughby said, "Anyway, the silly thing is that our washers had somehow run dry. Couldn't see a thing through all those sweet violets on the windscreen, so we left the keys with one of the traffic lads and thought we'd walk back here. Maybe take you up on the offer of coffee?" He raised his eyebrows and smiled. "Any chance?"

Sam glanced at George, who replied with a shrug of his shoulders. She said, "Coffee? Of course, inspector.

Shall we adjourn to the television lounge? Put the kettle on, sweetie. There's a dear."

Ten minutes later Alan placed the tray on the coffee table, then carefully handed a white coffee to Latimer and black to Willoughby and Sam. Willoughby was staring at Alan, who was wearing latex gloves and had a disposable face mask hanging around his neck. Heading for the door, Alan said, "Oops! Forgot I still had them on. Er, I'm allergic to Arabica."

Sam rolled her eyes and gave Alan a look which combined puzzlement and disbelief at his unconvincing excuse. She said, "Inspector Willoughby, I'm fascinated by this thing about tracing calls. You said that you'd like to be able to trace who sent you on the wild goose chase. Can you actually trace the call after it's been made? I thought you had to keep the person talking until the exchange did their clever stuff and traced the caller?"

"You mean like they do in all the detective stories?" said Willoughby, " Oh no, Miss Black. That was in the old days, before telephone exchanges were automated. Nowadays, all telephone calls are controlled by computers and they log details of who called who. If we really need to get a trace, we can get the information, but it costs a lot in terms of time and therefore, money."

"Even if the caller withholds his number?" said a very worried-looking George Wilson.

"Oh yes. But, like I say, it's only worthwhile in the most serious cases, like murder. It's subject to very strict rules. We don't live in a police state, yet. If we did, then the technology exists to keep all call details on computer file." Willoughby smiled and took a sip of coffee.

"That's fascinating," said Sam.

Alan, who had returned, bare of hand and maskless, had been standing near the door, but now walked over and sat on the arm of Sam's chair. He said, "What about fingerprints, inspector? Wouldn't your lives be easier if the police had everybody's prints on file?"

"Well, yes. It would make our job a lot simpler in some cases, but again, it's all dependent upon public acceptance. Do we want a police state? As it stands, we're not allowed to keep anybody's prints on file unless they've been convicted of an offence."

Latimer swallowed a mouthful of digestive and gulped down his coffee, which was quite cold – or more precisely, at exactly 36 degrees Celsius.

He said, "Well that's not strictly true, is it, sir? There's the staff elimination database."

Willoughby sighed at Latimer then said, "Okay, if you want to be pedantic, we *do* hold records of *unconvicted* police officers and staff on a separate database for elimination purposes, but we rarely get a match. It's there just in case there's a mistake made, like a Scene Of Crime Officer taking his gloves off and contaminating the crime scene."

Alan said, "So, do you always check this staff database when you find fingerprints at a crime scene?"

The inspector said, "Generally we do, but it depends on the importance we attach to the print."

Alan was leaning forward, hanging on every word. Sam said, "You'll have to forgive him, Inspector Willoughby, he does tend to ask a lot of silly questions."

269

Willoughby said, "It's alright. It's not as if I'm giving away any state secrets. As a matter of fact, we had an example in a recent case where we didn't need to check the staff database. We found an article on a dead body, with a couple of unknown prints. At first, we suspected that the deceased might have been unlawfully killed. We checked the offender database and didn't find a match. Then, as it happened, the coroner ruled that it was accidental death, so we had no reason to check the elimination database, because the case was closed. It was that case that you've been on about, Latimer."

Latimer said, "I think we need to re-open that case, sir. Maybe take some prints for elimination of you-know-who, and see what turns up. Of course, it could be that one of the SOCOs left his prints on the article. So, we'd have to run them past the staff database as well, but I'm confident that if we find whose prints are on the bottle, we'll have found our murderer." He surprised himself with a short involuntary laugh.

Alan said, "Well you know, sometimes it's better to let sleeping dogs lie. They don't like being disturbed and they *can* bite you."

Willoughby picked up a digestive and looked at Latimer. "Quite right, Mr Murray. Slow down a bit, constable. We'll discuss it later. It costs pennies to run the prints against the staff database, but when you start involving fingerprint officers taking elimination prints from everybody who had contact with the deceased, the costs mount up. And you don't want to be responsible for going over budget , do you? … Nice biscuits, Miss Black. Have you ever tried the chocolate coated ones?"

"They're a bit sweet for our tastes, and besides, they'd turn a cup of tea into cocoa if you dunked them," said Sam with a little chuckle.

The inspector laughed, then turned to Alan. "On the subject of sweet things, there's something I wanted to ask you, Mr Murray. It's been nagging me for some time. Why do you carry a little bag of sugar in your coat pocket?"

Alan looked at Sam and then back at Willoughby. His brain was functioning apace as he trotted out the words, "I'm ... I'm diabetic."

Unfortunately, Sam's brain ran a dead heat and she winced in pain, clutching her stomach and groin. She cried, "I think my waters have broken," then turning to Alan, "Eh?"

Alan, as composed as a Keystone cop, shouted in all directions, "She's pregnant. Call an ambulance! Quick!"

George sprang into action, took his mobile out of his pocket and extended the aerial. Fortunately, Sam recovered from her bout of extremely premature water-breaking as quickly as it had come on. She sat up straight, took a deep breath and exhaled with a smile. "False alarm. Yes of course ... He's diabetic ... Could go hypo at any time."

Completely confused, George pocketed his mobile.

271

Chapter 16

Thursday 8th June

The dark Audi pulled up outside the farmhouse. Two men got out and walked over the gravel to the front door. Both men were carrying brief cases. A bell started ringing and Sam opened the door. "Good morning, inspector. Back so soon? I'm afraid you're going to be disappointed. We still haven't got any chocolate digestives." Sam stared at the stern looking man with Willoughby. She said, "I see you've got a new bagman, inspector. Bagman, is that right term? That's what they say on the telly, isn't it?"

Willoughby said, "Well not quite, Miss Black, this gentleman isn't a serving police officer. May I introduce Mr. Carter, from the Police Complaints Authority."

Sam looked at Carter, shook her head, and said, "But we haven't made a complaint against the police."

The inspector said, "Maybe we could come inside and I'll explain?"

Alan appeared behind Sam. Gazing at Carter, he said, "What's up?"

Sam said, "The Police Complaints Authority are here. Better put the kettle on, sweetie."

As Sam and the two visitors got settled in the living room, Willoughby said, "I am here to conduct an interview and Mr. Carter is here in a supervisory role in the investigation, because a certain allegation has been made."

Sam said, "This all sounds very serious, inspector. What's it all about?"

"I'm not at liberty to say, madam."

"Oh. Well, go ahead then. Ask away."

Willoughby turned as the living room door opened and said, "It's not yourself I came to talk to, Miss Black. Won't you sit down, Mr. Murray? We've just a few questions to clear up a point or two."

Alan put the tray down on the coffee table. "Me? I haven't done anything."

Willoughby ignored the coffee and reached into his brief case. "I'm not accusing you of anything, sir. I just want to know if you recognise this." In Willoughby's hand was a plastic bag containing a large spanner.

"What do you mean? It's a spanner. About 20 millimetre, I'd say."

"Yes, sir. But could it be one of *your* spanners?" said Willoughby.

"I don't think so," said Alan, "It's dirty. What's all that brown stuff? Where did you get it from? What makes you think it's one of mine?"

"I'm not at liberty to say, sir. Now, could it be one of yours? Have you lost a spanner recently?"

Alan pulled a face and took the bag from Willoughby. Stretching the plastic, he read the characters cast into the steel. "Huh, Chrome Vanadium. No. It's not one of mine. I use professional tools, Chrome Moly. This looks like something you'd get free in a packet of cornflakes. It's a cheap import. Wouldn't last five minutes. You only get what you pay for."

Willoughby said, "So you're denying that it's your property. Is that correct, sir?"

"Like I just said. My set's much better quality, and I keep them clean. Do you want to see them? I can show you, if you want."

Willoughby looked at Carter, who nodded. The inspector said, "Yes, sir. That might help."

Alan said, "Come on down to the cellar. That's where I keep all of my tools."

Sam looked at Alan in disbelief, then covered her face with her hand and peeped through opened fingers as Alan led the two men out of the room.

In the cellar, Alan opened his tool cupboard and took out a large box. He unclipped it and showed the spanner set to the two men. Willoughby nodded and turned to Carter, who was writing in his notebook.

Alan said, "I've had these for about seven years. Never had one break on me yet. They're guaranteed for life, provided you look after them properly. If one of them ever did break, I could take it back and get it replaced, just like that." He tried to snap his fingers, but the layer of oil ensured that he failed miserably to make any noise.

Alan closed the spanner set and replaced the tools in the cupboard. The inspector said, "What's behind that door, sir? I thought I heard a noise."

As Willoughby pushed open the door, Alan turned and said, "Nothing really. It's just our plant room."

Willoughby looked in and said, "Plants? Oh, a chemical plant room? What's all that about then, sir?"

Alan ushered the two men in and waited while they took in the scene. The policeman's stare landed on the label of a plastic jar. "That's not really strychnine, is it? You'll need a licence for that. Just what exactly are you making here?"

Alan leaned over the computer desk and clicked the mouse a few times. "Just a minute, inspector." The printer, nearby, rattled into life and produced two A4 sheets of small print. "This is a biochemical pilot plant, inspector. Now, before I'm allowed to tell you anything further, you'll both have to sign these NDA documents."

Willoughby took one of the sheets and started to read. "Why do we have to sign this? It looks like an agreement not to disclose any information."

Alan said, "Precisely, inspector. We work as consultants for a pharmaceutical company. We have a non-disclosure agreement with them to protect their intellectual property. If we're compelled to give out any of that information to a third party, like the police, then we must first have that third party sign a similar agreement. Now if you'd just fill in your particulars there, and sign at the bottom, I'll be able to answer all of your questions."

The two third parties duly signed their papers and handed them back to Alan. He quickly checked the details and put the papers in a filing cabinet. "Samanal Pharm Limited, that's myself and Miss Black, have a contract with Falmer's to develop pilot production of a new drug, called Methyphenax Four. You might have heard about it in the news a while back."

Willoughby looked blank and shook his head. Carter ventured, "Isn't that some new wonder drug for cancer?"

275

"Yes, but unfortunately it's had some mixed results. It looks like it's going to be used in a niche market. Well, that's really all there is to it. That's what this plant makes," said Alan, clicking the mouse again to restore the plant control window to the screen. "Okay?" he said as he tried to show the two men out the room.

Willoughby stopped at the doorway and said, "But you haven't explained what the strychnine's for? Surely, it's not an ingredient of the drug? Wouldn't that make it deadly poisonous?"

Alan gave a short laugh. "Oh no. It's not mixed in with the ingredients, inspector. Making a drug like Meth 4 is done by using genetically modified bacteria. Basically, we have a fermenter which is maintained at a precise temperature with a sort of nutrient soup for the little tinkers to eat.

At a temperature of 31 degrees they convert their food into various chemical products, including a very small amount of the drug we are after. Any warmer, and the yield goes down. Above 36 degrees, all that the bacteria would make is a certain bi-product, which is no use to man or beast.

We keep the fermenter at the correct temperature and harvest the drug. It's mixed with the other compounds, so we have to purify it. The clever bit is separating the small amount of the drug from one bi-product in particular. The drug is pumped into a small storage tank and the bi-products are incinerated. Now, of course, bacteria will do what most red-blooded lifeforms like to do. They're like microscopic, supercharged bunny rabbits. In a very short time, you end up with lots more bacteria than you need. So, every few hours, the plant automatically removes a small proportion of the bacteria and kills them off. That's where the strychnine comes in. It's not really my field. Sam could probably explain better, but as I understand it, when this strain of bacteria was modified, they ended up being resistant to all known antibiotics. However, they're still susceptible to certain chemical toxins. The most effective way to guarantee their passage to bacterial heaven is to feed them a good dose of strychnine. Then we incinerate them just for good measure." With both hands Alan gestured. "Poof! And they're gone. Nothing survives my incinerator." He gave a mock mad scientist laugh.

Willoughby nodded and turned again to leave the room. "These bacteria. Are they dangerous? Could they make you ill?"

With his fingers crossed behind his back, Alan said, "No, they're incapable of causing disease. If I remember right, they were developed from the good bacteria in the human gut. They can't survive at low temperatures because they don't normally form cysts or spores. A few seconds in the air at room temperature would probably be enough to kill most of them. Of course, if they escaped this plant and ended up in someone's intestines, they might survive, but they would only produce some harmless chemicals."

Willoughby looked confused. "So why don't you just cool them down instead of using poison?"

"Health and Safety," said Alan, "We can't risk any of them surviving because they could mutate. Sam could tell you more, but you'd need a degree to understand it all. She tends to go on a bit."

"I still don't understand why Falmer's would get *you* to develop their drug, rather than doing it themselves.," said Willoughby.

"Oh, it's simple economics, inspector. It's cheaper for them to sub-contract the pilot production to us. We don't actually develop the drug. Falmer's have their own people for that, although Sam did have a hand in it. We're more concerned with ironing out the intricacies of the process of manufacturing the stuff. Falmer's had a round of down-sizing about six years ago, so Sam and I took redundancy to set up on our own. It was all very amicable and Falmer's were quite happy to be one of our clients. We've never looked back, since."

When the two men had gone, Alan returned to the living room. Sam said, "I thought you said that all mechy tools were the same. You wouldn't pay extra just for a top brand name. If the cheap one broke, you'd just buy another cheap one."

"Well, the other week I was reading about how the Institute had done a survey of tools and their conclusion was that Chrome Moly was far better, especially if you got one of the better American brands. Buying cheap far-East tools was false economy, so I treated myself to the best set of spanners you could buy and chucked my cheap ones away."

"So, did the coppers say why they wanted to know about your spanners? Nothing to do with brake pipes, was it?"

"Brake pipes? Are you mad?" Alan laughed, "No, that spanner they had in the bag was far too big for working on brakes. More like an offensive weapon than a tool. They seemed to be happy enough when I showed them my kit. But then they heard the incinerator pump going, so I had to let them see the plant. It might have looked suspicious if I tried to hide it from them. Then I gave them a load of guff about an NDA and got them to sign an agreement. Hopefully that should stop them talking about it too much."

Sam gave out a deep breathy sigh and said, "Well, all I can say is – It's a good thing we're all legal, now, with no more little secrets to hide."

"Yes, dear. No more little secrets."

Chapter 17

Some Months Later

Alan Murray stood at the foot of the wide staircase. Drawing aside the cuff of his overcoat, he checked the time on his expensive, Swiss-made watch. Just after half past seven. He screwed up his eyes to read the grandmother clock across the hall. Roughly twenty-eight minutes past. Squinting, he read the bright red digital display on the burglar alarm panel – 19:30. It was definitely half past seven, more or less. He'd been ready for an hour. It had only taken him fifteen minutes. A quick shower, a spray of *Real Man*, the anti-perspirant capable of turning any woman into a drooling, nympho wreck, and away you go. Why do women have to make such a fuss about washing? How long could it take to slap on a bit of lipstick and a flick of mascara? A couple of minutes should do it.

He sighed and looked around the hall. For the third time in five minutes, he walked over to the living room door, opened it and said, "Are you sure you'll be warm enough? I can turn the heating up if you want."

For the third time, the reply was, "We'll be fine. Go and enjoy yourselves."

He walked back to the base of the stairs, looked up and listened. There was still no sign of her.

"Taxi's here!" he shouted, stifling a snigger.

From above, there came the sound of a toilet flushing. A stair creaked and carpet-muffled footsteps hurried down the dog-leg flight.

Sam appeared, dressed in her black trouser suit. Her pace slowed as she came to the last few stairs.

"Keep it down," she said, standing on the bottom stair.

Alan said, "Have you checked the babies?"

"They're fine. The Dixies will hardly even know they're up there. I've made up the spare bed. I think the room's a lot better now. The musty smell's gone since you replaced the radiator and got the flashing fixed. You know, sweetie, I don't really see why we're going. It's not as if we'll know many people there."

"Come on, we deserve a night out. Let's enjoy ourselves. George will be there. It might be a laugh."

Sam said, "Well it's not as if we haven't seen much of uncle George. He's been round every week for the last year. And, I think he's leading you astray."

"Oh, a little flutter and a few beers on a Saturday afternoon. What's wrong with that? Besides, he really loves the kids. Just like they were his own."

Headlights momentarily illuminated the front window. A car horn sounded outside. Alan took Sam's coat from the stand and held it as she put her arms in.

She walked over to the living room and poked her head around the door. "It's really good of you to come tonight. We'll not be late. You've got my mobile number, just in case, and there's bottles made up for them. Georgina might wake up and need her nappy changing, but Angus should sleep through."

Wendy looked Sam in the eye and said, "Go on. We'll manage just fine."

281

John said, "Enjoy yourselves, but mind you don't go to any parties. Oh, and say hello to Sparky and Joan from us."

As the front door closed, Dixie and Wendy got back to watching their television programme. *True Crime Investigations'* featured the case of a drug-crazed, bent policeman who had murdered his girlfriend's brother in revenge for her having been abused by him as a child. The horrific murder involved torture, whereby the victim's thumb had been cut off, later to be found in the policeman's Land Rover, along with blood-stained secateurs. After being tortured, the victim had been pushed off a precipice into a disused quarry, where he fell to his death. In the victim's pocket was an empty bottle which the killer had planted to make the crime look as if it were drug related. Unfortunately for the killer, he had failed to wipe the bottle clean and his fingerprints were recovered.

The killer-cop had also tried to murder his superior officer after a long running dispute about professional incompetence. The blood-stained spanner, which the killer had used on his superior, was found in the Land Rover, next to the first victim's thumb. Again, fingerprint evidence had been recovered from the weapon, along with DNA, proving that the blood was the Chief Inspector's and that the killer cop had wielded the weapon. In the face of all the evidence against him the defendant had finally confessed and was detained in a secure hospital, having gone quite insane and now being permanently in what appeared to be a state of extreme euphoria.

The program ended with a conundrum posed by the presenter, "Why hadn't the DCI reported the incident? We may never know, as the senior officer had died of an emergent resistant strain of tetanus infection shortly after the attack. What is clear is that George Latimer, the killer-constable, was blackmailing the DCI over alleged sexual misconduct – the photographic evidence, recovered from the killer's flat, was damning. Maybe the inspector tried to silence the blackmailer and they fought. Who knows? He took the secret to his grave.

Now, what would you do if all of your neighbours were permanently high dopeheads and the police couldn't find any evidence of drug taking? We look into the extraordinary case of the village full of junkies the police can't touch. Tune in again next week for more *True Crime* …"

Suddenly the room went black, except for the dim afterglow of the screen. "Be careful!" said Wendy, as a heavy hand found its way to her crutch.

"Sorry, love. Can't see a thing."

"It's alright," she laughed, "Is it a power cut?"

"Yes. Looks like it, but don't worry. Alan was telling me that they kept the standby generator from the old pilot plant. It should kick in automatically after a few seconds. It won't be long now."

After a couple of minutes, Dixie stood up and felt around for the arm of the sofa. "Ooh! You naughty boy," said Wendy. "It's quite romantic, isn't it?" she giggled.

"Shush. What's that noise? At last! Sounds like the generator's starting up,"

"No, darling. That's Georgina. She's awake," sighed Wendy, "I can't see a thing. How long does it take for the bloody thing to get going? Do you think it's *ever* going to start?"

"Huh! Another nice mess you've got me into, Minty," said John Dixon.

Printed in Great Britain
by Amazon

54032210R00173